Anonymous

Memoirs of the Life of Sir Walter Scott, Bart.

By J.G. Lockhart "Memoirs of the life of sir Walter Scott, Bart." 9

Anonymous

Memoirs of the Life of Sir Walter Scott, Bart.
By J.G. Lockhart "Memoirs of the life of sir Walter Scott, Bart." 9

ISBN/EAN: 9783337393656

Printed in Europe, USA, Canada, Australia, Japan

Cover: Foto ©Raphael Reischuk / pixelio.de

More available books at **www.hansebooks.com**

MEMOIRS

OF THE

LIFE OF SIR WALTER SCOTT, BART.

BY

J. G. LOCKHART, ESQ.

VOL. IX.

EDINBURGH:
ADAM AND CHARLES BLACK.
1862.

CONTENTS

OF VOLUME NINTH.

CHAPTER LXXII.

CHAPTER LXXIII.

CHAPTER LXXVII.

CHAPTER LXXVIII.

MEMOIRS

OF THE

LIFE OF SIR WALTER SCOTT.

CHAPTER LXXII.

Journey to London and Paris — Scott's Diary — Rokeby — Burleigh — Imitators of the Waverley Novels — Southey's Peninsular War — Royal Lodge at Windsor — George IV. — Adelphi Theatre — Terry, Crofton Croker, Thomas Pringle, Allan Cunningham, Moore, Rogers, Lawrence, &c. — Calais, Montreuil, &c. — Paris — Pozzo di Borgo, Lord Granville, Marshals Macdonald and Marmont, Gallois, W. R. Spencer, Princess Galitzin, Charles X., Duchess of Angouleme, &c. — Enthusiastic recep-

*tion in Paris—Dover Cliff—Theodore Hooke,
Lydia White, Duke of Wellington, Peel, Canning, Croker, &c. &c.—Duke of York—Madame
D'Arblay— State of Politics — Oxford— Cheltenham — Abbotsford — Walker Street, Edinburgh.*

OCT.—DEC. 1826.

On the 12th of October, Sir Walter left Abbotsford for London, where he had been promised access to the papers in the Government offices ; and thence he proceeded to Paris, in the hope of gathering from various eminent persons authentic anecdotes concerning Napoleon. His Diary shows that he was successful in obtaining many valuable materials for the completion of his historical work ; and reflects, with sufficient distinctness, the very brilliant reception he, on this occasion, experienced both in London and Paris. The range of his society is strikingly (and unconsciously) exemplified in the record of one day, when we find him breakfasting at the Royal Lodge in Windsor Park, and supping on oysters and porter in " honest Dan Terry's house, like a squirrel's cage," above the Adelphi Theatre, in the Strand. There can be no doubt that this expedition was in many ways serviceable to his Life of Napoleon; and I think as little, that it was chiefly so by renerving his spirits. The deep and respectful sympathy with which his misfortunes, and gallant behaviour under them, had been regarded by all classes of men at home and abroad, was brought home to his perception in a way not to be mistaken. He was cheered and gratified, and returned to Scotland, with renewed hope and courage, for the prosecution of his marvellous course of industry.

EXTRACTS FROM DIARY.

" *Rokeby Park, October* 13.—We left Carlisle before seven, and, visiting Appleby Castle by the way (a most interesting and curious place), we got to Morritt's about half-past four, where we had as warm a welcome as one of the warmest hearts in the world could give an old friend. It was great pleasure to me to see Morritt happy in the middle of his family circle, undisturbed, as heretofore, by the sickness of any one dear to him. I may note that I found much pleasure in my companion's conversation, as well as in her mode of managing all her little concerns on the road. I am apt to judge of character by good-humour and alacrity in these petty concerns. I think the inconveniences of a journey seem greater to me than formerly; while, on the other hand, the pleasures it affords are rather less. The ascent of Stainmore seemed duller and longer than usual, and, on the other hand, Bowes, which used to strike me as a distinguished feature, seemed an ill-formed mass of rubbish, a great deal lower in height than I had supposed; yet I have seen it twenty times at least. On the other hand, what I lose in my own personal feelings I gain in those of my companion, who shows an intelligent curiosity and interest in what she sees. I enjoy, therefore, reflectively, *veluti in speculo*, the sort of pleasure to which I am now less accessible.— Saw in Morritt's possession the original miniature of Milton, by Cooper—a valuable thing indeed. The countenance is handsome and dignified, with a strong expression of genius.*

" *Grantham, October* 15.— Old England is no changeling. It is long since I travelled this road, having come up to town chiefly by sea of late years. One race of red-nosed innkeepers are gone, and their widows, eldest sons, or head-waiters, exercise hospitality in their room with the same bustle and importance. But other things seem, externally at least, much the same: the land is better ploughed; straight

* This precious miniature, executed by Cooper for Milton's favourite daughter, was long in the possession of Sir Joshua Reynolds, and bequeathed by him to the poet Mason, who was an intimate friend of Mr Morritt's father

ridges everywhere adopted in place of the old circumflex of twenty years ago. Three horses, however, or even four, are still often seen in a plough yoked one before the other. Ill habits do not go out at once.

" *Biggleswade, October* 16. — Visited Burleigh this morning; the first time I ever saw that grand place, where there are so many objects of interest and curiosity. The house is magnificent, in the style of James I.'s reign, and consequently in mixed Gothic. Of paintings I know nothing; so shall attempt to say nothing. But whether to connoisseurs, or to an ignorant admirer like myself, the Salvator Mundi, by Carlo Dolci, must seem worth a king's ransom. Lady Exeter, who was at home, had the goodness or curiosity to wish to see us. She is a beauty after my own heart; a great deal of liveliness in the face; an absence alike of form and of affected ease, and really courteous after a genuine and ladylike fashion.

" 25 *Pall-Mall, October* 17.—Here am I in this capital once more, after an April-weather meeting with my daughter and Lockhart. Too much grief in our first meeting to be joyful; too much pleasure to be distressing; a giddy sensation between the painful and the pleasurable. I will call another subject.

" I read with interest, during my journey, Sir John

Chiverton * and Brambletye House—novels, in what
I may surely claim as the style

> ' Which I was born to introduce —
> Refined it first, and show'd its use.

They are both clever books—one in imitation of the
days of chivalry—the other (by Horace Smith, one
of the authors of Rejected Addresses) dated in the
time of the Civil Wars, and introducing historical
characters.

" I believe, were I to publish the Canongate Chronicles without my name (*nomme de guerre*, I mean),
the event might be a corollary to the fable of the
peasant who made the real pig squeak against the
imitator, when the sapient audience killed the poor
grunter as if inferior to the biped in his own language. The peasant could, indeed, confute the long-
eared multitude by showing piggy; but were I to fail
as a knight with a white and maiden shield, and then
vindicate my claim to attention by putting ' By the
Author of Waverley' in the title, my good friend
Publicum would defend itself by stating I had tilted
so ill, that my course had not the least resemblance
to former doings, when indisputably I bore away the
garland. Therefore I am firmly and resolutely de-

---

* *Chiverton* was the first publication (anonymous) of Mr
William Harrison Ainsworth, the author of *Rookwood* and other
popular romances.   † Swift.

termined to tilt under my own cognizance. The hazard, indeed, remains of being beaten. But there is a prejudice (not an undue one neither) in favour of the original patentee; and Joe Manton's name has borne out many a sorry gun-barrel. More of this to-morrow.

Expense of journey, . . .	£41	0	0
Anne, pocket money, ...	. 5	0	0
Servants on journey, ...	2	0	0
Cash in purse (silver not reckoned), .	. 2	0	0
	£50	0	0

This is like to be an expensive trip; but if I can sell an early copy to a French translator, it should bring me home. Thank God, little Dohnnie Hoo, as he calls himself, is looking well, though the poor dear child is kept always in a prostrate posture.

" *October* 18.—I take up again my remarks on imitators. I am sure I mean the gentlemen no wrong by calling them so, and heartily wish they had followed a better model. But it serves to show me *veluti in speculo* my own errors, or, if you will, those of the *style*. One advantage, I think, I still have over all of them. They may do their fooling with better grace; but I, like Sir Andrew Aguecheek, do it more natural. They have to read old books, and consult antiquarian collections, to get their knowledge; I write because I have long since read such works, and possess, thanks to a strong memory, the information which they have to seek for. This leads to a dragging-in historical details by head and shoulders, so that the interest of the main piece is lost in minute descriptions of events which do not affect its progress. Perhaps I have sinned in this way myself; indeed, I am but too conscious of having considered the plot only as what Bayes calls the means of bringing in fine things; so that, in respect to the descriptions, it resembled the string of the showman's box, which he pulls to exhibit in succession, Kings, Queens, the Battle of Waterloo, Buonaparte at St Helena, Newmarket Races, and White-headed Bob floored by Jemmy from Town. All this I may have done, but I have repented of it; and in my better efforts, while I conducted my story through the agency of historical personages, and by connecting it with historical incidents, I have endeavoured to weave them pretty closely together, and in future I will study this more. Must not let the back-ground eclipse the principal figures—the frame overpower the picture.

" Another thing in my favour is, that my contemporaries steal too openly. Mr Smith has inserted in Brambletye House, whole pages from De Foe's ' Fire and Plague of London.'

' Steal! foh! a fico for the phrase—
Convey, the wise it call!'

When I *convey* an incident or so, I am at as much pains to avoid detection as if the offence could be indicted at the Old Bailey. But leaving this, hard pressed as I am by these imitators, who must put the thing out of fashion at last, I consider, like a fox at his shifts, whether there be a way to dodge them —some new device to throw them off, and have a mile or two of free ground while I have legs and wind left to use it. There is one way to give novelty; to depend for success on the interest of a well-contrived story. But, wo's me! that requires thought, consideration—the writing out a regular plan or plot—above all, the adhering to one—which I never can do, for the ideas rise as I write, and bear such a disproportioned extent to that which each occupied at the first concoction, that (cocksnowns!) I shall never be able to take the trouble ; and yet to make the world stare, and gain a new march ahead of them all! Well, something we still will do.

> ' Liberty's in every blow ;
> ' Let us do or die ! '

Poor Rob Burns! to tack thy fine strains of sublime patriotism! Better Tristram Shandy's vein. Hand me my cap and bells there. So now, I am equipped I open my raree-show with

> ' Ma'am, will you walk in, and fal de ral diddle?
> And, sir, will you stalk in, and fal de ral diddle?

> And, miss, will you pop in, and fal de ral diddle?
> And, master, pray hop in, and fal de ral diddle.

Query—How long is it since I heard that strain of dulcet mood, and where or how came I to pick it up? It is not mine, 'though by your smiling you seem to say so.'[*] Here is a proper morning's work! But I am childish with seeing them all well and happy here; and as I can neither whistle nor sing, I must let the giddy humour run to waste on paper.

"Sallied forth in the morning; bought a hat. Met Sir William Knighton,[†] from whose discourse I guess that Malachi has done me no prejudice in a certain quarter; with more indications of the times, which I need not set down. Sallied again after breakfast, and visited the Piccadilly ladies. Saw also the Duchess of Buckingham, and Lady Charlotte Bury, with a most beautiful little girl. Owen Rees breakfasted, and agreed I should have what the Frenchman has offered for the advantage of translating Napoleon, which will help my expenses to town and down again.

"*October* 19.—I rose at my usual time, but could not write; so read Southey's History of the Penin-

---

[*] *Hamlet, Act II. Scene 2.*

[†] Sir William was Private Secretary to King George IV. Sir Walter made his acquaintance in August 1822, and ever afterwards they corresponded with each other—sometimes very confidentially.

sular War. It is very good, indeed—honest English principle in every line; but there are many preju-dices, and there is a tendency to augment a work already too long, by saying all that can be said of the history of ancient times appertaining to every place mentioned. What care we whether Saragossa be derived from Cæsaria Augusta? Could he have proved it to be Numantium, there would have been a concatenation accordingly.*

" Breakfasted at Sam Rogers's with Sir Thomas Lawrence; Luttrel, the great London wit; Richard Sharp, &c. One of them made merry with some part of Rose's Ariosto; proposed that the Italian should be printed on the other side, for the sake of assisting the indolent reader to understand the Eng-lish; and complained of his using more than once the phrase of a lady having ' voided her saddle,' which would certainly sound extraordinary at Apo-thecaries' Hall. Well, well, Rose carries a dirk too. The morning was too dark for Westminster Abbey, which we had projected.

" I then went to Downing Street, and am put by Mr Wilmot Horton into the hands of a confiden-tial clerk, Mr Smith, who promises access to every-thing. Then saw Croker, who gave me a bundle of

* It is amusing to compare this criticism with Sir Walter's own anxiety to identify his daughter-in-law's place, *Lochore*, with the *Urbs Orrea* of the Roman writers. See Vol. VII. p. 352.

documents. Sir George Cockburn promises his despatches and journal. In short, I have ample prospect of materials. Dined with Mrs Coutts. Tragi-comic distress of my good friend on the marriage of her presumptive heir with a daughter of Lucien Buonaparte.

" *October* 20. — Commanded down to pass a day at Windsor. This is very kind of his Majesty. — At breakfast, Crofton Croker, author of the Irish Fairy Tales — little as a dwarf, keen-eyed as a hawk, and of easy, prepossessing manners — something like Tom Moore. Here were also Terry, Allan Cunningham, Newton, and others. Now I must go to work   Went down to Windsor, or rather to the Lodge in the Forest, which, though ridiculed by connoisseurs, seems to be no bad specimen of a royal retirement, and is delightfully situated. A kind of cottage, too large perhaps for the style, but yet so managed, that in the walks you only see parts of it at once, and these well composed and grouping with the immense trees. His Majesty received me with the same mixture of kindness and courtesy which has always distinguished his conduct towards me. There was no company besides the royal retinue — Lady Conyngham — her daughter — and two or three other ladies. After we left table, there was excellent music by the royal band, who lay ambushed in a green - house adjoining the apartment. The King made me sit beside him, and talk a great deal—*too much* perhaps—for he has the art of raising one's spirits, and making you forget the *retenue* which is prudent everywhere, especially at court. But he converses himself with so much ease and elegance, that you lose thoughts of the prince in admiring the well-bred and accomplished gentleman. He is in many respects the model of a British Monarch—has little inclination to try experiments on government otherwise than through his Ministers—sincerely, I believe, desires the good of his subjects—is kind towards the distressed, and moves and speaks ' every inch a king.'* I am sure such a man is fitter for us than one who would long to head armies, or be perpetually intermeddling with *la grande politique.* A sort of reserve, which creeps on him daily, and prevents his going to places of public resort, is a disadvantage, and prevents his being so generally popular as is earnestly to be desired. This, I think, was much increased by the behavour of the rabble in the brutal insanity of the Queen's trial, when John Bull, meaning the best in the world, made such a beastly figure.

" *October* 21.—Walked in the morning with Sir

* *King Lear, Act IV. Scene* 6.

William Knighton, and had much confidential chat, not fit to be here set down, in case of accidents. He undertook most kindly to recommend Charles, when he has taken his degree, to be attached to some of the diplomatic missions, which I think is best for the lad, after all. After breakfast, went to Windsor Castle, and examined the improvements going on there under Mr Wyattville, who appears to possess a great deal of taste and feeling for Gothic architecture. The old apartments, splendid enough in extent and proportion, are paltry in finishing. Instead of being lined with heart of oak, the palace of the British King is hung with paper, painted wainscot colour. There are some fine paintings, and some droll ones: Among the last are those of divers princes of the House of Mecklenburg-Strelitz, of which Queen Charlotte was descended. They are ill-coloured, orang-outang-looking figures, with black eyes and hook-noses, in old-fashioned uniforms. Returned to a hasty dinner in Pall-Mall, and then hurried away to see honest Dan Terry's theatre, called the Adelphi, where we saw the Pilot, from an American novel of that name. It is extremely popular, the dramatist having seized on the whole story, and turned the odious and ridiculous parts, assigned by the original author to the British, against the Yankees themselves. There is a quiet effrontery in this, that is of a rare and peculiar character. The

Americans were so much displeased, that they attempted a row—which rendered the piece doubly attractive to the seamen at Wapping, who came up and crowded the house night after night, to support the honour of the British flag. After all, one must deprecate whatever keeps up ill-will betwixt America and the mother country; and *we* in particular should avoid awakening painful recollections. Our high situation enables us to contemn petty insults, and to make advances towards cordiality. I was however, glad to see Dan's theatre as full seemingly as it could hold. The heat was dreadful, and Anne so unwell that she was obliged to be carried into Terry's house, a curious dwelling no larger than a squirrel's cage, which he has contrived to squeeze out of the vacant space of the theatre, and which is accessible by a most complicated combination of staircases and small passages. There we had rare good porter and oysters after the play, and found Anne much better.

" *October* 22.—This morning Mr Wilmot Horton, Under Secretary of State, breakfasted. He is full of some new plan of relieving the poor's-rates, by encouraging emigration.* But John Bull will think

* The Right Honourable Sir Robert Wilmot Horton, Bart. (lately Governor of Ceylon) has published various tracts on the important subject here alluded to. — [1839.]

this savours of Botany-Bay.   The attempt to look
the poor's-rates in the face is certainly meritorious.
Laboured in writing and marking extracts to be
copied, from breakfast to dinner—with the exception
of an hour spent in telling Johnnie the history of his
name-sake, Gilpin.   Tom Moore and Sir Thomas
Lawrence came in the evening, which made a pleasant *soirée.*   Smoke my French — Egad, it is time
to air some of my vocabulary.   It is, I find, cursedly
musty.

" *October* 23.—Sam Rogers and Moore breakfasted here, and we were very merry fellows.   Moore
seemed disposed to go to France with us.   I foresee
I shall be embarrassed with more communications
than I can use or trust to, coloured as they must
be by the passions of those who make them.   Thus
I have a statement from the Duchess d'Escars, to
which the Buonapartists would, I daresay, give no
credit.   If Talleyrand, for example, could be communicative, he must have ten thousand reasons for
perverting the truth, and yet a person receiving a
direct communication from him would be almost
barred from disputing it.

' Sing, tantarara, rogues all.'

" We dined at the Residentiary-house with good
Dr Hughes—Allan Cunningham, Sir Thomas Law-

rence, and young Mr Hughes. Thomas Pringle* is returned from the Cape. He might have done well there, could he have scoured his brains of politics, but he must needs publish a Whig journal at the Cape of Good Hope!! He is a worthy creature, but conceited withal—*hinc illæ lachrymæ*. He brought me some antlers and a skin, in addition to others he had sent to Abbotsford four years since.

" *October* 24.—Laboured in the morning. At breakfast, Dr Holland, and Cohen, whom they now call Palgrave, a mutation of names which confused my recollections. Item, Moore. I worked at the Colonial Office pretty hard. Dined with Mr Wilmot Horton, and his beautiful wife, the original of the ' *She walks in beauty*,' &c. of poor Byron.— *N. B.* The conversation is seldom excellent among

* Mr Pringle was a Roxburghshire farmer's son (lame from birth) who, in youth, attracted Sir Walter's notice by his poem called, " Scenes of Teviotdale." He was for a time Editor of Blackwood's Magazine, but the publisher and he had different politics, quarrelled, and parted. Sir Walter then gave Pringle strong recommendations to the late Lord Charles Somerset, Governor of the Cape of Good Hope, in which colony he settled, and for some years throve under the Governor's protection; but the newspaper alluded to in the text ruined his prospects at the Cape — he returned to England — became Secretary to an anti-slavery association — published a charming little volume entitled " African Sketches,"—and died, I fear in very distressed circumstances, in December 1834. He was a man of amiable feelings and elegant genius.

official people. So many topics are what Otaheitians call *taboo.* We hunted down a pun or two, which were turned out, like the stag at the Epping Hunt, for the pursuit of all and sundry. Came home early, and was in bed by eleven.

" *October* 25.— Kind Mr Wilson * and his wife at breakfast; also Sir Thomas Lawrence. Locker† came in afterwards, and made a proposal to me to give up his intended Life of George III. in my favour on cause shown. I declined the proposal, not being of opinion that my genius lies that way, and not relishing hunting in couples. Afterwards went to the Colonial Office, and had Robert Hay's assistance in my enquiries — then to the French Ambassador's for my passports. Picked up Sotheby, who endeavoured to saddle me for a review of his polyglott Virgil. I fear I shall scarce convince him that I know nothing of the Latin lingo. Sir R. H. Inglis, Richard Sharp, and other friends called. We dine at Miss Dumergue's, and spend a part of our soirée at Lydia White's. To-morrow,

'For France, for France, for it is more than need.' ‡

---

* William Wilson, Esq. of Wandsworth Common, formerly of Wilsontown, in Lanarkshire.

† E. H. Locker, Esq. then Secretary, now one of the Commissioners of Greenwich Hospital—an old and dear friend of Scott's

‡ *King John, Act I. Scene* 1.

" *Calais, October* 26.—Up at five, and in the packet by six. A fine passage—save at the conclusion, while we lay on and off the harbour of Calais. But the tossing made no impression on my companion or me; we ate and drank like dragoons the whole way, and were able to manage a good supper and best part of a bottle of Chablis, at the classic Dessein's, who received us with much courtesy.

" *October* 27.—Custom-house, &c. detained us till near ten o'clock, so we had time to walk on the Boulevards, and to see the fortifications, which must be very strong, all the country round being flat and marshy. Lost, as all know, by the bloody papist bitch (one must be vernacular when on French ground) Queen Mary, of red-hot memory. I would rather she had burned a score more of bishops. If she had kept it, her sister Bess would sooner have parted with her virginity. Charles I. had no temptation to part with it—it might, indeed, have been shuffled out of our hands during the Civil Wars, but Noll would have as soon let Monsieur draw one of his grinders—then Charles II. would hardly have dared to sell such an old possession, as he did Dunkirk; and after that the French had little chance till the Revolution. Even then, I think, we could have held a place that could be supplied from our own element the sea. *Cui bono?* None, I think, but to plague the rogues.——We dined at Cormont, and being stopped by Mr Canning, having taken up all the post-horses, could only reach Montreuil that night. I should have liked to have seen some more of this place, which is fortified; and as it stands on an elevated and rocky site, must present some fine points. But as we came in late, and left early, I can only bear witness to good treatment, good supper, good *vin de Barsac*, and excellent beds.

" *October* 28.——Breakfasted at Abbeville, and saw a very handsome Gothic church, and reached Grand-villiers at night. The house is but second-rate, though lauded by several English travellers for the moderation of its charges, as was recorded in a book presented to us by the landlady. There is no great patriotism in publishing that a traveller thinks the bills moderate——it serves usually as an intimation to mine host or hostess that John Bull will bear a little more squeezing. I gave my attestation, too, however, for the charges of the good lady resembled those elsewhere; and her anxiety to please was extreme. Folks must be harder hearted than I am to resist the *empressement*, which may, indeed, be venal, yet has in its expression a touch of cordiality.

" *Paris, October* 29.——Breakfasted at Beauvais, and saw its magnificent cathedral——unfinished it has

been left, and unfinished it will remain, of course,—
the fashion of cathedrals being passed away. But
even what exists is inimitable, the choir particularly,
and the grand front. Beauvais is called the *Pucelle*,
yet, so far as I can see, she wears no stays—I mean,
has no fortifications. On we run, however. *Vogue
la galère; et voila nous à Paris, Hotel de Windsor*
(Rue Rivoli), where we are well lodged. France, so
far as I can see, which is very little, has not undergone many changes. The image of war has, indeed,
passed away, and we no longer see troops cross-
ing the country in every direction—villages either
ruined or hastily fortified—inhabitants sheltered in
the woods and caves to escape the rapacity of the
soldiers,—all this has passed away. The inns, too,
much amended. There is no occasion for that ras-
cally practice of making a bargain—or *combien*-ing
your landlady, before you unharness your horses,
which formerly was matter of necessity. The general taste of the English seems to regulate the travelling—naturally enough, as the hotels, of which
there are two or three in each town, chiefly subsist
by them. We did not see one French equipage on
the road; the natives seem to travel entirely in the
diligence, and doubtless *à bon marché;* the road was
thronged with English. But in her great features
France is the same as ever. An oppressive air of
solitude seems to hover over these rich and extended

plains, while we are sensible, that whatever is the nature of the desolation, it cannot be sterility.   The towns are small, and have a poor appearance, and more frequently exhibit signs of decayed splendour than of increasing prosperity.   The chateau, the abode of the gentleman,—and the villa, the retreat of the thriving *negociant*,—are rarely seen till you come to Beaumont.   At this place, which well deserves its name of the fair mount, the prospect improves greatly, and country-seats are seen in abundance; also woods, sometimes deep and extensive, at other times scattered in groves and single trees.   Amidst these the oak seldom or never is found; England, lady of the ocean, seems to claim it exclusively as her own.   Neither are there any quantity of firs.   Poplars in abundance give a formal air to the landscape.   The forests chiefly consist of beeches, with some birches, and the roads are bordered by elms cruelly cropped and pollarded and switched.   The demand for fire-wood occasions these mutilations.   If I could waft by a wish the thinnings of Abbotsford here, it would make a little fortune of itself.   But then to switch and mutilate my trees! —not for a thousand francs.   Ay, but sour grapes, quoth the fox.

" *October* 30.—Finding ourselves snugly settled in our Hotel, we determined to remain here at fifteen francs per day   We are in the midst of what can be seen. This morning wet and surly. Sallied, however, by the assistance of a hired coach, and left cards for Count Pozzo di Borgo, Lord Granville, our ambassador, and M. Gallois, author of the History of Venice. Found no one at home, not even the old pirate Galignani, at whose den I ventured to call. Showed my companion the Louvre (which was closed unluckily), the fronts of the palace, with its courts, and all that splendid quarter which the fame of Paris rests upon in security. We can never do the like in Britain. Royal magnificence can only be displayed by despotic power.   In England, were the most splendid street or public building to be erected, the matter must be discussed in Parliament, or perhaps some sturdy cobbler holds out, and refuses to part with his stall, and the whole plan is disconcerted.   Long may such impediments exist! But then we should conform to circumstances, and assume in our public works a certain sober simplicity of character, which should point out that they were dictated by utility rather than show.   The affectation of an expensive style only places us at a disadvantageous contrast with other nations, and our substitution of plaster for freestone resembles the mean ambition which displays Bristol stones in default of diamonds.

" We went in the evening to the Comedie Française; *Rosamonde* the piece.   It is the composition

of a young man with a promising name — Emile de
Bonnechose; the story that of Fair Rosamond. There
were some good situations, and the actors in the
French taste seemed to be admirable, particularly
Mademoiselle Bourgoin. It would be absurd to cri-
ticise what I only half understood; but the piece was
well received, and produced a very strong effect. Two
or three ladies were carried out in hysterics; one
next to our box was frightfully ill. A Monsieur *à
belles moustaches*—the husband, I trust, though it is
likely they were *en partie fine* — was extremely and
affectionately assiduous. She was well worthy of the
trouble, being very pretty indeed; the face beautiful,
even amidst the involuntary convulsions. The after-
piece was *Femme Juge et Partie*, with which I was
less amused than I had expected, because I found I
understood the language less than I did ten or eleven
years since. Well, well, I am past the age of mending.

" Some of our friends in London had pretended
that at Paris I might stand some chance of being
encountered by the same sort of tumultuary reception
which I met in Ireland; but for this I see no ground
It is a point on which I am totally indifferent. As a
literary man I cannot affect to despise public applause;
as a private gentleman, I have always been embarrassed and displeased with popular clamours, even when
in my favour. I know very well the breath of which
such shouts are composed, and am sensible those who

applaud me to-day would be as ready to toss me to-morrow; and I would not have them think that I put such a value on their favour as would make me for an instant fear their displeasure. Now all this disclamation is sincere, and yet it sounds affected. It puts me in mind of an old woman, who, when Carlisle was taken by the Highlanders in 1745, chose to be particularly apprehensive of personal violence, and shut herself up in a closet, in order that she might escape ravishment. But no one came to disturb her solitude, and she began to be sensible that poor Donald was looking out for victuals, or seeking some small plunder, without bestowing a thought on the fair sex; by and by she popped her head out of her place of refuge with the pretty question, ' Good folks, can you tell when the ravishing is going to begin ?' I am sure I shall neither hide myself to avoid applause, which probably no one will think of conferring, nor have the meanness to do anything which can indicate any desire of ravishment. I have seen, when the late Lord Erskine entered the Edinburgh theatre, papers distributed in the boxes to mendicate a round of applause — the natural reward of a poor player.

" *October* 31. — At breakfast visited by M. Gallois, an elderly Frenchman (always the most agreeable class), full of information, courteous, and communicative. He had seen nearly, and remarked deeply.

and spoke frankly, though with due caution. He went with us to the Museum, where I think the Hall of Sculpture continues to be a fine thing — that of Pictures but tolerable, when we reflect upon 1815. A number of great French daubs (comparatively), by David and Gerard, cover the walls once occupied by the Italian *chefs-d'œuvre*. *Fiat justitia, ruat cœlum.* We then visited Nôtre Dame and the Palace of Justice. The latter is accounted the oldest building in Paris, being the work of St Louis. It is, however, in the interior, adapted to the taste of Louis XIV. We drove over the Pont Neuf, and visited the fine quays, which was all we could make out to-day, as I was afraid to fatigue Anne. When we returned home, I found Count Pozzo di Borgo waiting for me, a personable man, inclined to be rather corpulent — handsome features, with all the Corsican fire in his eyes. He was quite kind and communicative. Lord Granville had also called, and sent his Secretary to invite us to dinner to-morrow. In the evening at the Odeon, where we saw *Ivanhoe*. It was superbly got up, the Norman soldiers wearing pointed helmets and what resembled much hauberks of mail, which looked very well. The number of the attendants, and the skill with which they were moved and grouped on the stage, were well worthy of notice. It was an opera, and, of course, the story sadly mangled, and the dialogue, in great part, nonsense. Yet it was strange to hear anything like the words which I (then in agony of pain with spasms in my stomach) dictated to William Laidlaw at Abbotsford, now recited in a foreign tongue, and for the amusement of a strange people. I little thought to have survived the completing of this novel.

" *November* 1.—I suppose the ravishing is going to begin, for we have had the Dames des Halles, with a bouquet like a maypole, and a speech full of honey and oil, which cost me ten francs; also a small worshipper, who would not leave his name, but came *seulement pour avoir le plaisir, la felicité*, &c. &c. All this jargon I answer with corresponding *blarney* of my own, for have I not licked the black stone of that ancient castle? As to French, I speak it as it comes, and like Doeg in Absalom and Achitophel—

'————— dash on through thick and thin,
Through sense and nonsense, never out nor in.'

We went this morning with M. Gallois to the Church of St Genevieve, and thence to the College Henri IV., where I saw once more my old friend Chevalier. He was unwell, swathed in a turban of nightcaps and a multiplicity of *robes de chambre ;* but he had all the heart and vivacity of former times. I was truly glad to see the kind old man. We were unlucky in our day for sights, this being a high festival

—All Souls' Day. We were not allowed to scale the steeple of St Genevieve, neither could we see the animals at the Jardin des Plantes, who, though they have no souls, it is supposed, and no interest, of course, in the devotions·of the day, observe it in strict retreat, like the nuns of Kilkenny. I met, however, one lioness walking at large in the Jardin, and was introduced. This was Madame de Souza, the authoress of some well-known French romances of a very classical character, I am told, for I have never 'read them. She must have been beautiful, and is still well-looked. She is the mother of the handsome Count de Flahault, and had a very well-looking daughter with her, besides a son or two. She was very agreeable. We are to meet again. The day becoming decidedly rainy, we returned along the Boulevards by the Bridge of Austerlitz, but the weather spoiled the fine show.

" We dined at the Ambassador, Lord Granville's. He inhabits the same splendid house which Lord Castlereagh had in 1815, namely, Numero 30, Rue de Fauxbourg St Honoré. It once belonged to Pauline Borghese, and, if its walls could speak, they might tell us mighty curious stories. Without their having any tongue, they speak to my feelings ' with most miraculous organ.'* In these halls I had often seen and conversed familiarly with many of the great

* *Hamlet, Act II. Scene* 2.

and powerful, who won the world by their swords, and divided it by their counsel. There I saw very much of poor Lord Castlereagh—a man of sense, presence of mind, and fortitude, which carried him through many an affair of critical moment, when finer talents would have stuck in the mire. He had been, I think, indifferently educated, and his mode of speaking being far from logical or correct, he was sometimes in danger of becoming almost ridiculous, in despite of his lofty presence, which had all the grace of the Seymours, and his determined courage. But then he was always up to the occasion, and upon important matters was an orator to convince, if not to delight his hearers. He is gone, and my friend * * * * * * * also, whose kindness this town so strongly recalls. It is remarkable they were the only persons of sense and credibility who both attested supernatural appearances on their own evidence, and both died in the same melancholy manner. I shall always tremble when any friend of mine becomes visionary. I have seen in these rooms the Emperor Alexander, Platoff, Schwartzenberg, Old Blucher, Fouché, and many a marshal whose truncheon had guided armies—all now at peace, without subjects, without dominion, and where their past life, perhaps, seems but the recollection of a feverish dream. What a group would this band have made in the gloomy regions described in the Odyssey! But to lesser things

We were most kindly received by Lord and Lady Granville, and met many friends, some of them having been guests at Abbotsford; among these were Lords Ashley and Morpeth—there were also Charles Ellis (Lord Seaford now), *cum plurimis aliis.* Anne saw for the first time an entertainment *à la mode de France,* where the gentlemen left the parlour with the ladies. In diplomatic houses it is a good way of preventing political discussion, which John Bull is always apt to introduce with the second bottle. We left early, and came home at ten, much pleased with Lord and Lady Granville's kindness, though it was to be expected, as our recommendation came from Windsor.

" *November* 2.—Another gloomy day—a pize upon it!—and we have settled to go to St Cloud, and dine, if possible, with the Drummonds at Auteuil. Besides, I expect poor Spencer* to breakfast. There is another thought which depresses me. Well —but let us jot down a little politics, as my book

* The late Honourable William Robert Spencer, the best writer of *vers de societé* in our time, and one of the most charming of companions, was exactly Sir Walter's contemporary, and like him first attracted notice by a version of Bürger's *Lenore.* Like him, too, this remarkable man fell into pecuniary distress in the disastrous year 1825, and he was now an involuntary resident in Paris, where he died in October 1834, *ann. ætat* 65.

has a pretty firm lock.   The Whigs may say what they please, but I think the Bourbons will stand. M. * * * *, no great Royalist, says that the Duke of Orleans lives on the best terms with the reigning family, which is wise on his part, for the golden fruit may ripen and fall of itself, but it would be dangerous to

' Lend the crowd his arm to shake the tree.' *

The army, which was Buonaparte's strength, is now very much changed by the gradual influence of time, which has removed many, and made invalids of many more.   The artisans are neutral, and if the King will govern according to the Charte, and, what is still more, according to the habits of the people, he will sit firm enough, and the constitution will gradually attain more and more reverence as age gives it authority, and distinguishes it from those temporary and ephemeral governments, which seemed only set up to be pulled down.   The most dangerous point in the present state of France is that of religion.   It is, no doubt, excellent in the Bourbons to desire to make France a religious country; but they begin, I think, at the wrong end.   To press the observancy and ritual of religion on those who are not influenced by its doctrines, is planting the growing tree with

* Dryden's *Absalom and Achitophel* — Character of Shaftesbury.

its head downwards.   Rites are sanctified by belief;
but belief can never arise out of an enforced observance of ceremonies; it only makes men detest what
is imposed on them by compulsion.   Then these
Jesuits, who constitute emphatically an *imperium in
imperio*, labouring first for the benefit of their own
order, and next for that of the Roman See — what
is it but the introduction into France of a foreign
influence, whose interest may often run counter to
the general welfare of the kingdom?

"We have enough of ravishment.   M. Meurice
writes me that he is ready to hang himself that we
did not find accommodation at his hotel; and Madame
Mirbel came almost on her knees to have permission
to take my portrait.   I was cruel; but, seeing her
weeping ripe, consented she should come to-morrow
and work while I wrote.   A Russian Princess Galitzin, too, demands to see me, in the heroic vein;
"*Elle vouloit traverser les mers pour aller voir
S. W. S.,*"* &c.—and offers me a rendezvous at my

---

* S. W. S. stands very often in this Diary for *Sir Walter Scott.*
This is done in sportive allusion to the following trait of Tom
Purdie: — The morning after the news of Scott's baronetcy
reached Abbotsford, Tom was not to be found in any of his usual
haunts: he remained absent the whole day — and when he returned at night the mystery was thus explained. He and the head
shepherd (who, by the by, was also butcher in ordinary), viz.
Robert Hogg (a brother of the Bard of Ettrick), had been spending the day on the hill busily employed in prefixing a large S. for

hotel. This is precious tom-foolery; however, it is better than being neglected like a fallen sky-rocket, which seemed like to be my fate last year.

" We went to St Cloud with my old friend Mr Drummond, now living at a pretty *maison de campagne* at Auteuil. St Cloud, besides its unequalled views, is rich in remembrances. I did not fail to visit the *Orangerie*, out of which Boney expelled the Council of Five-Hundred. I thought I saw the scoundrels jumping the windows, with the bayonet at their rumps. What a pity the house was not two stories high! I asked the Swiss some questions on the *locale*, which he answered with becoming caution, saying, however, that ' he was not present at the time.' There are also new remembrances. A separate garden, laid out as a play-ground for the royal children, is called Trocadero, from the siege of Cadiz. But the Bourbons should not take military ground —it is firing a pop-gun in answer to a battery of cannon. All within the house is deranged. Every trace of Nap. or his reign totally done away, as if traced in sand over which the tide has passed. Mo-

---

Sir to the W. S. which previously appeared on the backs of the sheep. It was afterwards found that honest Tom had taken it upon him to order a mason to carve a similar honourable augmentation on the stones which marked the line of division between his master's moor and that of the Laird of Kippilaw.

reau and Pichegru's portraits hang in the royal ante-chamber. The former has a mean physiognomy; the latter has been a strong and stern-looking man. I looked at him, and thought of his death-struggles. In the guard-room were the heroes of La Vendeé, Charette with his white bonnet, the two La Roche Jacquelins, l'Escures, in an attitude of prayer, Stof-flet, the gamekeeper, with others.

"*November* 3.— Sat to Mad. Mirbel — Spencer at breakfast. Went out and had a long interview with Marshal Macdonald, the purport of which I have put down elsewhere. Visited Princess Galitzin, and also Cooper, the American novelist. This man, who has shown so much genius, has a good deal of the manners, or want of manners, peculiar to his countrymen. He proposed to me a mode of publish-ing in America, by entering the book as the property of a citizen. I will think of this. Every little helps, as the tod says, when, &c. At night, at the Theatre de Madame, where we saw two petit pieces, *Le Mar-riage de Raison,* and *Le plus beau jour de Ma Vie* —both excellently played. Afterwards, at Lady Granville's rout, which was as splendid as any I ever saw — and I have seen *beaucoup dans ce genre.* A great number of ladies of the first rank were present, and if honeyed words from pretty lips could surfeit, I had enough of them. One can swallow a great deal of whipped cream, to be sure, and it does not hurt an old stomach.

" *November* 4.—After ten I went with Anne to the Tuileries, where we saw the royal family pass through the Glass Gallery as they went to chapel. We were ver much looked at in our turn, and the King, on passing out, did me the honour to say a few civil words, which produced a great sensation. Mad. la Dauphine and Mad. de Berri curtsied, smiled, and looked extremely gracious; and smiles, bows, and curtsies rained on us like odours, from all the courtiers and ladies of the train. We were conducted by an officer of the Royal Gardes du Corps to a convenient place in the chapel, where we had the pleasure of hearing the mass performed with excellent music.

" I had a perfect view of the royal family. The King is the same in age as I knew him in youth at Holyroodhouse,—debonair and courteous in the highest degree. Mad. Dauphine resembles very much the prints of Marie Antoinette, in the profile especially. She is not, however, beautiful, her features being too strong, but they announce a great deal of character, and the Princess whom Buonaparte used to call the *man* of the family. She seemed very attentive to her devotions. The Duchess of Berri seemed less immersed in the ceremony, and yawned once or twice. She is a lively-looking blonde—looks

as if she were good-humoured and happy, by no
means pretty, and has a cast with her eyes; splendidly
adorned with diamonds, however. After this, gave
Mad. Mirbel a sitting, where I encountered a general officer, her uncle, who was chef de l'etat major
to Buonaparte. He was very communicative, and
seemed an interesting person, by no means over much
prepossessed in favour of his late master, whom he
judged impartially, though with affection. We came
home and dined in quiet, having refused all tempta-
tions to go out in the evening; this on Anne's account as well as my own. It is not quite gospel,
though Solomon says it — The eye *can* be tired with
seeing, whatever he may allege in the contrary. And
then there are so many compliments. I wish for a
little of the old Scotch causticity. I am something
like the bee that sips treacle.

" *November* 5. — I believe I must give up my
journal till I leave Paris. The French are literally
outrageous in their civilities — bounce in at all hours,
and drive one half mad with compliments. I am
ungracious not to be so entirely thankful as I ought
to this kind and merry people. We breakfasted with
Mad. Mirbel, where were the Dukes of Fitz-James
and Duras, &c. &c.; goodly company — but all's one
for that. I made rather an impatient sitter, wishing
to talk much more than was agreeable to Madame.

Afterwards we went to the Champs Elysées, where a balloon was let off, and all sorts of frolics performed for the benefit of the *bons gens de Paris* — besides stuffing them with victuals. I wonder how such a civic festival would go off in London or Edinburgh, or especially in Dublin. To be sure, they would not introduce their shilelahs! But, in the classic taste of the French, there were no such gladiatorial doings. To be sure, they have a natural good-humour and gaiety which inclines them to be pleased with themselves, and everything about them. We dined at the Ambassador's, where was a large party, Lord Morpeth, the Duke of Devonshire, and others — all very kind. Pozzo di Borgo there, and disposed to be communicative. A large soirée. Home at eleven These hours are early, however.

" *November* 6. — Cooper came to breakfast, but we were *obsedés partout*. Such a number of French men bounced in successively, and exploded (I mean discharged) their compliments, that I could hardly find an opportunity to speak a word, or entertain Mr Cooper at all. After this we sat again for our por-- traits. Mad. Mirbel took care not to have any one to divert my attention, but I contrived to amuse myself with some masons finishing a façade opposite to me, who placed their stones, not like Inigo Jones, but in the most lubberly way in the world, with the

help of a large wheel, and the application of strength
of hand.   John Smith of Darnick, and two of his
men, would have done more with a block and pulley
than the whole score of them.   The French seem
far behind in machinery.   We are almost eaten up
with kindness, but that will have its end.   I have had
to parry several presents of busts, and so forth.   The
funny thing was the airs of my little friend.   We had
a most affectionate parting — wet, wet cheeks on the
lady's side.   Pebble-hearted, and shed as few tears as
Crab of doggish memory.*

" Went to Galignani's, where the brothers, after
some palaver, offered £105 for the sheets of Napoleon, to be reprinted at Paris in English.   I told them
I would think of it.   I suppose Treuttel and Würtz
had apprehended something of this kind, for they write
me that they had made a bargain with my publisher
(Cadell, I suppose) for the publishing of my book in
all sorts of ways.   I must look into this.

" Dined with Marshal Macdonald† and a splendid
party ; amongst others, Marshal Marmont — middle
size, stout made, dark complexion, and looks sensible.
The French hate him much for his conduct in 1814,
but it is only making him the scape-goat.   Also I

* See the *Two Gentlemen of Verona*, *Act II. Scene 3.*

† The Marshal had visited Scotland in 1825 — and the Diarist
then saw a good deal of him under the roof of his kinsman, Mr
Macdonald Buchanan.

saw Mons. de Molé, but especially the Marquis de Lauriston, who received mé most kindly. He is personally like my cousin Colonel Russell. I learned that his brother, Louis Law,* my old friend, was alive, and the father of a large family. I was most kindly treated, and had my vanity much flattered by the men who had acted such important parts talking to me in the most frank manner.

" In the evening to Princess Galitzin, where were a whole covey of Princesses of Russia arrayed in *tartan*, with music and singing to boot. The person in whom I was most interested was Mad. de Boufflers, upwards of eighty, very polite, very pleasant, and with all the acquirements of a French court lady of the time of Mad. Sevigné, or of the correspondent rather of Horace Walpole. Cooper was there, so the Scotch and American lions took the field together.— Home, and settled our affairs to depart.

---

* Lauriston, the ancient seat of the Laws, so famous in French history, is very near Edinburgh, and the estate was in their possession at the time of the Revolution. Two or three cadets of the family were of the first emigration, and one of them (M. Louis Law) was a frequent guest of the poet's father, and afterwards corresponded during many years with himself. I am not sure whether it was M. Louis Law whose French designation so much amused the people of Edinburgh. One brother of the Marquis de Lauriston, however, was styled *Le Chevalier de Mutton-hole* — this being the name of a village on the Scotch property.

"*November* 7.—Off at seven—breakfasted at Beauvais, and pushed on to Amiens. This being a forced march, we had bad lodgings, wet wood, uncomfortable supper, damp beds, and an extravagant charge. I was never colder in my life than when I waked with the sheets clinging around me like a shroud.

"*November* 8.—We started at six in the morning, having no need to be called twice, so heartily was I weary of my comfortless couch. Breakfasted at Abbeville—then pushed on to Boulogne, expecting to find the packet ready to start next morning, and so to have had the advantage of the easterly tide. But, lo ye! the packet was not to sail till next day. So, after shrugging our shoulders—being the solace *à la mode de France*—and recruiting ourselves with a pullet and a bottle of Chablis *à la mode d'Angleterre,* we set off for Calais after supper, and it was betwixt three and four in the morning before we got to Dessein's, when the house was full, or reported to be so. We could only get two wretched brick-paved garrets, as cold and moist as those of Amiens, instead of the comforts which we were received with at our arrival.* But I was better prepared. Stripped

---

* A room in Dessein's hotel is now inscribed " Chambre de Walter Scott "— another has long been marked " Chambre de Sterne."

off the sheets, and lay down in my dressing-gown, and so roughed it out—*tant bien que mal.*

" *November 9.*— At four in the morning we were called—at six we got on board the packet, where I found a sensible and conversible man, a very pleasant circumstance. At Dover Mr Ward came with the lieutenant-governor of the castle, and wished us to visit that ancient fortress. I regretted much that our time was short, and the weather did not admit of our seeing views, so we could only thank the gentlemen in declining their civility. The castle, partly ruinous, seems to have been very fine. The Cliff, to which Shakspeare gave his immortal name, is, as all the world knows, a great deal lower than his description implies. Our Dover friends, justly jealous of the reputation of their Cliff, impute this diminution of its consequence to its having fallen in repeatedly since the poet's time. I think it more likely that the imagination of Shakspeare, writing perhaps at a period long after he may have seen the rock, had described it such as he conceived it to have been. Besides, Shakspeare was born in a flat country, and Dover Cliff is at least lofty enough to have suggested the exaggerated features to his fancy. At all events, it has maintained its reputation better than the Tarpeian Rock—no man could leap from it and live. Left Dover after a hot luncheon about four o'clock, and reached London at half-past three in the morning. So adieu to *la belle France*, and welcome merry England.

" *Pall - Mall, November* 10. — Ere I leave *la belle France*, however, it is fit I should express my gratitude for the unwontedly kind reception which I met with at all hands. It would be an unworthy piece of affectation did I not allow that I have been pleased — highly pleased — to find a species of literature intended only for my own country, has met such an extensive and favourable reception in a foreign land, where there was so much *à priori* to oppose its progress. For my work I think I have done a good deal; but, above all, I have been confirmed strongly in the impressions I had previously formed of the character of Nap., and may attempt to draw him with a firmer hand.

" The succession of new people and unusual incidents has had a favourable effect on my mind, which was becoming rutted like an ill-kept highway. My thoughts have for sometime flowed in another and pleasanter channel than through the melancholy course into which my solitary and deprived state had long driven them, and which gave often pain to be endured without complaint, and without sympathy. ' For this relief,' as Marcellus says in Hamlet, ' much thanks.'

" To-day I visited the public offices, and prosecuted my researches. Left enquiries for the Duke of York, who has recovered from a most desperate state. His legs had been threatened with mortification; but he was saved by a critical discharge;— also visited the Duke of Wellington, Lord Melville, and others, besides the ladies in Piccadilly. Dined and spent the evening quietly in Pall-Mall.

" *November* 11.—Croker came to breakfast, and we were soon after joined by Theodore Hook, *alias (on dit)* John Bull —he has got as fat as the actual monarch of the herd. Lockhart sat still with us, and we had, as Gil Blas says, a delicious morning, spent in abusing our neighbours, at which my three neighbours are no novices any more than I am myself, though (like Puss in Boots, who only caught mice for his amusement) I am only a chamber counsel in matters of scandal. The fact is, I have refrained, as much as human frailty will permit, from all satirical composition. Here is an ample subject for a little black-balling in the case of Joseph Hume, the great accountant, who has managed the Greek loan so egregiously. I do not lack personal provocation (see 13th March last), yet I won't attack him — at present at least—but *qu'il se garde de moi :*

> ' I'm not a king, nor nae sic thing,
> My word it may not stand;

> But Joseph may a buffet bide,
> Come he beneath my brand.'

" At dinner we had a little blow-out on Sophia's part. Lord Dudley, Mr Hay, Under Secretary of State, Sir Thomas Lawrence, &c. *Mistress*, as she now calls herself, Joanna Baillie, and her sister, came in the evening. The whole went off pleasantly.

" *November* 12.—Went to sit to Sir T. L. to finish the picture for his Majesty, which every one says is a very fine one. I think so myself; and wonder how Sir Thomas has made so much out of an old weather-beaten block. But I believe the hard features of old Dons like myself are more within the compass of the artist's skill than the lovely face and delicate complexion of females. Came home after a heavy shower. I had a long conversation about * * with * * * *—all that was whispered is true —a sign how much better our domestics are acquainted with the private affairs of our neighbours than we are. A dreadful tale of incest and seduction, and nearly of blood also — horrible beyond expression in its complications and events — ' And yet the end is not;' — and this man was amiable, and seemed the soul of honour—laughed, too, and was the soul of society. It is a mercy our own thoughts are concealed from each other. Oh! if, at our social table we could see what passes in each bosom around, we would seek dens and caverns to shun human society! To see the projector trembling for his falling speculations—the voluptuary rueing the event of his debauchery—the miser wearing out his soul for the loss of a guinea,—all—all bent upon vain hopes and vainer regrets,—we should not need to go to the hall of the Caliph Vathek to see men's hearts broiling under their black veils. Lord keep us from all temptation, for we cannot be our own shepherd!

" We dined to-day at Lady Stafford's, at Westhill. Lord S. looks very poorly, but better than I expected. No company, excepting Sam Rogers and Mr Thomas Grenville, a very amiable and accomplished man whom I knew better about twenty years since. Age has touched him, as it has doubtless affected me. The great lady received us with the most cordial kindness, and expressed herself, I am sure sincerely, desirous to be of service to Sophia.

" *November* 13.—I consider Charles's business as settled by a private intimation which I had to that effect from Sir W. K., so I need negotiate no farther, but wait the event. Breakfasted at home, and somebody with us, but the whirl of visits so great that I have already forgot the party. Lockhart and I dined at an official person's, where there was a little too much of that sort of flippant wit, or rather smartness, which becomes the parochial Joe Miller of boards and offices. You must not be grave, because it might lead to improper discussions; and to laugh without a joke is a hard task. Your professed wags are treasures to this species of company. Gil Blas was right in eschewing the literary society of his friend Fabricio; but nevertheless one or two of the mess could greatly have improved the conversation of his *Commis.* Went to poor Lydia White's, and found her extended on a couch, frightfully swelled, unable to stir, rouged, jesting, and dying. She has a good heart, and is really a clever creature, but unhappily, or rather happily, she has set up the whole staff of her rest in keeping literary society about her. The world has not neglected her. It is not always so bad as it is called. She can always make up her circle, and generally has some people of real talent and distinction. She is wealthy, to be sure, and gives petit dinners, but not in a style to carry the point *à force d'argent.* In her case the world is good-natured, and, perhaps it is more frequently so than is generally supposed.

" *November* 14.—We breakfasted at honest Allan Cunningham's—honest Allan—a leal and true Scotsman of the old cast. A man of genius, besides, who only requires the tact of knowing when and where to stop, to attain the universal praise which ought to follow it. I look upon the alteration of ' It's hame and it's hame,' and ' A wet sheet and a flowing sea,' as among the best songs going. His prose has often admirable passages ; but he is obscure, and overlays his meaning, which will not do now-a-days, when he who runs must read.

" Dined at Croker's, at Kensington, with his family, the Speaker,* and the facetious Theodore Hook.

" We came away rather early, that Anne and I might visit Mrs Arbuthnot to meet the Duke of Wellington. In all my life I never saw him better. He has a dozen of campaigns in his body—and tough ones. Anne was delighted with the frank manners of this unequalled pride of British war, and me he received with all his usual kindness. He talked away about Buonaparte, Russia, and France.

" *November* 15.—I went to the Colonial Office, where I laboured hard. Dined with the Duke of Wellington. Anne could not look enough at the *vainqueur du vainqueur de la terre.* The party were Mr and Mrs Peel and Mr and Mrs Arbuthnot, Vesey Fitzgerald, Banks, and Croker, with Lady Bathurst and Lady Georgina. One gentleman took much of the conversation, and gave us, with unnecessary emphasis, and at superfluous length, his opinion of a late gambling transaction. This spoiled the evening. I

* The Right Honourable Sir Charles Manners Sutton, now Viscount Canterbury.—[1839.]

am sorry for the occurrence though, for Lord * * * is fetlock deep in it, and it looks like a vile bog. This misfortune, with the foolish incident at * * *, will not be suffered to fall to the ground, but will be used as a counterpoise to the Greek loan. Peel asked me, in private, my opinion of three candidates for the Scotch gown, and I gave it him candidly. We shall see if it has weight.* I begin to tire of my gaieties ; and the late hours and constant feasting disagree with me. I wish for a sheep's-head and whisky-toddy against all the French cookery and champaign in the world. Well, I suppose I might have been a Judge of Session by this time—attained, in short, the grand goal proposed to the ambition of a Scottish lawyer. It is better, however, as it is, while, at least, I can maintain my literary reputation.

" *November* 16.—Breakfasted with Rogers, with my daughters and Lockhart. R. was exceedingly entertaining, in his dry, quiet, sarcastic manner. At eleven to the Duke of Wellington, who gave me a bundle of remarks on Buonaparte's Russian campaign, written in his carriage during his late mission to St Petersburgh. It is furiously scrawled, and the Russian names hard to distinguish, but it *shall* do me yeoman's service. Thence I passed to the Colonial

---

* Sir Walter's early friend Cranstoun was placed on the Scotch Bench, as Lord Corehouse, in 1826.

Office, where I concluded my extracts. Lockhart and I dined with Croker at the Admiralty *au grand couvert*. No less than five Cabinet Ministers were present—Canning, Huskisson, Melville, Peel, and Wellington, with sub-secretaries by the bushel. The cheer was excellent, but the presence of too many men of distinguished rank and power always freezes the conversation. Each lamp shines brightest when placed by itself; when too close, they neutralize each other.*

" *November* 17.—Sir John Malcolm at breakfast. Saw the Duke of York. The change on H. R. H. is most wonderful. From a big, burly, stout man, with a thick and sometimes an inarticulate mode of speaking, he has sunk into a thin-faced, slender-looking old man, who seems diminished in his very size. I could hardly believe I saw the same person, though I was received with his usual kindness. He speaks much more distinctly than formerly; his complexion is clearer; in short, H. R. H. seems, on the whole, more healthy after this crisis than when in the stall-fed state, for such it seemed to be, in which I remember him, God grant it !—his life is of infinite value to the King and country—it is a breakwater behind the throne.

* In returning from this dinner Sir Walter said, " I have seen some of these great men at the same table *for the last time.*"

" *November* 18.—Was introduced by Rogers to Mad. D'Arblay, the celebrated authoress of Evelina and Cecilia—an elderly lady, with no remains of personal beauty, but with a simple and gentle manner, a pleasing expression of countenance, and apparently quick feelings. She told me she had wished to see two persons—myself, of course, being one, the other George Canning. This was really a compliment to be pleased with—a nice little handsome pat of butter made up by a ' neat-handed Phillis'* of a dairy-maid, instead of the grease, fit only for cart-wheels, which one is dosed with by the pound.

" Mad. D'Arblay told us that the common story of Dr Burney, her father, having brought home her own first work, and recommended it to her perusal, was erroneous. Her father was in the secret of Evelina being printed. But the following circumstances may have given rise to the story:—Dr Burney was at Streatham soon after the publication, where he found Mrs Thrale recovering from her confinement, low at the moment, and out of spirits. While they were talking together, Johnson, who sat beside in a kind of reverie, suddenly broke out—' You should read this new work, madam—you should read Evelina ; every one says it is excellent, and they are right.' The delighted father obtained a commission from Mrs

* Milton's *L'Allegro.*

Thrale to purchase his daughter's work, and retired the happiest of men. Mad. D'Arblay said she was wild with joy at this decisive evidence of her literary success, and that she could only give vent to her rapture by dancing and skipping round a mulberry-tree in the garden. She was very young at this time. I trust I shall see this lady again.

" Dined at Mr Peel's with Lord Liverpool, Duke of Wellington, Croker, &c. The conversation very good, Peel taking the lead in his own house, which he will not do elsewhere. . . . . Should have been at the play, but sat too long at Peel's. So ends my campaign amongst these magnificoes and ' potent seigniors,'* with whom I have found, as usual, the warmest acceptation.

" *November* 20.—I ended this morning my sittings to Lawrence, and am heartily sorry there should be another picture of me except that which he has finished. The person is remarkably like, and conveys the idea of the stout blunt carle that cares for few things, and fears nothing. He has represented the author as in the act of composition, yet has effectually discharged all affectation from the manner and attitude. He dined with us at Peel's yesterday, where, by the way, we saw the celebrated Chapeau de Paille, which is not a Chapeau de Paille

* *Othello.*

at all.   I also saw this morning the Duke of Wellington and the Duke of York; the former so communicative, that I regretted extremely the length of time,* but have agreed on a correspondence with him. *Trop d'honneur pour moi.* The Duke of York seems still mending, and spoke of state affairs as a high Tory.   Were his health good, his spirit is as strong as ever.   H. R. H. has a devout horror of the Liberals.   Having the Duke of Wellington, the Chancellor, and (perhaps) a still greater person on his side, he might make a great fight when they split, as split they will.   But Canning, Huskisson, and a mitigated party of Liberaux, will probably beat them.   Canning's wit and eloquence are almost invincible.   But then the Church, justly alarmed for their property, which is plainly struck at, and the bulk of the landed interest, will scarce brook even a mild infusion of Whiggery into the Administration. Well, time will show.

" We visited our friends Peel, Lord Gwydir, Mr Arbuthnot, &c. and left our tickets of adieu.   In no instance, during my former visits to London, did I ever meet with such general attention and respect on all sides.

" Lady Louisa Stuart dined—also Wright and Mr and Mrs Christie.   Dr and Mrs Hughes came

* Sir Walter no doubt means that he regretted not having seen the Duke at an earlier period of his historical labours.

in the evening; so ended pleasantly our last night in London.

" *Oxford, November* 20.—Left London after a comfortable breakfast, and an adieu to the Lockhart family. If I had had but comfortable hopes of their poor, pale, prostrate child, so clever and so interesting, I should have parted easily on this occasion; but these misgivings overcloud the prospect. We reached Oxford by six o'clock, and found Charles and his friend young Surtees waiting for us, with a good fire in the chimney, and a good dinner ready to be placed on the table. We had struggled through a cold, sulky, drizzly day, which deprived of all charms even the beautiful country near Henley. So we came from cold and darkness into light, and warmth, and society.—*N. B.* We had neither daylight nor moon-light to see the view of Oxford from the Maudlin Bridge, which I used to think one of the most beautiful in the world.

" The expense of travelling has mounted high. I am too old to rough it, and scrub it, nor could I have saved fifty pounds by doing so. I have gained, however, in health and spirits, in a new stock of ideas, new combinations, and new views. My self-consequence is raised, I hope not unduly, by the many flattering circumstances attending my reception in the two capitals, and I feel confident in propor-

tion.   In Scotland I shall find time for labour and
for economy.

" *Cheltenham, November* 21.—Breakfasted with
Charles in his chambers at Brazen-nose, where he
had everything very neat.   How pleasant it is for a
father to sit at his child's board! It is like the aged
man reclining under the shadow of the oak which
he has planted.   My poor plant has some storms to
undergo, but were this expedition conducive to no
more than his entrance into life under suitable aus-
pices, I should consider the toil and the expense well
bestowed. We then sallied out to see the lions. Remembering the ecstatic feelings with which I visited
Oxford more than twenty-five years since, I was
surprised at the comparative indifference with which
I revisited the same scenes.   Reginald Heber, then
composing his Prize Poem, and imping his wings
for a long flight of honourable distinction, is now
dead in a foreign land—Hodgson * and other able
men all entombed.   The towers and halls remain,
but the voices which fill them are of modern days.
Besides, the eye becomes saturated with sights, as
the full soul loathes the honeycomb.   I admired indeed, but my admiration was void of the enthusiasm which I formerly felt.   I remember particularly

* Dr Frodsham Hodgson, the late excellent Master of Brazen-
nose College.

having felt, while in the Bodleian, like the Persian
magician who visited the enchanted library in the
bowels of the mountain, and willingly suffered himself
to be enclosed in its recesses, while less eager sages
retired in alarm. Now I had some base thoughts
concerning luncheon, which was most munificently
supplied by Surtees, at his rooms in University College, with the aid of the best ale I ever drank in my
life, the real wine of Ceres, and worth that of Bac-
chus. Dr Jenkyns,* the vice-chancellor, did me the
honour to call, but I saw him not. Before three set
out for Cheltenham, a long and uninteresting drive,
which we achieved by nine o'clock. My sister-in-
law, Mrs Thomas Scott, and her daughter, instantly
came to the hotel, and seem in excellent health and
spirits.

" *November* 22. — Breakfasted and dined with
Mrs Scott, and leaving Cheltenham at seven, pushed
on to Worcester to sleep. — *Nov.* 23. Breakfasted at
Birmingham and slept at Macclesfield. As we came
in between ten and eleven, the people of the inn
expressed surprise at our travelling so late, as the
general distress of the manufacturers has rendered
many of the lower classes desperately outrageous. —
Nov. 24. Breakfasted at Manchester — pressed on —

* Dr Richard Jenkyns, Master of Balliol College

and by dint of exertion reached Kendal to sleep; thus getting out of the region of the stern, sullen, unwashed artificers, whom you see lounging sulkily along the streets in Lancashire. God's justice is requiting, and will yet farther requite, those who have blown up this country into a state of unsubstantial opulence, at the expense of the health and morals of the lower classes.

" *Abbotsford, November* 26.— Consulting my purse, found my good £60 diminished to Quarter less Ten. In purse, £8. Naturally reflected how much expense has increased since I first travelled.. My uncle's servant, during the jaunts we made together while I was a boy, used to have his option of a shilling per diem for board wages, and usually preferred it to having his charges borne. A servant now-a-days, to be comfortable on the road, should have 4s. or 4s. 6d. board wages, which before 1790 would have maintained his master. But if this be pitiful, it is still more so to find the alteration in my own temper. When young, on returning from such a trip as I have just had, my mind would have loved to dwell on all I had seen that was rich and rare, or have been placing, perhaps, in order, the various additions with which I had supplied my stock of information—and now, like a stupid boy blundering over an arithmetical question half obliterated on his slate, I go stumbling on upon the audit of pounds, shillings, and pence. Well,—the skirmish has cost me £200. I wished for information—and I have had to pay for it."——

On proceeding to Edinburgh to resume his official duties, Sir Walter established himself in a furnished house in Walker Street, it being impossible for him to leave his daughter alone in the country, and the aspect of his affairs being so much ameliorated that he did not think it necessary to carry the young lady to such a place as Mrs Brown's lodgings. During the six ensuing months, however, he led much the same life of toil and seclusion from company which that of Abbotsford had been during the preceding autumn—very rarely dining abroad, except with one or two intimate friends, *en famille*—still more rarely receiving even a single guest at home; and, when there was no such interruption, giving his night as well as his morning to the desk.*

* Here ended the 6th Volume of the First Edition.

CHAPTER LXXIII.

*Life of Napoleon, and Chronicles of the Canongate
in progress —Reviewals of Mackenzie's Edition
of Home, and of Hoffman's Tales—Rheumatic
attacks — Theatrical Fund Dinner — Avowal
of the sole Authorship of the Waverley Novels —
Letter from Goethe — Reply — Deaths of the
Duke of York, Mr Gifford, Sir George Beaumont, &c.—Mr Canning Minister—Completion
of the Life of Buonaparte—Reminiscences of an
Amanuensis—Goethe's Remarks on the Work
— its pecuniary results.*

DEC. 1826 — JUNE 1827.

DURING the winter of 1826-7, Sir Walter suffered
great pain (enough to have disturbed effectually any
other man's labours, whether official or literary) from
successive attacks of rheumatism, which seems to
have been fixed on him by the wet sheets of one of

his French inns; and his Diary contains, besides, various indications that his constitution was already shaking under the fatigue to which he had subjected it. Formerly, however great the quantity of work he put through his hands, his evenings were almost always reserved for the light reading of an elbow-chair, or the enjoyment of his family and friends. Now he seemed to grudge every minute that was not spent at the desk. The little that he read of new books, or for mere amusement, was done by snatches in the course of his meals; and to walk, when he could walk at all, to the Parliament House, and back again through the Prince's Street Gardens, was his only exercise and his only relaxation. Every ailment, of whatever sort, ended in aggravating his lameness; and, perhaps, the severest test his philosophy encountered was the feeling of bodily helplessness that from week to week crept upon him. The winter, to make bad worse, was a very cold and stormy one. The growing sluggishness of his blood showed itself in chilblains, not only on the feet but the fingers, and his handwriting becomes more and more cramped and confused. I shall not pain the reader by extracting merely medical entries from his Diary; but the following give characteristic sketches of his temperament and reflections :—

" *December* 16.—Another bad night. I remember

I used to think a slight illness was a luxurious thing. My pillow was then softened by the hand of affection, and the little cares put in exercise to soothe the languor or pain, were more flattering and pleasing than the consequences of the illness were disagreeable. It was a new scene to be watched and attended, and I used to think that the *malade imaginaire* gained something by his humour. It is different in the latter stages — the old post-chaise gets more shattered and out of order at every turn; windows will not be pulled up, doors refuse to open, or being open will not shut again — which last is rather my case. There is some new subject of complaint every moment — your sicknesses come thicker and thicker — your comforting and sympathizing friends fewer and fewer — for why should they sorrow for the course of nature? The recollection of youth, health, and uninterrupted powers of activity, neither improved nor enjoyed, is a poor strain of comfort. The best is, the long halt will arrive at last, and cure all. This was a day of labour, agreeably varied by a pain which rendered it scarce possible to sit upright. My journal is getting a vile chirurgical aspect. I begin to be afraid of the odd consequences complaints in the *post equitem* are said to produce. I shall tire of my journal. In my better days I had stories to tell; but death has closed the long dark avenue upon loves and friendships, and I look at them as through the grated door of a burial-place filled with monuments of those who were once dear to me, with no insincere wish that it may open for me at no distant period, provided such be the will of God. My pains were those of the heart, and had something flattering in their character; if in the head, it was from the blow of a bludgeon gallantly received, and well paid back. I think I shall not live to the usual verge of human existence; I shall never see the threescore and ten, and shall be summed up at a discount. No help for it, and no matter either.

" *December* 18. — Sir Adam Fergusson breakfasted — one of the few old friends left out of the number of my youthful companions. In youth, we have many companions, few friends perhaps; in age, companionship is ended, except rarely, and by appointment. Old men, by a kind of instinct, seek younger associates, who listen to their stories, honour their grey hairs while present, and mimic and laugh at them when their backs are turned. At least that was the way in our day, and I warrant our chicks of the present brood crow to the same tune. Of all the friends that I have left here, there is none who has any decided attachment to literature. So either I must talk on that subject to young people — in other words, turn proser — or I must turn tea-table talker and converse with ladies. I am too old and too proud for either character, so I'll live alone and be contented.   Lockhart's departure for London was a loss to me in this way."

He spent a few days at Abbotsford at Christmas, and several weeks during the spring vacation; but the frequent Saturday excursions were now out of the question — if for no other reason, on account of the quantity of books which he must have by him while working at his Napoleon.   He says on the 30th of December — " Wrote hard.   Last day of an eventful year; much evil — and some good, but especially the courage to endure what Fortune sends without becoming a pipe for her fingers.*   It is *not* the last day of the year; but to-morrow being Sunday, we hold our festival to-day. — The Fergussons came, and we had the usual appliances of mirth and good cheer.   Yet our party, like the chariot-wheels of Pharoah in the Red Sea, dragged heavily. — It must be allowed that the regular recurrence of annual festivals among the same individuals has, as life advances, something in it that is melancholy.   We meet like the survivors of some perilous expedition, wounded and weakened ourselves, and looking through diminished ranks to think of those who are no more.   Or they are like the feasts of the Caribs,

* *Hamlet, Act III. Scene. 2.*

in which they held that the pale and speechless phantoms of the deceased appeared and mingled with the living. Yet where shall we fly from vain repining?—or why should we give up the comfort of seeing our friends, because they can no longer be to us, or we to them, what we once were to each other?

" *January* 1, 1827.—God make this a happy new year to the King and country, and to all honest men.

" I went to dine as usual at the kind house of Huntly-Burn; but the cloud still had its influence. The effect of grief upon persons who, like myself and Sir Adam, are highly susceptible of humour, has, I think, been finely touched by Wordsworth in the character of the merry village teacher Matthew, whom Jeffrey profanely calls " a half crazy sentimental person."* But, with my friend Jeffrey's pardon, I think he loves to see imagination best when it is bitted and managed, and ridden upon the *grand pas.* He does not make allowance for starts and sallies, and bounds, when Pegasus is beautiful to behold, though sometimes perilous to his rider. Not that I think the amiable bard of Ryedale shows judgment in choosing such subjects as the popular

* See *Edinburgh Review*, No. xxiii. p. 135.

mind cannot sympathize in. It is unwise and unjust
to himself. I do not compare myself, in point of
imagination, with Wordsworth—far from it; for
his is naturally exquisite, and highly cultivated from
constant exercise. But I can see as many castles in
the clouds as any man, as many genii in the curling
smoke of a steam-engine, as perfect a Persepolis in
the embers of a sea-coal fire. My life has been spent
in such day-dreams. But I cry no roast-meat. There
are times a man should remember what Rousseau
used to say, *Tais-toi, Jean Jacques, car on ne t'en-
tend pas!*

" Talking of Wordsworth, he told Anne a story,
the object of which, as she understood it, was to
show that Crabbe had no imagination. Crabbe, Sir
George Beaumont, and Wordsworth, were sitting
together in Murray's room in Albemarle Street. Sir
George, after sealing a letter, blew out the candle
which had enabled him to do so, and exchanging a
look with Wordsworth, began to admire in silence
the undulating thread of smoke which slowly arose
from the expiring wick, when Crabbe put on the
extinguisher. Anne laughed at the instance, and enquired if the taper was wax, and being answered in
the negative, seemed to think that there was no call
on Mr Crabbe to sacrifice his sense of smell to their
admiration of beautiful and evanescent forms. In
two other men I should have said, ' Why it is affec-

tations,' with Sir Hugh Evans;* but Sir George is the man in the world most void of affectation; and then he is an exquisite painter, and no doubt saw where the *incident* would have succeeded in painting. The error is not in you yourself receiving deep impressions from slight hints, but in supposing that precisely the same sort of impression must arise in the mind of men, otherwise of kindred feeling, or that the common-place folk of the world can derive such inductions at any time or under any circumstances.

" *January* 13.—The Fergussons, with my neighbours Mr Scrope and Mr Bainbridge, ate a haunch of venison from Drummond Castle, and seemed happy. We had music and a little dancing, and enjoyed in others the buoyancy of spirit that we no longer possess ourselves. Yet I do not think the young people of this age so gay as we were. There is a turn for persiflage, a fear of ridicule among them, which stifles the honest emotions of gaiety and lightness of spirit; and people, when they give in the least to the expansion of their natural feelings, are always kept under by the fear of becoming ludicrous. To restrain your feelings and check your enthusiasm in the cause even of pleasure, is now a rule among

* *Merry Wives of Windsor, Act I. Scene* 1.

people of fashion, as much as it used to be among philosophers.

"*Edinburgh, January* 15.—Off we came, and in despite of rheumatism I got through the journey tolerably.   Coming through Galashiels, we met the Laird of Torwoodlee, who, on hearing how long I had been confined, asked how I bore it, observing that he had *once* in his life—Torwoodlee must be between sixty and seventy—been confined for five days to the house, and was like to hang himself.   I regret God's free air as much as any man, but I could amuse myself were it in the Bastile.

"*February* 19.—Very cold weather.   What says Dean Swift?—

> ' When frost and snow come both together,
> Then sit by the fire and save shoe leather.

I read and wrote at the bitter account of the French retreat from Moscow, in 1812, till the little room and coal fire seemed snug by comparison.   I felt cold in its rigour in my childhood and boyhood, but not since.   In youth and middle life I was yet less sensible to it than now—but I remember thinking it worse than hunger.   Uninterrupted to-day, and did eight leaves.*

---

* One page of his MS. answers to from four to five of the close-printed pages of the original edition of his Buonaparte.

" *March* 3.—Very severe weather, and home covered with snow. White as a frosted plum-cake. by jingo. No matter; I am not sorry to find I can stand a brush of weather yet. I like to see Arthur's Seat and the stern old Castle with their white watchcloaks on. But, as Byron said to Moore, d——n it, Tom, don't be poetical I settled to Boney, and wrote right long and well.

" *Abbotsford, March* 12.—Away we set, and came safely to Abbotsford amid all the dulness of a great thaw, which has set the rivers a streaming in full tide. The wind is high, but for my part

' I like this rocking of the battlements.' *

I was received by old Tom and the dogs with the unsophisticated feelings of good-will. I have been trying to read a new novel which I had heard praised. It is called *Almacks*, and the author has so well succeeded in describing the cold selfish fopperies of the time, that the copy is almost as dull as the original. I think I shall take up my bundle of Sheriff-Court processes instead of Almacks, as the more entertaining avocation of the two.

" *March* 13.—Before breakfast, prepared and forwarded the processes to Selkirk. Had a pleasant

* Zanga, in " *The Revenge,*" *Act I. Scene* 1.

walk to the thicket, though my ideas were olla-podrida-ish. I expect this will not be a day of work but of idleness, for my books are not come. Would to God I could make it light, thoughtless idleness, such as I used to have when the silly smart fancies ran in my brain like the bubbles in a glass of champaign—as brilliant to my thinking, as intoxicating, as evanescent. But the wine is somewhat on the lees. Perhaps it was but indifferent cyder after all. Yet I am happy in this place, where everything looks friendly from old Tom to young Nym.[*] After all, he has little to complain of who has left so many things that like him.

" *March* 21.——Wrote till twelve, then out upon the heights, though the day was stormy, and faced the gale bravely. Tom Purdie was not with me. He would have obliged me to keep the sheltered ground. There is a touch of the old spirit in me yet, that bids me brave the tempest—the spirit that, in spite of manifold infirmities, made me a roaring boy in my youth, a desperate climber, a bold rider, a deep drinker, and a stout player at single-stick, of all which valuable qualities there are now but slender remains. I worked hard when I came in, and finished five pages.

" *March* 26.——Despatched packets Colonel and

* Nimrod — a stag-hound.

Captain Fergusson arrived to breakfast. I had previously determined to give myself a day to write letters; and this day will do as well as another. I cannot keep up with the world without shying a letter now and then. It is true, the greatest happiness I could think of would be to be rid of the world entirely. Excepting my own family, I have little pleasure in the world, less business in it, and am heartily careless about all its concerns.

" *April* 24.— Still deep snow — a foot thick in the court-yard, I daresay. Severe welcome for the poor lambs now coming into the world. But what signifies whether they die just now, or a little while after to be united with sallad at luncheon time ? It signifies a good deal too. There is a period, though a short one, when they dance among the gowans, and seem happy. As for your aged sheep or wether, the sooner they pass to the *Norman* side of the vocabulary, the better. They are like some old dowager ladies and gentlemen of my acquaintance—no one cares about them till they come to be *cut up*, and then we see how the tallow lies on the kidneys and the chine.

" *May* 13.— A most idle and dissipated day. I did not rise till half-past eight o'clock. Col. and Capt. Fergusson came to breakfast. I walked half-

way home with them, then turned back and spent the
day, which was delightful, wandering from place to
place in the woods, sometimes reading the new and
interesting volumes of *Cyril Thornton*, sometimes
' chewing the cud of sweet and bitter fancies' which
alternated in my mind, idly stirred by the succession
of a thousand vague thoughts and fears, the gay
strangely mingled with those of dismal melancholy;
tears which seemed ready to flow unbidden; smiles
which approached to those of insanity; all that wild
variety of mood which solitude engenders. I scrib-
bled some verses, or rather composed them in my
memory. The contrast at leaving Abbotsford to
former departures, is of an agitating and violent description. Assorting papers, and so forth. I never
could help admiring the concatenation between Ahi-
thophel's setting his house in order and hanging himself.* The one seems to follow the other as a matter
of course. But what frightens and disgusts me is
those fearful letters from those who have been long
dead, to those who linger on their wayfare through
the valley of tears. Those fine lines of Spencer came
into my head —

> " The shade of youthful Hope is there,
>   That lingered long, and latest died;
>   Ambition all dissolved to air,
>   With phantom Honours by his side.

---

* 2d Sam. xvii. 23.

> " What empty shadows glimmer nigh?
>   They once were Friendship, Truth, and *Love* !
>   Oh die to thought, to memory die,
>   Since lifeless to my heart ye prove." *

Ay, and can I forget the Author—the frightful moral of his own vision? What is this world?—a dream within a dream: as we grow older, each step is an awakening. The youth awakes, as he thinks, from childhood—the full-grown man despises the pursuits of youth as visionary—the old man looks on manhood as a feverish dream. The grave the last sleep? No; it is the last and final awakening.

" *Edinburgh, May* 15.—It is impossible not to compare this return to Edinburgh with others in more happy times. But we should rather recollect under what distress of mind I took up my lodgings in Mrs Brown's last summer.—Went to Court and resumed old habits. Heard the true history of ———.† Imagination renders us liable to be the victims of occasional low spirits. All belonging to this gifted, as it is called, but often unhappy class, must have felt, that but for the dictates of religion, or the na-

---

* Poems by the late Honourable W. R. Spencer, London, 1835, p. 45. See *ante*, p. 29.

† Sir Walter had this morning heard of the suicide of a man of warm imagination, to whom, at an earlier period, he was much attached.

tural recoil of the mind from the idea of dissolution, there have been times when they would have been willing to throw away life as a child does a broken toy. I am sure I know one who has often felt so. O God! what are we?— Lords of nature?— Why, a tile drops from a house-top, which an elephant would not feel more than the fall of a sheet of pasteboard, and there lies his lordship. Or something of inconceivably minute origin—the pressure of a bone, or the inflamation of a particle of the brain—takes place, and the emblem of the Deity destroys himself or some one else. We hold our health and our reason on terms slighter than one would desire, were it in their choice, to hold an Irish cabin."

These are melancholy entries. Most of those from which they have been selected begin with R. for Rheumatism, or R.R. for Rheumatism Redoubled, and then mark the number of leaves sent to James Ballantyne—the proof-sheets corrected for press— or the calculations on which he reluctantly made up his mind to extend the life of Buonaparte from six to seven, from seven to eight, and finally from eight to nine thick and closely printed volumes.

During the early months of 1827, however, he executed various minor tracts also: for the Quarterly Review, an article on Mackenzie's Life and Works of John Home, author of Douglas, which is, in fact,

a rich chapter of Scott's own early reminiscences,
and gives many interesting sketches of the literary
society of Scotland in the age of which Mackenzie
was the last honoured relic; * and for the Foreign
Review, then newly started under the editorship of
Mr R. P. Gillies, an ingenious and elaborate paper
on the writings of the German Novelist Hoffman.†
This article, it is proper to observe, was a benefaction to Mr Gillies, whose pecuniary affairs rendered
such assistance very desirable.   Scott's generosity in
this matter—for it was exactly giving a poor brother
author £100 at the expense of considerable time and
drudgery to himself—I think it necessary to mention; the date of the exertion requires it of me.   But
such, in fact, had been in numberless instances his
method of serving literary persons, who had little or
no claim on him, except that they were of that class.
I have not conceived it delicate to specify many instances of this kind; but I am at liberty to state,
that when he wrote his first article for the Encyclo-
pædia Supplement, and the Editor of that work, Mr
Macvey Napier (a Whig in politics, and with whom
he had hardly any personal acquaintance), brought
him £100 as his remuneration, Sir Walter said—
" Now tell me frankly, if I don't take this money,
does it go into your pocket or your publisher's, for it

* See Miscellaneous Prose Works, vol. xix. p. 283.
† *Ibid.* vol. xviii. p. 270.

is impossible for me to accept a penny of it from a literary brother." Mr Napier assured him that the arrangements of the work were such, that the Editor had nothing to do with the fund destined for contributions:—Scott then pocketed his due, with the observation, that " he had trees to plant, and no conscience as to the purse of his fat friend"—to wit, Constable.

At this period, Sir Walter's Diary very seldom mentions anything that could be called a dinner-party. He and his daughter partook generally once in every week the family meal of Mr and Mrs Skene; and they did the like occasionally with a few other old friends, chiefly those of the Clerks' table. When an exception occurs, it is easy to see that the scene of social gaiety was doubly grateful from its rarity. Thus one entry, referring to a party at Mr J. A. Murray's,* says—" Went to dine with John Murray, where met his brother (Henderland), Jeffrey, Cockburn, Rutherford, and others of that file. Very pleasant—capital good cheer and excellent wine—much laugh and fun. I do not know how it is, but when I am out with a party of my Opposition friends, the day is often merrier than when with our own set. Is it because they are cleverer? Jeffrey and Harry Cockburn are to be sure very extraordinary men; yet it is not owing to that entirely. I

* Afterwards Lord Advocate, and now a Judge of the Court of Session, by the title of Lord Murray.—[1839.]

believe both parties meet with the feeling of something like novelty. We have not worn out our jests in daily contact. There is also a disposition on such occasions to be courteous, and of course to be pleased."

Another evening, spent in Rose Court with his old friend, Mr Clerk, seems to have given him especial delight. He says—" This being a blank day at the Court, I wrote hard till dressing time, when I went to Will Clerk's to dinner. As a bachelor, and keeping a small establishment, he does not do these things often, but they are proportionally pleasant when they come round. He had trusted Sir Adam to bespeak his dinner, who did it *con amore*, so we had excellent cheer, and the wines were various and capital. As I before hinted, it is not every day that M'Nab mounts on horseback,* and so our landlord had a little of that solicitude that the party should go off well, which is very flattering to the guests. We had a very pleasant evening. The Chief Commissioner was there, Admiral Adam, J. A. Murray, Tom Thomson, &c. &c.—Sir Adam predominating at the head, and dancing what he calls his merry-andrada in great style. In short, we really laughed, and real

---

* That singular personage, the late M'Nab of *that ilk*, spent his life almost entirely in a district where a boat was the usual conveyance. I suspect, however, there is an allusion to some particular anecdote which I have not recovered.

laughter is a thing as rare as real tears. I must say, too, there was a *heart*, a kindly feeling prevailed over the party. Can London give such a dinner?—it may, but I never saw one—they are too cold and critical to be easily pleased.——I hope the Banna-tyne Club will be really useful and creditable. Thomson is superintending a capital edition of Sir James Melville's Memoirs. It is brave to see how he wags his Scots tongue, and what a difference there is in the form and firmness of the language, compared to the mincing English edition in which he has hitherto been alone known."

No wonder that it should be a sweet relief from Buonaparte and Blucher to see M'Nab on horseback, and Sir Adam Fergusson in his merry-andrada ex altation, and laugh over old Scotch stories with the Chief-Commissioner, and hear Mr Thomas Thomson report progress as to the doings of the Bannatyne Club. But I apprehend every reader will see that Sir Walter was misled by his own modesty, when he doubted whether London could afford symposia of the same sort. He forgets that he had never mixed in the society of London except in the capacity of a stranger, a rare visiter, the unrivalled literary marvel of the time, and that every party at which he dined was got up expressly on his account, and constituted, whoever might be the landlord, on the natural prin-ciple of bringing together as many as the table could hold—to see and hear Sir Walter Scott. Hence, if he dined with a Minister of State, he was likely to find himself seated with half the Cabinet—if with a Bishop, half the Bench had been collected. As a matter of course, every man was anxious to gratify on so rare an occasion as many as he could of those who, in case they were uninvited, would be likely to reproach him for the omission. The result was a crowding together of too many rival eminences; and he very seldom, indeed, witnessed the delightful result so constantly produced in London by the intermingling of distinguished persons of various classes, full of facts and views new to each other—and neither chilled nor perplexed by the pernicious and degrading trickery of lionizing. But, besides, it was unfair to institute any comparison between the society of comparative strangers and that of old friends dear from boyhood. He could not have his Clerks and Fergussons both in Edinburgh and in London. Enough, however, of commentary on a very plain text.

That season was further enlivened by one public dinner, and this, though very briefly noticed in Scott's Diary, occupied a large space in public attention at the time, and, I believe I may add, several columns in every newspaper printed in Europe. His good friend William Murray, manager of the Edinburgh Theatre, invited him to preside at the first festival of a charitable fund then instituted for the behoof of decayed performers. He agreed, and says in his Journal—" There are 300 tickets given out. I fear it will be uncomfortable; and whatever the stoics may say, a bad dinner throws cold water on charity. I have agreed to preside—a situation in which I have been rather felicitous, not by much superiority of art or wisdom, far less of eloquence; but by two or three simple rules, which I put down here for the benefit of my posterity :—

" 1st, Always hurry the bottle round for five or six rounds, without prosing yourself, or permitting others to prose. A slight fillip of wine inclines people to be pleased, and removes the nervousness which prevents men from speaking—disposes them, in short, to be amusing and to be amused.

" 2d, Push on, keep moving, as Young Rapid says.* Do not think of saying fine things—nobody cares for them any more than for fine music, which is often too liberally bestowed on such occasions.— Speak at all ventures, and attempt the *mot pour rire.* You will find people satisfied with wonderfully indifferent jokes, if you can but hit' the taste of the company, which depends much on its character. Even a very high party, primed with all the cold irony and *non est tanti* feelings or no feelings of fashionable folks, may be stormed by a jovial, rough, round, and ready preses. Choose your text with discretion —

* Morton's comedy of *A Cure for the Heart-Ache.*

the sermon may be as you like.   Should a drunkard or an ass break in with anything out of joint, if you can parry it with a jest, good and well—if not, do not exert your serious authority, unless it is something very bad.   The authority even of a chairman ought to be very cautiously exercised.   With patience you will have the support of every one.

" 3*dly*, When you have drunk a few glasses to play the good-fellow, and banish modesty—(if you are unlucky enough to have such a troublesome companion)—then beware of the cup too much.   Nothing is so ridiculous as a drunken preses.

" *Lastly*, always speak short, and *Skeoch doch na skiel*—cut a tale with a drink.

> ' This is the purpose and intent
> Of gude Schir Walter's testament.' *

This dinner took place on Friday the 23d February. Sir Walter took the chair, being supported by the Earl of Fife, Lord Meadowbank, Sir John Hope of Pinkie, Admiral Adam, Robert Dundas of Arniston, *Peter* Robertson, and many other personal friends. Lord Meadowbank had come on short notice, and was asked abruptly on his arrival to take a toast which had been destined for a noble person who had not

---

* Sir Walter parodies the conclusion of King Robert the Bruce's " Maxims, or Political Testament." See Hailes's Annals, A. D 1311,— or Fordun's Scoti-chronicon,—XII. 10.

been able to appear.   He knew that this was the first
public dinner at which the object of this toast had appeared since his misfortunes, and taking him aside in
the anteroom, asked him whether he would consider
it indelicate to hazard a distinct reference to the pa-
rentage of the Waverley Novels, as to which there
had, in point of fact, ceased to be any obscurity from
the hour of Constable's failure.   Sir Walter smiled,
and said, " Do just as you like—only don't say much
about so old a story."— In the course of the evening
the Judge rose accordingly, and said—*

" I would beg leave to propose a toast — the health of one of
the Patrons — a great and distinguished individual, whose name
must always stand by itself, and which, in an assembly such as
this, or in any other assembly of Scotsmen, must ever be received,
I will not say with ordinary feelings of pleasure or of delight, but
with those of rapture and enthusiasm. In doing this I feel that I
stand in a somewhat new situation. Whoever had been called
upon to propose the health of my Hon. Friend some time ago,
would have found himself enabled, from the mystery in which
certain matters were involved, to gratify himself and his auditors
by allusions sure to find a responding chord in their own feelings,
and to deal in the language, the sincere language, of panegyric,
without intruding on the modesty of the great individual to whom
I refer. But it is no longer possible, consistently with the respect
due to my auditors, to use upon this subject terms either of mys-

---

* By the favour of a friend, who took notes at this dinner, I
am enabled to give a better report of these speeches than that of
the contemporary newspapers.

tification, or of obscure or indirect allusion. The clouds have been dispelled — the *darkness visible* has been cleared away — and the Great Unknown — the minstrel of our native land — the mighty magician who has rolled back the current of time, and conjured up before our living senses the men and the manners of days which have long passed away, stands revealed to the eyes and the hearts of his affectionate and admiring countrymen. If I were capable of imagining all that belongs to this mighty subject — were I able to give utterance to all that as a man, as a Scotsman, and as a friend, I must feel regarding it, yet knowing, as I well do, that this illustrious individual is not more distinguished for his towering talents, than for those feelings which render such allusions ungrateful to himself, however sparingly introduced, I would on that account still refrain from doing what would otherwise be no less pleasing to myself than to those who hear me. But this I hope I may be allowed to say — (my auditors would not pardon me were I to say less) — we owe to him, as a people, a large and heavy debt of gratitude. He it is who has opened to foreigners the grand and characteristic beauties of our country. It is to him that we owe that our gallant ancestors and illustrious patriots — who fought and bled in order to obtain and secure that independence and that liberty we now enjoy — have obtained a fame no longer confined to the boundaries of a remote and comparatively obscure country — it is *He* who has called down upon their struggles for glory and freedom the admiration of foreign lands. He it is who has conferred a new reputation on our national character, and bestowed on Scotland an imperishable name, were it only by her having given birth to himself. I propose the health of Sir Walter Scott."

Long before Lord Meadowbank ceased speaking, the company had got upon chairs and tables, and the storm of applause that ensued was deafening. When they recovered from the first fever of their raptures, Sir Walter spoke as follows :—

" I certainly did not think, in coming here to-day, that I should have the task of acknowledging, before 300 gentlemen, a secret which, considering that it was communicated to more than twenty people, has been remarkably well kept. I am now at the bar of my country, and may be understood to be on trial before Lord Meadowbank as an offender; and so quietly did all who were *airt and pairt* conduct themselves, that I am sure that, were the *panel* now to stand on his defence, every impartial jury would bring in a verdict of *Not Proven*. I am willing, however, to plead *guilty* — nor shall I detain the Court by a long explanation why my confession has been so long deferred. Perhaps caprice might have a considerable share in the matter. I have now to say, however, that the merits of these works, if they had any, and their faults, are all entirely imputable to myself. Like another Scottish criminal of more consequence, one Macbeth,

> ' I am afraid to think what I have done ;
> Look on't again I dare not.'

" I have thus far unbosomed myself, and I know that my confession will be reported to the public. I mean, then, seriously to state, that when I say I am the author, I mean the total and undivided author. With the exception of quotations, there is not a single word that was not derived from myself, or suggested in the course of my reading. The wand is now broken, and the book buried. You will allow me further to say, with Prospero, it is your breath that has filled my sails, and to crave one single toast in the capacity of the author of these novels. I would fain dedicate a bumper to the health of one who has represented several of those characters, of which I had endeavoured to give the skeleton, with a truth and liveliness for which I may well be grateful.　I beg leave to propose the health of my friend Bailie Nicol Jarvie —and I am sure, that when the author of Waverley and Rob Roy drinks to Nicol Jarvie, it will be received with the just applause to which that gentleman has always been accustomed,—nay, that you will take care that on the present occasion it shall be PRO— DI—GI—OUS!" (Long and vehement applause.)

MR MACKAY.—" My conscience! My worthy father the deacon could never have believed that his son would hae sic a compliment paid to h:m by the Great Unknown!"

SIR WALTER SCOTT. — " The Small Known now, Mr Bailie." &c. &c.

Shortly after resuming his chair, Sir Walter (I am told) sent a slip of paper to Mr Robertson, begging him to " confess something too,—why not the murder of Begbie?" (See *ante*, Vol. IV. p. 70.) But if Peter complied with the hint, it was long after the senior dignitaries had left the room.

The " sensation" produced by this scene was, in newspaper phrase, " unprecedented." Sir Walter's Diary merely says—" *February* 24. I carried my own instructions into effect the best I could, and if our jests were not good, our laughter was abundant. I think I will hardly take the chair again when the company is so miscellaneous; though they all behaved perfectly well. Meadowbank taxed me with the novels, and to end that farce at once, I pleaded guilty; so that splore is ended. As to the collection—it has been much cry and little woo, as the deil said when he shore the sow. I got away at ten at night. The performers performed very like gentlemen, especially Will Murray.——*March* 2.—Clerk walked home with me from the Court. I was scarce able to keep up with him; could once have done it well enough. Funny thing at the Theatre last night. Among the discourse in High Life below Stairs, one of the ladies' ladies asks who wrote Shakspeare. One says, ' Ben Jonson ;' another, ' Finis.' ' No,' said Will Murray,* ' it is Sir Walter Scott; he confessed it at a public meeting the other day.'"

The reader may, perhaps, expect that I should endeavour to name the " upwards of twenty persons' whom Sir Walter alluded to on this occasion as having been put into the secret of the Waverley Novels, previously, and without reference, to the catastrophe of 1826. I am by no means sure that I can give the complete list: but in addition to the immediate members of the author's own family — (including his mother and his brother Thomas) — there were Constable, Cadell, the two Ballantynes, — two persons employed in the printing-office, namely Daniel M'Corkindale and Daniel Robertson — Mr Terry, Mr Laidlaw, Mr Train, and Mr. G. H. Gordon; Charles Duke of Buccleuch, Lady Louisa Stuart, Lord Montagu, Lord and Lady Polwarth, Lord

---

* For *W. Murray*, read *Jones.* — *Note by Mr Andrew Short-rede.*—[1839.]

Kinnedder, Sir Adam Fergusson, Mr. Morritt, Mr and Mrs Skene, Mr William Clerk, Mr. Hay Donaldson, Mr Thomas Shortreed, Mr John Richardson, and Mr Thomas Moore.

The entries in Scott's Diary on contemporary literature are at this time very few; nor are there many on the public events of the day, though the period was a very stirring one. He seems, in fact, to have rarely seen, even when in town, any newspaper except the Edinburgh Weekly Journal. At his age, it is not wonderful that when that sheet reached him it for the most part contained the announcement of a death which interested his feelings; and several of the following passages refer to incidents of this melancholy class :—

"*January* 9.—This morning received the long-expected news of the Duke of York's death. I am sorry both on public and private accounts. His R. H. was, while he occupied the situation of next in succession, a *Breakwater* behind the throne. I fear his brother of Clarence's opinions may be different, and that he may hoist a standard under which men of desperate hopes and evil designs will rendezvous. I am sorry, too, on my own account. The Duke of York was uniformly kind to me, and though I never tasked his friendship, yet I find a powerful friend is gone. His virtues were honour, good sense, integrity; and by exertion of these qualities, he raised the British army from a very low ebb to be the pride and dread of Europe. His errors were those of a sanguine and social temper—he could not resist the tempta tion of deep play, which was fatally allied with a disposition to the bottle. This last is incident to his complaint, which vinous influence soothes for the time, while it insidiously increases it in the end.

" *January* 17.—I observe in the papers my old friend Gifford's funeral. He was a man of rare attainments and many excellent qualities. His Juvenal is one of the best versions ever made of a classical author, and his satire of the Baviad and Mæviad squabashed at one blow a set of coxcombs, who might have humbugged the world long enough. As a commentator he was capital, could he but have suppressed his rancours against those who had preceded him in the task; but a misconstruction or misinterpretation, nay, the misplacing of a comma, was in Gifford's eyes a crime worthy of the most severe animadversion. The same fault of extreme severity went through his critical labours, and in general he flagellated with so little pity, that people lost their sense of the criminal's guilt in dislike of the savage pleasure which the executioner seemed to take in inflicting the punishment. This lack of temper probably arose from indifferent health, for he was very valetudinary, and realized two verses, wherein he says Fortune assigned him—

    ———— ' One eye not over good,
Two sides that to their cost have stood
    A ten years' hectic cough,
Aches, stitches, all the various ills
That swell the devilish doctor's bills,
    And sweep poor mortals off.'

But he might also justly claim, as his gift, the moral qualities expressed in the next fine stanza—

    ———————————— ' A soul
That spurns the crowd's malign control,
    A firm contempt of wrong;
Spirits above affliction's power,
And skill to soothe the lingering hour
    With no inglorious song.'

He was a little man, dumpled up together, and so ill made as to seem almost deformed, but with a singular expression of talent in his countenance. Though so little of an athlete, he nevertheless beat off Dr Wolcott, when that celebrated person, the most unsparing calumniator of his time, chose to be offended with Gifford for satirizing him in his turn. Peter Pindar made a most vehement attack, but Gifford had the best of the affray,* and remained, I think, in tri-

* See Epistle to Peter Pindar, Gifford's *Baviad and Mæviad,*
pp. 181–191, ed. 1812.

umphant possession of the field of action, and of the assailant's cane.   G. had one singular custom.   He used always to have a duenna of a housekeeper to sit in his study with him while he wrote.   This female companion died when I was in London, and his distress was extreme.   I afterwards heard he got her place supplied.   I believe there was no scandal in all this.

" This is another vile day of darkness and rain, with a heavy yellow mist that might become Charing Cross—one of the benefits of our extended city; for that in our atmosphere was unknown till the extent of the buildings below Queen Street.

" *January* 28.—Hear of Miss White's death. Poor Lydia! she gave a dinner on the Friday before, and had written with her own hand invitations for another party.   Twenty years ago she used to tease me with her youthful affectations—her dressing like the Queen of Chimney-sweeps on May-day morning, &c.; and sometimes with letting her wit run wild. But she *was* a woman of wit, and had a feeling and kind heart.   Poor Lydia! I saw the Duke of York and her in London, when Death, it seems, was brandishing his dart over them.

' The view o't gave them little fright.' *

---

* Burns's ' Twa Dogs.'

" *February* 10.—I got a present of Lord Francis Gower's printed but unpublished Tale of the Mill. It is a fine tale of terror in itself, and very happily brought out. He has certainly a true taste for poetry. I do not know why, but from my childhood I have seen something fearful, or melancholy at least, about a mill. Whether I had been frightened at the machinery when very young, of which, I think, I have some shadowy remembrance—whether I had heard the stories of the Miller of Thirlestane, and similar molendinar tragedies, I cannot tell; but not even recollections of the Lass of Patie's Mill, or the Miller of Mansfield, or ' he who dwelt on the river Dee,' have ever got over my inclination to connect gloom with a mill, especially when the sun is setting. So I entered into the spirit of the terror with which Lord Francis has invested his haunted spot.

" *February* 14.—' Death's gi'en the art an unco devel.' * Sir George Beaumont's dead; by far the most sensible and pleasing man I ever knew—kind, too, in his nature, and generous—gentle in society, and of those mild manners which tend to soften the causticity of the general London tone of persiflage and personal satire. As an amateur painter, he was

---

* " Death's gi'en the lodge an unco devel,
  Tam Sampson's dead."—*Burns.*

of the very highest distinction; and though I know nothing of the matter, yet I should hold him a perfect critic on painting, for he always made his criticisms intelligible, and used no slang. I am very sorry—as much as it is in my nature to be for one whom I could see but seldom. He was the great friend of Wordsworth, and understood his poetry, which is a rare thing, for it is more easy to see his peculiarities than to feel his great merit, or follow his abstract ideas.

" A woman of rather the better class, a farmer's wife, was tried a few days ago for poisoning her maid-servant. There seems to have been little doubt of her guilt; but the motive was peculiar. The unfortunate girl had an intrigue with her son, which this Mrs Smith (I think that is the name) was desirous to conceal, from some ill-advised Puritanic notions, and also for fear of her husband. She could find no better way of hiding the shame than giving the girl (with her own knowledge and consent, I believe) potions to cause abortion, which she afterwards changed for arsenic, as the more effectual silencing medicine. In the course of the trial one of the jury fell down in an epileptic fit, and on his recovery was far too much disordered to permit the trial to proceed. With only fourteen jurymen, it was impossible to go on. The Advocate says she shall be tried anew, since she has not *tholed ane assize*. *Sic Paulus ait*

.—*et recte quidem.* But, having been half-tried, I think she should have some benefit of it, as far as saving her life, if convicted on the second indictment. Lord Advocate declares, however, that she shall be hanged, as certainly she deserves. Yet it looks something like hanging up a man who has been recovered by the surgeons, which has always been accounted harsh justice.

" *February* 20.—At Court, and waited to see the poisoning woman tried. She is clearly guilty, but as one or two witnesses said the poor wench hinted an intention to poison herself, the jury gave that bastard verdict, *Not proven.* I hate that Caledonian *medium quid.* One who is not *proved guilty*, is innocent in the eyes of law. It was a face to do or die, or perhaps to do to die. Thin features, which had been handsome, a flashing eye, an acute and aquiline nose, lips much marked as arguing decision, and I think, bad temper — they were thin, and habitually compressed, rather turned down at the corners, as one of a rather melancholy disposition. There was an awful crowd; but, sitting within the bar, I had the pleasure of seeing much at my ease; the constables knocking the other folks about, which was of course very entertaining.

" I have a letter from Baron von Goethe, which I must have read to me; for though I know Ger-

man, I have forgot their written hand. I make it a
rule seldom to read, and never to answer foreign letters from literary folks. It leads to nothing but the
battledore and shuttle-cock intercourse of compliments, as light as cork and feathers. But Goethe
is different, and a wonderful fellow — the Ariosto at
once, and almost the Voltaire of Germany. Who
could have told me thirty years ago I should corre-
spond and be on something like an equal footing with
the author of the Goetz?   Ay, and who could have
told me fifty things else that have befallen me ?"

Goethe's letter (as nearly as the Editor can render
it) runs thus : —

" *To Sir Walter Scott, Bart., Edinburgh.*

"Weimar, January 12th, 1827.

Mr H——, well known to me as a collector of
objects of art, has given me a likeness, I hope authentic and accurate, of the late Lord Byron, and it
awakens anew the sorrow which I could not but feel
for the loss of one whom all the world prized, and I
in particular : since how could I fail to be delighted
with the many expressions of partiality for me which
his writings contain ?

" Meantime the best consolation for us, the survivors, is to look around us, and consider, that as

the departed is not *alone*, but has joined the noble spiritual company of high-hearted men, capable of love, friendship, and confidence, that had left this sphere before him, so we have still kindred spirits on earth, with whom, though not visible any more than the blessed shades of past ages, we have a right to feel a brotherlike connexion—which is indeed our richest inheritance.

" And so, as Mr H—— informs me he expects to be soon in Edinburgh, I thus acquit myself, mine honoured sir, of a duty which I had long ago felt to be incumbent on me—to acknowledge the lively interest I have during many years taken in your wonderful pictures of human life. I have not wanted external stimulants enough to keep my attention awake on this subject, since not only have translations abounded in the German, but the works are largely read here in the original, and valued according as different men are capable of comprehending their spirit and genius.

" Can I remember that such a man in his youth made himself acquainted with my writings, and even (unless I have been misinformed) introduced them in part to the knowledge of his own nation, and yet defer any longer, at my now very advanced years, to express my sense of such an honour? It becomes me, on the contrary, not to lose the opportunity now offered of praying for a continuance of your kindly regard, and telling you how much a direct assurance of good-will from your own hand would gratify my old age.

" With high and grateful respect I salute you,

J. W. v. GOETHE."

This letter might well delight Scott. Goethe, in writing soon afterwards to his friend Mr Thomas Carlyle (the translator of the Wilhelm Meister), described the answer as " cheering and warm-hearted."

" *To the Baron von Goethe, &c. &c., Weimar.*

·' Venerable and much respected Sir,

" I received your highly-valued token of esteem by Mr H——, and have been rarely so much gratified as by finding that any of my productions have been fortunate enough to attract the attention of Baron von Goethe, of whom I have been an admirer ever since the year 1798, when I became a little acquainted with the German language : and soon after gave an example at once of my good taste and consummate assurance, by an attempt to translate Goetz of Berlichingen,— entirely forgetting that it is necessary not only to be delighted with a work of genius, but to be well acquainted with the language in which it is written, before we attempt to communicate its beauty to others.   I still set a value on my early translation, however, because it serves to show that I knew at least how to select an object worthy of admiration, although, from the terrible blunders into which I fell, from imperfect acquaintance with the language, it was plain I had not adopted the best way of expressing my admiration.

" I have heard of you often from my son-in-law Lockhart—I do not believe you have a more devout admirer than this young connexion of mine. My friend, Sir John Hope of Pinkie has had more lately the honour of seeing you; and I hoped to have written to you—indeed, *did* use that freedom—by two of his kinsmen who were to travel in Germany, but illness intervened and prevented their journey, and my letter was returned after it was two or three months old; — so that I had presumed to claim the acquaintance of Baron von Goethe even before the flattering notice which he has been pleased to bestow on me.   It gives to all admirers of genius and litera-ture delight, to know that one of the greatest Euro-pean models enjoys a happy and dignified retirement during an age which is so universally honoured and respected.   Fate destined a premature close to that of poor Lord Byron, who was cut off when his life was in the flower, and when so much was hoped and expected from him.   He esteemed himself, as I have reason to know, happy in the honour which you did him, and not unconscious of the obligations which he owed to ONE to whom all the authors of this generation have been so much obliged, that they are bound to look up to him with filial reverence.

" I have given another instance that, like other barristers, I am not encumbered with too much modesty, since I have entreated Messrs Treuttel and Würtz to find some means of conveying to you a hasty, and, of course, rather a tedious attempt to give an account of that remarkable person Napoleon, who had for so many years such a terrible influence in the world. I do not know but what I owe him some obligations, since he put me in arms for twelve years, during which I served in one of our corps of Yeomanry, and notwithstanding an early lameness, became a good horseman, a hunter, and a shooter. Of late these faculties have failed me a little, as the rheumatism, that sad torment of our northern climate, has had its influence on *my* bones. But I cannot complain, since I see my sons pursuing the sport I have given up. My eldest has a troop of Hussars, which is high in our army for a young man of twenty-five; my youngest son has just been made Bachelor of Arts at Oxford, and is returned to spend some months with me before going out into the world. God having been pleased to deprive me of their mother, my youngest daughter keeps my household in order, my eldest being married, and having a family of her own. Such are the domestic circumstances of the person you so kindly enquired after: for the rest, I have enough to live on in the way I like, notwithstanding some very heavy losses; and I have a stately antique chateau (modern antique), to which any friend of Baron von Goethe will be at all times most welcome, with an entrance hall filled with armour, which might have become Jaxthausen itself, and a gigantic blood-hound to guard the entrance.

" I have forgot, however, one who did not use to be forgotten when he was alive:—I hope you will forgive the faults of the composition, in consideration of the author's wish to be as candid toward the memory of this extraordinary man, as his own prejudices would permit. As this opportunity of addressing you opens suddenly by a chance traveller, and must be instantly embraced, I have not time to say more than to wish Baron von Goethe a continuance of health and tranquillity, and to subscribe myself, with sincerity and profound respect, his much honoured and obliged humble servant,

WALTER SCOTT." *

---

* I am indebted [1839] to the politeness of Goethe's accomplished friend Mrs Jameson for a copy of this hasty letter; and I may quote in connexion with it the following passage from that lady's *Winter Studies and Rambles in Canada* (1838), vol. i. p. 246:—" Everywhere Goethe speaks of Sir Walter Scott with the utmost enthusiasm of admiration, as the greatest writer of his time:

I now insert a few entries from Sir Walter's Diary, intermixed with extracts from his letters to myself and Mr Morritt, which will give the reader sufficient information as to the completion of his Life of Buonaparte, and also as to his impressions on hearing of the illness of Lord Liverpool, the consequent dissolution of the Cabinet, and the formation of a new Ministry under Mr Canning.

DIARY—" *February* 21. — Lord Liverpool is ill of an apoplexy. I am sorry for it. He will be missed. Who will be got for Premier? If Peel would consent to be made a peer, he would do; but I doubt his ambition will prefer the House of Commons. Wrought a good deal.

" *April* 16.—A day of work and exercise. In the evening a letter from L., with the wonderful news that the Ministry has broken up, and apparently for no cause that any one can explain. The old grudge, I suppose, which has gone on like a crack in the

---

he speaks of him as being without his *like*, as without his equal. I remember Goethe's daughter-in-law saying to me playfully— ' When my father got hold of one of Scott's romances, there was no speaking to him till he had finished the third volume; he was worse than any girl at a boarding-school with her first novel!'"

Mrs Jameson says—" All Goethe's family recollect the exceeding pleasure which Sir Walter's letter gave him."

side of a house, enlarging from day to day, till down goes the whole."

———————

" *To John Lockhart, Esq., Wimbledon.*

. . . . " Your letter has given me the vertigo—my head turns round like a chariot-wheel, and I am on the point of asking

' Why, how now? Am I Giles, or am I not?'

The Duke of Wellington out?—bad news at home, and worse abroad. Lord Anglesea in his situation? —does not much mend the matter. Duke of Clarence in the Navy?—wild work. Lord Melville, I suppose, falls of course—perhaps *cum totâ sequelâ,* about which *sequela,* unless Sir W. Rae and the Solicitor, I care little. The whole is glamour to one who reads no papers, and has none to read. I must get one, though, if this work is to go on, for it is quite bursting in ignorance. Canning is haughty and prejudiced—but, I think, honourable as well as able —*nous verrons.* I fear Croker will shake, and heartily sorry I should feel for that." . . . .

———————

DIARY—" *April* 25.—I have now got Boney pegg'd up in the knotty entrails of St Helena, and may make a short pause. So I finished the review of John Home's works, which, after all, are poorer than I thought them. Good blank verse, and stately sentiment, but something luke-warmish, excepting Douglas, which is certainly a masterpiece. Even that does not stand the closet. Its merits are for the stage; and it is certainly one of the best acting plays going. Perhaps a play to act well should not be too poetical.

" *April* 26.—The snow still profusely distributed, and the surface as our hair used to be in youth, after we had played at some active game, half black, half white, all in large patches. I finished the criticism on Home, adding a string of Jacobite anecdotes, like that which boys put to a kite's tail. Received a great cargo of papers from Bernadotte—some curious, and would have been inestimable two months back, but now my task is almost done. And then my feelings for poor Count Itterberg, the lineal and legitimate, make me averse to have much to do with this child of the revolution."

———————

" *To J. G. Lockhart, Esq.*

" April 26.

. . . . " The news you send is certainly the most wonderful of my time, in a party point of view, especially as I can't but think all has turned on personal likings and dislikings. I hope they won't let in the Whigs at the breach, for I suppose, if Lansdowne come in, he must be admitted with a tail on, and Lauderdale will have the weight in Scotland. How our tough Tories may like that, I wot not; but they will do much to keep the key of the corn-chest within reach. The Advocate has not used me extremely kindly, but I shall be sorry if he suffers in this State tempest. For me, I remain, like the Lilliputian poet—' In amaze—Lost I gaze'—or rather as some other bard sings—

> ' So folks beholding at a distance
> *Seven* men flung out of a casement,
> They never stir to their assistance,
> But just afford them their amazement.' *

—You ask why the wheels of Napoleon tarry; not by my fault, I swear;

> ' We daily are jogging,
> While whistling and flogging,
> While whistling and flogging,
> The coachman drives on,
> With a hey hoy, gee up gee ho,' &c. &c. &c.

To use a more classical simile—

---

* *Crazy Tales*, by John Hall Stevenson.

> ‘ Wilds immeasurably spread
> Seem lengthening as I go.’ *

I have just got some very curious papers from Sweden. I have wrought myself blind between writing and collating, and, except about three or four hours for food and exercise, I have not till to-day *devauled*† from my task. . . . .

> O, Boney, I’ll owe you a curse, if Hereafter
>   To my vision your tyrannous spectre shall show,
> But I doubt you’ll be pinned on old Nick’s reddest rafter,
>   While the vulgar of Tophet howl back from below. . . .

I shall, however, displease Ultras such as Croker, on the subject of Boney, who was certainly a great man, though far from a good man, and still farther from a good king. But the stupidest Roitelet in Europe has his ambition and selfishness, and where will you find his talents? I own I think Ultra-writing only disgusts people, unless it is in the way of a downright invective, and that in history you had much better keep the safe side, and avoid colouring too highly. After all, I suspect, were Croker in presence of Boney to-morrow, he might exclaim, as Captain T. did at one of the Elba levees, ‘ Well, Boney’s a d——d good fellow after all.’ ”

---

* Goldsmith’s *Hermit.*   † Anglice — *Ceased.*

" To the Same.

" Abbotsford, May 10, 1827.

. . . . . " To speak seriously of these political movements, I cannot say that I approve of the dissidents. I understand Peel had from the King *carte blanche* for an Anti-Catholic Administration, and that he could not accept it because there was not strength enough to form such. What is this but saying in plain words that the Catholics had the country and the Question? And because they are defeated in a single question, and one which, were it to entail no farther consequences, is of wonderfully little import, they have abandoned the King's service—given up the citadel because an exterior work was carried, and marched out into Opposition. I can't think this was right. They ought either to have made a stand without Canning, or a stand with him; for to abdicate as they have done was the way to subject the country to all the future experiments which this Catholic Emancipation may lead those that now carry it to attempt, and which may prove worse, far worse, than anything connected with the Question itself. Thus says the old Scotch Tory. But *I* for one do not believe it was the question of Emancipation, or any public question, which carried them out. I believe the predominant motive in the bosom of every one of them

was personal hostility to Canning; and that with more
prudence, less arbitrary manners, and more attention
to the feelings of his colleagues, he would have stepped
nem. con. into the situation of Prime Minister, for
which his eloquence and talent naturally point him
out. They objected to the man more than the statesman, and the Duke of Wellington, more frank than
the rest, almost owns that the quarrel was personal.
Now, acting upon that, which was, I am convinced,
the *real* ground, I cannot think the dissidents acted
well and wisely. It is very possible that they might
not have been able to go on with Canning; but I
think they were bound, as loyal subjects and patriots,
to ascertain that continuing in the Cabinet with him
as Premier was impossible, before they took a step
which may change the whole policy, perhaps even-
tually the whole destiny of the realm, and lead to the
prevalence of those principles which the dissidents
have uniformly represented as destructive to the interests of Britain. I think they were bound to have
made a trial before throwing Canning — and, alas!
both the King and the country — into the hand of the
Whigs. These are the sort of truths more visible
to the lookers-on than to those who play.

" As for Canning, with his immense talent, wit, and
eloquence, he unhappily wants prudence and patience,
and in his eager desire to scramble to the highest
point, is not sufficiently select as to his assistants.

The Queen's affair is an example of this — Lord Castlereagh's was another. In both he threw himself back by an over-eager desire to press forward, and something of the kind must have been employed now. It cannot be denied that he has placed himself (perhaps more from compulsion than choice) in a situation which greatly endangers his character. Still, however, he has that character to maintain, and unluckily it is all we have to rest upon as things go. The sons of Zeruiah would be otherwise too many for us.*   It is possible, though I doubt it, that the Whigs will be satisfied with their share of *orts* and *grains*, and content themselves with feeding out of the trough without overturning it. My feeling, were I in the House of Commons, would lead me to stand up and declare that I supported Canning so far, and so far only, as he continued to preserve and maintain the principles which he had hitherto professed — that my allegiance could not be irredeemably pledged to him, because his camp was filled with those against whom I had formerly waged battle under his command — that, however, it should not be mere apprehension of evil that would make me start off — reserving to myself to do what should be called for when the crisis arrived. I think, if a number of intelligent and able men were to hold by Canning on

* 2d Samuel, ii. 18.

these grounds, they might yet enable him to collect a Tory force around him, sufficient to check at least, if not on all points to resist the course of innovation. 'If my old friend is wise he will wish to organize such a force, for nothing is more certain than that if the champion of Anti-Jacobinism should stoop to become the tool of the Whigs, it is not all his brilliancy of talents, eloquence, and wit, which can support him in such a glaring want of consistency. *Meliora spero.* I do not think Canning can rely on his Whig confederates, and some door of reconciliation may open itself as unexpectedly as the present confusion has arisen."

DIARY — " *May* 11. — The boar of the Forest called this morning to converse about trying to get him on the pecuniary list of the Royal Literary Society. Certainly he deserves it, if genius and necessity can do so. But I do not belong to the society, nor do I propose to enter it as a coadjutor. I do not like your royal academies of this kind; they almost always fall into jobs, and the members are seldom those who do credit to the literature of a country. It affected, too, to comprehend those men of letters who are specially attached to the Crown, and though I love and honour my King as much as any of them can, yet I hold it best, in this free country, to preserve the exterior of independence, that my loyalty may be the more impressive, and tell more effectually. Yet I wish sincerely to help poor Hogg, and have written to Lockhart about it. It may be my own desolate feelings — it may be the apprehension of evil from this political hocus-pocus; but I have seldom felt more moody and uncomfortable than while writing these lines. I have walked, too, but without effect. W. Laidlaw, whose very ingenious mind is delighted with all novelties, talked nonsense about the new government, in which men are to resign principle, I fear, on both sides.

" Parliament House a queer sight. Looked as if people were singing to each other the noble song of ' The sky's falling — chickie diddle.' Thinks I to myself, I'll keep a calm sough.

> ' Betwixt both sides I unconcerned stand by —
> Hurt can I laugh, and harmless need I cry ? '

" *May* 15. — I dined at a great dinner given by Sir George Clerk to his electors, the freeholders of Mid-Lothian; a great attendance of Whig and Tory, huzzaing each other's toasts. *If* is a good peacemaker, but quarter-day is a better. I have a guess the best game-cocks would call a truce, if a handful or two of oats were scattered among them.

" *May* 27. — I got ducked in coming home from

the Court. Made a hard day of it. Scarce stirred from one room to another, but by bed-time finished a handsome handful of copy. I have quoted Gourgaud's evidence; I suppose he will be in a rare passion, and may be addicted to vengeance, like a long-moustached son of a French bitch as he is.

> ' Frenchman, Devil, or Don,
>   Damn him let him come on,
>   He shan't scare a son of the Island.' *

" *May* 28.—Another day of uninterrupted study; two such would finish the work with a murrain. What shall I have to think of when I lie down at night and awake in the morning? What will be my plague and my pastime—my curse and my blessing —as ideas come and the pulse rises, or as they flag and something like a snow-haze covers my whole imagination?—I have my Highland Tales—and then—never mind—sufficient for the day is the evil thereof.—Letter from John touching public affairs; don't half like them, and am afraid we shall have the Whig alliance turn out like the calling in of the Saxons. I told this to Jeffrey, who said they would convert us as the Saxons did the British. I shall die in my Paganism for one. I don't like a bone of them as a party. Ugly reports of the King's health; God

---

* Sir W. *varies* a verse of " *The tight little Island.*"

pity this poor country should that be so, but I hope it is a thing devised by the enemy.

" *June* 3.—Wrought hard.   I thought I had but a trifle to do, but new things cast up; we get beyond the Life, however, for I have killed him to-day.   The newspapers are very saucy; the *Sun* says I have got £4000 for suffering a Frenchman to look over my manuscript.   Here is a proper fellow for you!   I wonder what he thinks Frenchmen are made of— walking money bags, doubtless.   ' Now,' as Sir Fretful Plagiary says, ' another person would be vexed at this,' but I care not one brass farthing.

" *June* 5.—Proofs.   Parliament House till two. Commenced the character of Buonaparte.   To-morrow being a Teind-day, I may hope to get it finished.

" *June* 10.—Rose with the odd consciousness of being free of my daily task.   I have heard that the fish-women go to church of a Sunday with their creels new washed, and a few stones in them for ballast, just because they cannot walk steadily without their usual load.   I feel something like them, and rather inclined to take up some light task, than to be altogether idle. I have my proof-sheets, to be sure; but what are these to a whole day?   A good thought came in my head to write Stories for little Johnnie Lockhart, from the History of Scotland, like those taken from the History of England.   But I will not write mine quite so simply as Croker has done.*   I am persuaded both children and the lower class of readers hate books which are written *down* to their capacity, and love those that are composed more for their elders and betters.   I will make, if possible, a book that a child shall understand, yet a man will feel some temptation to peruse should he chance to take it up. It will require, however, a simplicity of style not quite my own.   The grand and interesting consists in ideas, not in words.   A clever thing of this kind might have a race."

* * *

" *To John B. S. Morritt, Esq., Portland Place, London.*

"Edinburgh, June 10, 1827.

" My Dear Morritt,

" Napoleon has been an absolute millstone about my neck, not permitting me for many a long day to

---

* The following note accompanied a copy of the First Series of the Tales of a Grandfather : —

" *To the Right Hon. J. W. Croker.*

" My Dear Croker, — I have been stealing from you, and as it seems the fashion to compound felony, I send you a sample of the *swag*, by way of stopping your mouth. . . . . Always yours, W. Scott."

think my own thoughts, to work my own work, or to write my own letters—which last clause of prohibition has rendered me thus long your debtor. I am now finished—*valeat quod valere potest*—and as usual not very anxious about the opinion of the public, as I have never been able to see that such anxiety has any effect in mollifying the minds of the readers, while it renders that of the author very uncomfortable—so *vogue la galère.*

" How are you, as a moderate pro-Catholic, satisfied with this strange alliance in the Cabinet ? I own I look upon it with doubt at best, and with apprehensions. At the same time I cannot approve of the late Ministers leaving the King's councils in such a hurry. They could hardly suppose that Canning's fame, talent, and firm disposition would be satisfied with less than the condition of Premier, and such being the case—

> ' To fly the boar before the boar pursued,
> Was to incense the boar to follow them.' *

On the other hand, his allying himself so closely and so hastily with the party against whom he had maintained war from youth to age seems to me, at this distance, to argue one of two things ;—either that the Minister has been hoodwinked by ambition and

* *King Richard III. Act III. Scene 2.*

anger — or that he looks upon the attachment of
those gentlemen to the opinions which he has always
opposed as so slight, unsubstantial, and unreal, that
they will not insist upon them, or any of them,
provided they are gratified personally with a certain
portion of the benefits of place and revenue. Now,
not being disposed to think over well of the Whigs,
I cannot suppose that a large class of British statesmen, not deficient certainly in talents, can be willing
to renounce all the political maxims and measures
which they have been insisting upon for thirty years,
merely to become placeholders under Canning. The
supposition is too profligate. But then, if they come
in the same Whigs we have known them, where,
how, or when are they to execute their favourite
notions of Reform of Parliament? and what sort of
amendments will they be which are to be brought
forward when the proper time comes? or how is
Canning to conduct himself when the Saxons, whom
he has called in for his assistance, draw out to fight
for a share of the power which they have assisted
him to obtain? When such strange and unwonted
bedfellows are packed up together, will they not kick
and struggle for the better share of the coverlid and
blankets? Perhaps you will say that I look gloomily
on all this, and have forgotten the way of the world,
which sooner or later shows that the principles of
statesmen are regulated by their advance towards, or

retreat from power; and that from men who are always acting upon the emergencies of the moment, it is in vain to expect consistency. Perfect consistency, I agree, we cannot look for—it is inconsistent with humanity. But that gross inconsistency which induces men to clasp to their bosom the man whom they most hated, and to hold up to admiration the principles which they have most forcibly opposed, may gain a temporary triumph, but will never found a strong Ministry or a settled Government. My old friend Canning, with his talents and oratory, ought not, I think, to have leagued himself with any party, but might have awaited, well assured that the general voice must have carried him into full possession of power. I am sorry he has acted otherwise, and argue no good from it, though when or how the evil is to come I cannot pretend to say.

" My best compliments wait on your fireside.—I conclude you see Lady Louisa Stuart very often, which is a happiness to be envied.

Ever yours, most kindly,

WALTER SCOTT."

I received, some years ago, from a very modest and intelligent young man, the late Mr Robert Hogg (a nephew of the Ettrick Shepherd), employed in 1827 as a *reader* in Ballantyne's printing-office, a letter for which this is perhaps the most proper place.

" *To J. G. Lockhart, Esq.*

" Edinburgh, 16th February 1833.

" Sir,

" Having been for a few days employed by Sir Walter Scott, when he was finishing his Life of Buonaparte, to copy papers connected with that work, and to write occasionally to his dictation, it may perhaps be in my power to mention some circumstances relative to Sir Walter's habits of composition, which could not full under the observation of any one except a person in the same situation with myself, and which are therefore not unlikely to pass altogether without notice.

" When, at Sir Walter's request, I waited upon him to be informed of the business in which he needed my assistance, after stating it, he asked me if I was an early riser, and added that it would be no great hardship for me, being a young man, to attend him the next morning at six o'clock. I was punctual, and found Sir Walter already busy writing. He appointed my tasks, and again sat down at his own desk. We continued to write during the regular work hours tlil six o'clock in the evening, without interruption, except to take breakfast and dinner, which were served in the room beside us, so that no time was lost;—we rose from our desks when everything was ready, and resumed our labours when the meals were over. I need not tell you, that during these intervals Sir Walter conversed with me as if I had been on a level of perfect equality with himself.

" I had no notion it was possible for any man to undergo the fatigue of composition for so long a time at once, and Sir Walter acknowledged he did not usually subject himself to so much exertion, though it seemed to be only the manual part of the operation that occasioned him any inconvenience. Once or twice he desired me to relieve him, and dictated while I wrote with as much rapidity as I was able. I have performed the same service to several other persons most of whom walked up and down the apartment while excogitating what was to be committed to writing; they sometimes stopt too, and, like those who fail in a leap and return upon their course to take the advantage of another race, endeavoured to hit upon something additional by perusing over my shoulder what was already set down, — mending a phrase, perhaps, or recasting a sentence, till they should recover their wind. None of these aids were necessary to Sir Walter: his thoughts flowed easily and felicitously, without any difficulty

to lay hold of them, or to find appropriate language;
which was evident by the absence of all solicitude
(miseria cogitandi) from his countenance. He sat
in his chair, from which he rose now and then, took
a volume from the bookcase, consulted it, and restored it to the shelf—all without intermission in
the current of ideas, which continued to be delivered
with no less readiness than if his mind had been
wholly occupied with the words he was uttering. It
soon became apparent to me, however, that he was
carrying on two distinct trains of thought, one of
which was already arranged, and in the act of being
spoken, while at the same time he was in advance
considering what was afterwards to be said. This
I discovered by his sometimes introducing a word
which was wholly out of place—*entertained* instead
of *denied*, for example,—but which I presently found
to belong to the next sentence, perhaps four or five
lines farther on, which he had been preparing at the
very moment that he gave me the words of the one
that preceded it. Extemporaneous orators of course,
and no doubt many writers, think as rapidly as was
done by Sir Walter; but the mind is wholly occupied with what the lips are uttering or the pen is
tracing. I do not remember any other instance in
which it could be said that two threads were kept
hold of at once—connected with each other indeed,
but grasped at different points. I was, as I have

said, two or three days beside Sir Walter, and had repeated opportunities of observing the same thing —I am, Sir, respectfully your obliged humble servant,   ROBERT HOGG."

The Life of Buonaparte, then, was at last published about the middle of June 1827. Two years had elapsed since Scott began it; but, by a careful comparison of dates, I have arrived at the conclusion that, his expeditions to Ireland and Paris, and the composition of novels and critical miscellanies being duly allowed for, the historical task occupied hardly more than twelve months. The book was closely printed; in fact, those nine volumes contain as much letter-press as Waverley, Guy Mannering, the Antiquary, the Monastery, and the Legend of Montrose, all put together. If it had been printed on the original model of those novels, the Life of Buonaparte would have filled from thirteen to fourteen volumes. —the work of one twelvemonth—done in the midst of pain, sorrow, and ruin.

The magnitude of the theme, and the copious detail with which it was treated, appear to have frightened the critics of the time. None of our great Reviews grappled with the book at all; nor am I so presumptuous as to undertake what they shrunk from.

The general curiosity with which it was expected, and the satisfaction with which high and candid minds perused it, cannot I believe be better described than in the words of the author's most illustrious literary contemporary.

" Walter Scott," says Goethe, " passed his childhood among the stirring scenes of the American War, and was a youth of seventeen or eighteen when the French Revolution broke out. Now well advanced in the fifties, having all along been favourably placed for observation, he proposes to lay before us his views and recollections of the important events through which he has lived. The richest, the easiest, the most celebrated narrator of the century, undertakes to write the history of his own time.

" What expectations the announcement of such a work must have excited in me, will be understood by any one who remembers that I, twenty years older than Scott, conversed with Paoli in the twentieth year of my age, and with Napoleon himself in the sixtieth.

" Through that long series of years, coming more or less into contact with the great doings of the world, I failed not to think seriously on what was passing around me, and, after my own fashion, to connect so many extraordinary mutations into something like arrangement and interdependence.

" What could now be more delightful to me, than leisurely and calmly to sit down and listen to the discourse of such a man, while clearly, truly, and with all the skill of a great artist, he recalls to me the incidents on which through life I have meditated, and the influence of which is still daily in operation? " — *Kunst und Altherthum*.

The lofty impartiality with which Scott treats the

personal character of Buonaparte was, of course, sure to make all ultra-politicians at home and abroad condemn his representation; and an equally general and better founded exception was taken to the lavish imagery of his historical style. He despised the former clamour—to the latter he bowed submissive. He could not, whatever character he might wish to assume, cease to be one of the greatest of poets. Metaphorical illustrations, which men born with prose in their souls hunt for painfully, and find only to murder, were to him the natural and necessary offspring and playthings of ever-teeming fancy. He could not write a note to his printer—he could not speak to himself in his Diary—without introducing them. Few will say that his historical style is, on the whole, excellent; none that it is perfect; but it is completely unaffected, and therefore excites nothing of the unpleasant feeling with which we consider the elaborate artifices of a far greater historian—the greatest that our literature can boast—Gibbon. The rapidity of the execution infers many inaccuracies as to minor matters of fact; but it is nevertheless true that no inaccuracy in the smallest degree affecting the character of the book as a fair record of great events, has to this hour been detected even by the malevolent ingenuity of Jacobin and Buonapartist pamphleteers. Even the most hostile examiners were obliged to acknowledge that the gigantic career of their idol had been traced, in its leading features, with wonderful truth and spirit. No civilian, it was universally admitted, had ever before described modern battles and campaigns with any approach to his daring and comprehensive felicity. The public, ever unwilling to concede a new species of honour to a name already covered with distinction, listened eagerly for a while to the indignant reclamations of nobodies, whose share in mighty transactions had been omitted, or slightly misrepresented; but, ere long, all these pompous rectifications were summed up—and found to constitute nothing but a contemptible monument of self-deluding vanity. The work, devoured at first with breathless delight, had a shade thrown over it for a time by the pertinacious blustering of these angry Lilliputians; but it has now emerged, slowly and surely, from the mist of suspicion—and few, whose opinions deserve much attention, hesitate to avow their conviction that, whoever may be the Polybius of the modern Hannibal, posterity will recognise his Livy in Scott.

Woodstock, as we have seen, placed upwards of £8000 in the hands of Sir Walter's creditors. The Napoleon (first and second editions) produced for them a sum which it even now startles me to mention—£18,000. As by the time the historical work was published, nearly half of the First Series of Chronicles of the Canongate had been written, it is obvious that the amount to which Scott's literary industry, from the close of 1825, to the 10th of June 1827, had diminished his debt, cannot be stated at less than £28,000. Had health been spared him, how soon must he have freed himself from all his encumbrances!

CHAPTER LXXIV.

Excursion to St Andrews—Deaths of Lady Diana Scott, Constable, and Canning—Extract from Mr Adolphus's Memoranda—Affair of General Gourgaud—Letter to Mr Clerk—Blythswood—Corehouse—Duke of Wellington's Visit to Durham—Dinner in the Castle—Sunderland—Ravensworth—Alnwick—Verses to Sir Cuthbert Sharp—Affair of Abud & Co.—Publication of the Chronicles of the Canongate, series first—and of the first Tales of a Grandfather—Essay on Planting, &c.—Miscellaneous prose works collected—Sale of the Waverley Copyrights—Dividend to Creditors.

JUNE—DEC. 1827.

MY wife and I spent the summer of 1827, partly at a sea-bathing place near Edinburgh, and partly in Roxburghshire; and I shall, in my account of tne sequel of this year, draw, as it may happen, on Sir Walter's Diary, his letters, the memoranda of friendly visitors, or my own recollections. The arrival of his daughter and her children at Portobello was a source of constant refreshment to him during June; for every other day he came down and dined there, and strolled about afterwards on the beach; thus interrupting, beneficially for his health, and I doubt not for the result of his labours also, the new custom of regular night-work, or, as he called it, of serving double-tides. When the Court released him, and he returned to Abbotsford, his family did what they could to keep him to his ancient evening habits; but nothing was so useful as the presence of his invalid grandson. The poor child was at this time so far restored as to be able to sit his pony again; and Sir Walter, who had, as the reader observed, conceived, the very day he finished Napoleon, the notion of putting together a series of stories on the history of Scotland, somewhat in the manner of Mr Croker's on that of that England, rode daily among the woods with his " Hugh Littlejohn," and told the tale, and ascertained that it suited the comprehension of boyhood, before he reduced it to writing. Sibyl Grey had been dismissed in consequence of the accident at the Catrail; and he had now stooped his pride to a sober, steady creature, of very humble blood; dun, with black mane and legs; by name Douce Davie, *alias* the Covenanter. This, the last of his steeds, by the way, had been previously in the possession of a jolly old laird in a neighbouring county, and acquired a distinguished reputation by its skill in carrying him home safely when dead drunk. Douce Davie, on such occasions, accommodated himself to the swerving balance of his rider with such nice discrimination, that, on the laird's death, the country people expected a vigorous competition for the sagacious animal; but the club-companions of the defunct stood off to a man when it was understood that the Sheriff coveted the succession.

The Chronicles of the Canongate proceeded *pari passu* with these historical tales; and both works were published before the end of the year. He also superintended, at the same time, the first collection of his Prose Miscellanies, in six volumes 8vo.—several articles being remodelled and extended to adapt them for a more permanent sort of existence than had been originally thought of. Moreover, Sir Walter penned, that autumn, his beautiful and instructive paper on the Planting of Waste Lands, which is indeed no other than a precious chapter of his autobiography, for the Quarterly Review.* What he wrote of new matter between June and December, fills from five to six volumes in the late uniform

* See Miscellaneous Prose Works (edition 1836) vol. xxi.

edition of his works; but all this was light and easy after the perilous drudgery of the preceding eighteen months.

The Blair-Adam Club, this year, had their head-quarters at Charleton, in Fife—the seat of the founder's son-in-law, Mr Anstruther Thomson; and one of their drives was to the two ancient mansions of Ely and Balcaskie. "The latter," says Sir Walter in his Diary, "put me in mind of poor Philip Anstruther, dead and gone many a long year since. He was a fine, gallant, light-hearted young sailor. I remember the story of his drawing on his father for some cash, which produced an angry letter from old Sir Robert, to which Philip replied, that if he did not know how to write like a gentleman, he did not desire any more of his correspondence. Balcaskie is much dilapidated; but they are restoring the house in the good old style, with its terraces and yew hedges."

Another morning was given to St Andrew's, which one of the party had never before visited. "The ruins," he says, "have been lately cleared out. They had been chiefly magnificent from their size, not their richness in ornament.*   I did not go up to St Rule's

* I believe there is no doubt that the Metropolitan Cathedral of St. Andrews had been the *longest* in Europe—a very remarkable fact, when one thinks of the smallness and poverty of the country. It is stated, with minute calculations, and much exultation, by an old Scotch writer — *Volusenus* (i. e. Wilson) — in his once celebrated treatise *De Tranquillitate Animi.*

Tower, as on former occasions ; this is a falling off, for when before did 1 remain sitting below when there was a steeple to be ascended ? But the rheumatism has begun to change that vein for some time past, though I think this is the first decided sign of acquiescence in my lot. I sat down on a grave-stone, and recollected the first visit I made to St Andrew's, now thirty-four years ago. What changes in my feelings and my fortunes have since then taken place! — some for the better, many for the worse. I remembered the name I then carved in runic characters on the turf beside the castle-gate, and I asked why it should still agitate my heart. But my friends came down from the tower, and the foolish idea was chased away."

On the 22d of July, his Diary bears the date of *Minto.* . He then says—" We rubbed up some recollections of twenty years ago, when I was more intimate in the family, till Whig and Tory separated us for a time. By the way, nobody talks Whig or Tory just now, and the fighting men on each side go about muzzled and mute, like dogs after a proclamation about canine madness. Am I sorry for this truce or not? Half and half. It is all we have left to stir the blood, this little political brawling. But better too little of it than too much.—Here I have received news of two deaths at once ; Lady Die Scott, my very old friend, and Archibald Constable, the bookseller."—He adds next day—" Yes! they are both, for very different reasons, subjects of reflection. Lady Diana Scott, widow of Walter Scott of Harden, was the last person whom I recollect so much older than myself, that she kept always at the same distance in point of age, so that she scarce seemed older to me (relatively) two years ago, when in her ninety-second year, than fifty years before. She was the daughter (alone remaining) of Pope's Earl of Marchmont, and, like her father, had an acute mind, and an eager temper. She was always kind to me, remarkably so indeed when I was a boy.— Constable's death might have been a most important thing to me if it had happened some years ago, and I should then have lamented it much. He has lived to do me some injury; yet, excepting the last £5000. I think most unintentionally. He was a prince of booksellers; his views sharp, powerful, and liberal; too sanguine, however, and like many bold and successful schemers, never knowing when to stand or stop, and not always calculating 'his means to his object with mercantile accuracy. He was very vain, for which he had some reason, having raised himself to great commercial eminence, as he might also, with good management, have attained great wealth. He knew, I think, more of the business of a bookseller, in planning and executing popular works, than any man of his time. In books themselves, he had much bibliographical information, but none whatever that could be termed literary. He knew the rare volumes of his library, not only by the eye, but by the touch, when blindfolded. Thomas Thomson saw him make this experiment, and that it might be complete, placed in his hand an ordinary volume instead of one of these *libri rariores*. He said he had over-estimated his memory; he could not recollect that volume. Constable was a violent tempered man with those he dared use freedom with. He was easily overawed by people of consequence; but, as usual, took it out of those whom poverty made subservient to him. Yet he was generous, and far from bad-hearted:— in person good-looking, but very corpulent latterly; a large feeder, and deep drinker, till his health became weak. He died of water in the chest, which the natural strength of his constitution set long at defiance. I have no great reason to regret him; yet I do. If he deceived me, he also deceived himself."

Constable's spirit had been effectually broken by his downfall. To stoop from being *primus absque secundo* among the Edinburgh booksellers, to be the occupant of an obscure closet of a shop, without capital, without credit, all his mighty undertakings abandoned or gone into other hands, except indeed his Miscellany, which he had now no resources for pushing on in the fashion he once contemplated—

this reverse was too much for that proud heart. He no longer opposed a determined mind to the ailments of the body, and sunk on the 21st of this month, having, as I am told, looked, long ere he took to his bed, at least ten years older than he was. He died in his 54th year; but into that space he had crowded vastly more than the usual average of zeal and energy, of hilarity and triumph, and perhaps of anxiety and misery.

About this time the rumour became prevalent that Mr Canning's health was breaking up among toils and mortifications of another order, and Scott's Diary has some striking entries on this painful subject. Meeting Lord Melville casually at the seat of a common friend towards the end of July, he says —" I was sorry to see my very old friend, this upright statesman and honourable gentleman, deprived of his power, and his official income, which the number of his family must render a matter of importance. He was cheerful, not affectedly so, and bore his declension like a wise and brave man. Canning said the office of Premier was his by inheritance; he could not, from constitution, hold it above two years, and then it would descend to Peel. Such is ambition! Old friends forsaken — old principles changed — every effort used to give the vessel of the State a new direction, and all to be Palinurus for two years!"

Of the 10th of August — when the news of Mr Canning's death reached Abbotsford — and the day following, are these entries: — " The death of the Premier is announced — late George Canning — the witty, the accomplished, the ambitious; — he who had toiled thirty years,. and involved himself in the most harassing discussions, to attain this dizzy height; he who had held it for three months of intrigue and obloquy — and now a heap of dust, and that is all. He was an early and familiar friend of. mine, through my intimacy with George Ellis. No man possessed a gayer and more playful wit in society; no one, since Pitt's time, had more commanding sarcasm in debate; in the House of Commons he was the terror of that species of orators called the Yelpers. His lash fetched away both skin and flesh, and would have penetrated the hide of a rhinoceros. In his conduct as a statesman he had a great fault; he lent himself too willingly to intrigue. Thus he got into his quarrel with Lord Castlereagh, and lost credit with the country for want of openness. Thus, too, he got involved with the Queen's party to such an extent, that it fettered him upon that miserable occasion, and obliged him to butter Sir Robert Wilson with *dear friend,* and *gallant general,* and so forth. The last composition with the Whigs was a sacrifice of principle on both sides. I have some reason to think they counted on getting rid of him in two or three years. To me Canning was always personally most kind. I saw, with pain, a great change in his health when I met him at Colonel Bolton's, at Storrs, in 1825. In London last year I thought him looking better. My nerves have for these two or three last days been susceptible of an acute excitement from the slightest causes; the beauty of the evening, the sighing of the summer breeze, bring the tears into my eyes not unpleasantly. But I must take exercise, and case-harden myself. There is no use in encouraging these moods of the mind.

" *August* 11.— Wrote nearly five pages; then walked. A visit from Henry Scott; nothing known as yet about politics. A High Tory Administration would be a great evil at this time. There are repairs in the structure of our constitution which ought to be made at this season, and without which the people will not long be silent. A pure Whig Administration would probably play the devil by attempting a thorough repair. As to a compound, or melo-dramatic Ministry, the parts out of which such a one could be organised just now are at a terrible discount in public estimation, nor will they be at par in a hurry again. The public were generally shocked at the complete lack of principle testified on the late occasion, and by some who till then had high credit.

The Duke of Wellington has risen by his firmness on
the one side, Earl Grey on the other."

He received, about this time, a third visit from
Mr J. L. Adolphus. The second occurred in August
1824, and since that time they had not met. I tran-
scribe a few paragraphs from my friend's memoranda,
on which I formerly drew so largely: He says—

" Calamity had borne heavily upon Sir Walter in
the interval; but the painful and anxious feeling with
which a friend is approached for the first time under
such circumstances, gave way at once to the unas-
sumed serenity of his manner. There were some
signs of age about him which the mere lapse of time
would scarcely have accounted for; but his spirits
were abated only, not broken; if they had sunk, they
had sunk equably and gently. It was a declining,
not a clouded sun. I do not remember, at this period,
hearing him make any reference to the afflictions he
had suffered, except once, when, speaking of his Life
of Napoleon, he said ' he knew that it had some
inaccuracies, but he believed it would be found right
in all essential points;' and then added, in a quiet,
but affecting tone, ' I could have done it better, if I
could have written at more leisure, and with a mind
more at ease.' One morning a party was made to

breakfast at Chiefswood; and any one who on that
occasion looked at and heard Sir Walter Scott, in the
midst of his children, and grandchildren, and friends,
must have rejoiced to see that life still yielded him a
store of pleasures, and that his heart was as open to
their influence as ever.

"I was much struck by a few words which fell
from him on this subject a short time afterwards.
After mentioning an accident which had spoiled the
promised pleasure of a visit to his daughter in London, he then added—'I am like Seged, Lord of
Ethiopia, in the Rambler, who said that he would
have ten happy days, and all turned to disappointment. But, however, I have had as much happiness
in my time as most men, and I must not complain
now.' I said, that whatever had been his share of
happiness, no man could have laboured better for it.
He answered—'I consider the capacity to labour as
part of the happiness I have enjoyed.'

"Abbotsford was not much altered since 1824.
I had then seen it complete even to the statue of
Maida at the door, though in 1824 old Maida was
still alive, and now and then raised a majestic bark
from behind the house. It was one of the little
scenes of Abbotsford life which should have been pre-
served by a painter, when Sir Walter strolled out in
a sunny morning to caress poor Maida, and condole
with him upon being so 'very frail;' the aged hound

dragging his gaunt limbs forward, painfully, yet with some remains of dignity, to meet the hand and catch the deep affectionate tones of his master.

" The greatest observable difference which the last three years had made in the outward appearance of Abbotsford, was in the advanced growth of the plantations. Sir Walter now showed me some rails and palisades, made of their wood, with more self-complacency than I ever saw him betray on any other subject. The garden did not appear to interest him so much, and the ' mavis and merle' were, upon principle, allowed to use their discretion as to the fruit. His favourite afternoon exercise was to ramble through his grounds, conversing with those who accompanied him, and trimming his young trees with a large knife. Never have I received an invitation more gladly than when he has said — ' If you like a walk in the plantations, I will bestow my tediousness upon you after one o'clock.' His conversation at such times ran in that natural, easy, desultory course, which accords so well with the irregular movements of a walk over hill and woodland, and which he has himself described so well in his epistle to Mr Skene.* I remember with particular pleasure one of our walks through the romantic little ravine of the Huntly-Burn. Our progress was leisurely, for the path was

* *See Marmion — Poetical Works*, vol. vii. p. 182.

somewhat difficult to him.   Occasionally he would stop, and, leaning on his walking-stick and fixing his eyes on those of the hearer, pour forth some sonorous stanza of an old poem applicable to the scene, or to the last subject of the conversation.   Several times we paused to admire the good taste, as it seemed, with which his great Highland staghound Nimrod always displayed himself on those prominent points of the little glen, where his figure, in combination with the scenery, had the most picturesque effect. Sir Walter accounted for this by observing that the situations were of that kind which the dog's instinct would probably draw him to if looking out for game. In speaking of the Huntly-Burn I used the word ' brook.'   ' It is hardly that,' said he, ' it is just a runnel.'   Emerging into a more open country, we saw a road a little below us, on each side of which were some feathery saplings.   ' I like,' he said, ' that way of giving an eyelash to the road.'   Independently of the recollections called up by particular objects, his eye and mind always seemed to dwell with a perfect complacency on his own portion of the vale of Tweed : he used to say that he did not know a more ' liveable' country.

" A substitute for walking, which he always very cheerfully used, and which at last became his only resource for any distant excursion, was a ride in a four-wheeled open carriage, holding four persons, but

not absolutely limited to that number on an emer-
gency.   Tame as this exercise might be in comparison with riding on horseback, or with walking under
propitious circumstances, yet as he was rolled along
to Melrose, or Bowhill, or Yair, his spirits always
freshened ; the air, the sounds, the familiar yet romantic scenes, wakened up all the poetry of his
thoughts, and happy were they who heard it resolve
itself into words.   At the sight of certain objects —
for example, in passing the green foundations of the
little chapel of Lindean, where the body of the ' Dark
Knight of Liddesdale' was deposited, on its way to
Melrose, it would, I suppose, have been impossible
for him, unless with a companion hopelessly unsus-
ceptible or pre-occupied, to forbear some passing
comment, some harping (if the word may be favourably used) on the tradition of the place.   This was,
perhaps, what he called ' bestowing his tediousness ;'
but if any one could think these effusions tedious
because they often broke forth, such a man might
have objected against the rushing of the Tweed, or
the stirring of the trees in the wind, or any other
natural melody, that he had heard the same thing
before.

" Some days of my visit were marked by an almost
perpetual confinement to the house ; the rain being
incessant.   But the evenings were as bright and
cheerful as the atmosphere of the days was dreary.

Not that the gloomiest morning could ever be weari-
some under a roof where, independently of the resources in society which the house afforded, the
visiter might ransack a library, unique, I suppose,
in some of its collections, and in all its departments
interesting and characteristic of the founder. So many
of the volumes were enriched with anecdotes or com-
ments in his own hand, that to look over his books
was in some degree conversing with him. And sometimes this occupation was pleasantly interrupted by a
snatch of actual conversation with himself, when he
entered from his own room, to consult or take away
a book. How often have I heard with pleasure, after
a long silence, the uneven step, the point of the stick
striking against the floor, and then seen the poet himself emerge from his study, with a face of thought
but yet of cheerfulness, followed perhaps by Nimrod,
who stretched his limbs and yawned, as if tired out
with some abstruse investigation.

" On one of the rainy days I have alluded to,
when walking at the usual hour became hopeless,
Sir Walter asked me to sit with him while he continued his morning occupation, giving me, for my
own employment, the publications of the Bannatyne
Club. His study, as I recollect it, was strictly a
work-room, though an elegant one. It has been
fancifully decked out in pictures, but it had, I think,
very few articles of mere ornament. The chief of

these was the print of Stothard's Canterbury Pilgrims, which hung over the chimneypiece, and, from
the place assigned to it, must have been in great
favour, though Sir Walter made the characteristic
criticism upon it, that, if the procession were to
move, the young squire who is prancing in the fore-
ground would in another minute be over his horse's
head.   The shelves were stored with serviceable
books; one door opened into the great library, and
a hanging-stair within the room itself communicated
with his bedroom. It would have been a good lesson
to a desultory student, or even to a moderately active
amanuensis, to see the unintermitted energy with
which Sir Walter Scott applied himself to his work.
I conjectured that he was at this time writing the
Tales of a Grandfather.   When we had sat down to
our respective employments, the stillness of the room
was unbroken, except by the light rattle of the rain
against the windows, and the dashing trot of Sir
Walter's pen over his paper; sounds not very unlike
each other, and which seemed to vie together in rapidity and continuance. Sometimes, when he stopped
to consult a book, a short dialogue would take place
upon the subjects with which I was occupied; about
Mary Queen of Scots, perhaps, or Viscount Dundee;
or, again, the silence might be broken for a moment
by some merry outcry in the hall, from one of the
little grandchildren, which would half waken Nim-

rod, or Bran, or Spice, as they slept at Sir Walter's feet, and produce a growl or a stifled bark, not in anger, but by way of protest. For matters like these, work did not proceed the worse, nor, as it seemed to me, did Sir Walter feel at all discomposed by such interruptions as a message, or the entrance of a visiter. One door of his study opened into the hall, and there did not appear to be any understanding that he should not be disturbed. At the end of our morning we attempted a sortie, but had made only a little way in the shrubbery-walks overlooking the Tweed, when the rain drove us back. The river, swollen and discoloured, swept by majestically, and the sight drew from Sir Walter his favourite lines—

' I've seen Tweed's silver streams, glittering in the sunny beams,
   Turn drumly and dark, as they roll'd on their way.'

There could not have been a better moment for ap preciating the imagery of the last line. I think it was in this short walk that he mentioned to me, with great satisfaction, the favourable prospects of his literary industry, and spoke sanguinely of retrieving his ' losses with the booksellers.'

" Those who have seen Abbotsford will remember that there is at the end of the hall, opposite to the entrance of the library, an arched door-way leading to other rooms. One night some of the party observed that, by an arrangement of light, easily to be imagined, a luminous space was formed upon the library door, in which the shadow of a person standing in the opposite archway made a very imposing appearance, the body of the hall remaining quite dark. Sir Walter had some time before told his friends of the deception of sight (mentioned in his Demonology) which made him for a moment imagine a figure of Lord Byron standing in the same hall.*

* " Not long after the death of a late illustrious poet, who had filled, while living, a great station in the eye of the public, a literary friend, to whom the deceased had been well known, was engaged, during the darkening twilight of an autumn evening, in perusing one of the publications which professed to detail the habits and opinions of the distinguished individual who was now no more. As the reader had enjoyed the intimacy of the deceased to a considerable degree, he was deeply interested in the publication, which contained some particulars relating to himself and other friends. A visiter was sitting in the apartment, who was also engaged in reading. Their sitting-room opened into an entrance-hall, rather fantastically fitted up with articles of armour, skins of wild animals, and the like. It was when laying down his book, and passing into this hall, through which the moon was beginning to shine, that the individual of whom I speak, saw right before him, and in a standing posture, the exact representation of his departed friend, whose recollection had been so strongly brought to his imagination. He stopped for a single moment, so as to notice the wonderful accuracy with which fancy had impressed upon the bodily eye the peculiarities of dress and posture of the illustrious poet. Sensible, however, of the delusion, he felt no sentiment save that of wonder at the extraordinary accuracy of the resemblance, and stepped onwards towards

The discoverers of the little phantasmagoria which I have just described, called to him to come and see *their* ghost. Whether he thought that raising ghosts at a man's door was not a comely amusement, or whether the parody upon a circumstance which had made some impression upon his own fancy was a little too strong, he certainly did not enter into the jest.

" On the subjects commonly designated as the ' marvellous,' his mind was susceptible, and it was delicate. He loved to handle them in his own manner and at his own season, not to be pressed with them, or brought to anything like a test of belief or disbelief respecting them. There is, perhaps, in most minds, a point more or less advanced, at which incredulity on these subjects may be found to waver. Sir Walter Scott, as it seemed to me, never cared to ascertain very precisely where this point lay in his

---

the figure, which resolved itself, as he approached, into the various materials of which it was composed. These were merely a screen, occupied by great-coats, shawls, plaids, and such other articles as usually are found in a country entrance-hall. The spectator returned to the spot from which he had seen the illusion, and endeavoured, with all his power, to recall the image which had been so singularly vivid. But this was beyond his capacity; and the person who had witnessed the apparition, or, more properly, whose excited state had been the means of raising it, had only to return into the apartment, and tell his young friend under what a striking hallucination he had for a moment laboured." — Scott's *Letters on Demonology and Witchcraft,* pp. 38–9.

own mental constitution; still less, I suppose, did he
wish the investigation to be seriously pursued by
others. In no instance, however, was his colloquial
eloquence more striking than when he was well
launched in some ‘ tale of wonder.’ The story came
from him with an equally good grace, whether it
was to receive a natural solution, to be smiled at as
merely fantastical, or to take its chance of a serious
reception.”

About the close of August Sir Walter’s Diary is
chiefly occupied with an affair which, as the reader
of the previous chapter is aware, did not come altogether unexpectedly on him. Among the documents
laid before him in the Colonial Office, when he was
in London at the close of 1826, were some which
represented one of Buonaparte’s attendants at St
Helena, General Gourgaud, as having been guilty
of gross unfairness, giving the English Government
private information that the Emperor’s complaints
of ill-usage were utterly unfounded, and yet then,
and afterwards, aiding and assisting the delusion in
France as to the harshness of Sir Hudson Lowe’s
conduct towards his captive. Sir Walter, when using
these remarkable documents, guessed that Gourgaud
might be inclined to fix a personal quarrel on him-

self; and there now appeared in the newspapers a succession of hints that the General was seriously bent on this purpose. He applied, as " *Colonel Grogg*" would have done forty years before, to " *The Baronet.*"

DIARY — " *August* 27. — A singular letter from a lady, requesting me to father a novel of hers. That won't pass. Cadell transmits a notice from the French papers that Gourgaud has gone, or is going, to London; and the bibliopolist is in a great funk. I lack some part of his instinct. I have done Gourgaud no wrong. I have written to Will Clerk, who has mettle in him, and will think of my honour as well as my safety."

" *To William Clerk, Esq., Rose Court, Edinburgh.*

" Abbotsford, 27th August 1827.
" My Dear Clerk,
" I am about to claim an especial service from you in the name of our long and intimate friendship. I understand, from a passage in the French papers, that General Gourgaud has, or is about to set out for London, to *verify* the facts averred concerning him in my history of Napoleon. Now, in case of a personal appeal to me, I have to say that his confes-

sions to Baron Sturmer, Count Balmain, and others at St Helena, confirmed by him in various recorded conversations with Mr Goulburn, then Under Secretary of State—were documents of a historical nature which I found with others in the Colonial Office, and was therefore perfectly entitled to use. If his language has been misrepresented, he has certainly been very unfortunate; for it has been misrepresented by four or five different people to whom he said the same things, true or false he knows best. I also acted with delicacy towards him, leaving out whatever related to his private quarrels with Bertrand, &c., so that, in fact, he has no reason to complain of me, since it is ridiculous to suppose I was to suppress historical evidence, furnished by him voluntarily, because his present sentiments render it unpleasing for him that those which he formerly entertained should be known. Still, like a man who finds himself in a scrape, General Gourgaud may wish to fight himself out of it, and if the quarrel should be thrust on me—why, *I will not baulk him, Jackie.* He shall not dishonour the country through my sides I can assure him. I have. of course, no wish to bring the thing to such an arbitrement. Now, in this case, I shall have occasion for a sensible and resolute friend, and I naturally look for him in the companion of my youth, on whose firmness and sagacity I can with such perfect confidence rely. If you can do me this office of friendship,

will you have the kindness to let me know where or
how we can form a speedy junction, should circumstances require it.

"After all, the matter may be a Parisian *on dit*.
But it is best to be prepared. The passages are in
the ninth volume of the book. Pray look at them.
I have an official copy of the principal communication.
Of the others I have abridged extracts. Should he
desire to see them, I conceive I cannot refuse to give
him copies, as it is likely they may not admit him to
the Colonial Office. But if he asks any apology or
explanation for having made use of his name, it is my
purpose to decline it and stand to consequences. I
am aware I could march off upon the privileges of
literature, and so forth, but I have no taste for that
species of retreat; and if a gentleman says to me I
have injured him, however captious the quarrel may
be, I certainly do not think, as a man of honour, I
can avoid giving him satisfaction, without doing intolerable injury to my own feelings, and giving rise
to the most malignant animadversions. I need not
say that I shall be anxious to hear from you, and that
I always am, dear Clerk, affectionately yours,

WALTER SCOTT."

DIARY— "*September* 4.—William Clerk quite
ready and willing to stand my friend if Gourgaud
should come my road. He agrees with me that there

is no reason why he should turn on me, but that if
he does, reason or none, it is best to stand buff to
him.   It appears to me that what is least forgiven in
a man of any mark or likelihood, is want of that article blackguardly called *pluck.* All the fine qualities
of genius cannot make amends for it.   We are told
the genius of poets, especially, is irreconcilable with
this species of grenadier accomplishment.   If so, *quel
chien de genre!*

" *September* 10.— Gourgaud's wrath has burst
forth in a very distant clap of thunder, in which he
accuses me of contriving, with the Ministry, to slander his rag of a reputation.   He be d——d for a fool,
to make his case worse by stirring.   I shall only revenge myself by publishing the whole extracts I made
from the records of the Colonial Office, in which he
will find enough to make him bite his nails.

" *September* 17.—Received from James Ballantyne the proofs of my Reply, with some cautious balaam from mine honest friend, alarmed by a Highland
colonel, who had described Gourgaud as a *mauvais
garçon,* famous fencer, marksman, and so forth.   I
wrote, in answer, which is true, that I hoped all my
friends would trust to my acting with proper caution
and advice ; but that if I were capable, in a moment
of weakness, of doing anything short of what my

honour demanded, I should die the death of a poi-
soned rat in a hole, out of mere sense of my own
degradation. God knows, that, though life is placid
enough with me, I do not feel anything to attach me
to it so strongly as to occasion my avoiding any risk
which duty to my character may demand from me.—
I set to work with the Tales of a Grandfather, second
volume, and finished four pages."

" To the Editor of the Edinburgh Weekly Journal.

" Abbotsford, Sept. 14, 1827.

" Sir,—I observed in the London papers which I
received yesterday, a letter from General Gourgaud,
which I beg you will have the goodness to reprint,
with this communication and the papers accompany-
ing it.

" It appears, that the General is greatly displeased,
because, availing myself of formal official documents,
I have represented him, in my Life of Buonaparte,
as communicating to the British Government and the
representatives of others of the Allied Powers, cer
tain statements in matter, which he seems at present
desirous to deny or disavow, though in what degree,
or to what extent, he has not explicitly stated.

" Upon these grounds, for I can discover no other,
General Gourgaud has been pleased to charge me, in

the most intemperate terms, as the agent of a plot, contrived by the late British Ministers, to slander and dishonour him.   I will not attempt to imitate the General either in his eloquence or his invective, but confine myself to the simple fact, that his accusation against me is as void of truth as it is of plausibility. I undertook, and carried on, the task of writing the Life of Napoleon Buonaparte, without the least intercourse with, or encouragement from, the Ministry of the time, or any person connected with them; nor was it until my task was very far advanced, that I asked and obtained permission from the Earl Bathurst, then Secretary for the Colonial Department, to consult such documents as his office afforded, concerning the residence of Napoleon at St Helena.   His Lordship's liberality, with that of Mr Hay, the Under Secretary, permitted me, in the month of October last, personal access to the official records, when I inspected more than sixteen quarto volumes of letters, from which I made memoranda or extracts at my own discretion, unactuated by any feeling excepting the wish to do justice to all parties.

" The papers relating to General Gourgaud and his communications were not pointed out to me by any one.   They occurred, in the course of my researches, like other pieces of information, and were of too serious and important a character, verified as they were, to be omitted in the history.   The idea that, dated and authenticated as they are, they could have been false documents, framed to mislead future historians, seems as absurd, as it is positively false that they were fabricated on any understanding with me, who had not at the time of their date the slightest knowledge of their existence.

" To me, evidence, *ex facie* the most unquestionable, bore, that General Gourgaud had attested certain facts of importance to different persons, at different times and places; and it did not, I own, occur to me that what he is stated to have made the subject of grave assertion and attestation, could or ought to be received as matter of doubt, because it rested only on a verbal communication made before responsible witnesses, and was not concluded by any formal signature of the party. I have been accustomed to consider a gentleman's word as equally worthy of credit with his handwriting.

" At the same time, in availing myself of these documents, I felt it a duty to confine myself entirely to those particulars which concerned the history of Napoleon, his person and his situation at St Helena; omitting all subordinate matters in which General Gourgaud, in his communications with our Ministers and others, referred to transactions of a more private character, personal to himself and other gentlemen residing at St Helena. I shall observe the same degree of restraint as far as possible, out of the sincere respect I entertain for the honour and fidelity of General Gourgaud's companions in exile, who might justly complain of me for reviving the memory of petty altercations; but out of no deference to General Gourgaud, to whom I owe none. The line which General Gourgaud has adopted, obliges me now, in respect to my own character, to lay the full evidence before the public—subject only to the above restriction—that it may appear how far it bears out the account given of those transactions in my History of Napoleon. I should have been equally willing to have communicated my authorities to General Gour gaud in private, had he made such a request, according to the ordinary courtesies of society.

" I trust that, upon reference to the Life of Napoleon, I shall be found to have used the information these documents afforded with becoming respect to private feelings, and, at the same time, with the courage and candour due to the truth of history. If I were capable of failing in either respect, I should despise myself as much, if possible, as I do the re sentment of General Gourgaud. The historian's task of exculpation is of course ended, when he has published authorities of apparent authenticity. If General Gourgaud shall undertake to prove that the subjoined documents are false and forged, in whole or in part, the burden of the proof will lie with himself; and something better than the assertion of the party interested will be necessary to overcome the testimony of Mr Goulburn and the other evidence.

" There is indeed another course. General Gourgaud may represent the whole of his communications as a trick played off upon the English Ministers, in order to induce them to grant his personal liberty. But I cannot imitate the General's disregard of common civility, so far as to suppose him capable of a total departure from veracity, when giving evidence upon his word of honour. In representing the Ex-Emperor's health as good, his finances as ample, his means of escape as easy and frequent, while he knew his condition to be the reverse in every particular, General Gourgaud must have been sensible, that the deceptive views thus impressed on the British Ministers must have had the natural effect of adding to the rigours of his patron's confinement. Napoleon, it must be recollected, would receive the visits of no English physician in whom Sir Hudson Lowe seemed to repose confidence, and he shunned, as much as possible, all intercourse with the British. Whom, therefore, were Sir Hudson Lowe and the British Ministers to believe concerning the real state of his health and circumstances, if they were to refuse credit to his own aide-de-camp, an officer of distinction, whom no one could suppose guilty of slandering his master for the purpose of obtaining a straight passage to England for himself, instead of being subjected to the inconvenience of going round by the Cape of Good Hope?   And again, when General Gourgaud, having arrived in London, and the purpose of his supposed deception being fully attained, continued to represent Napoleon as feigning poverty whilst in affluence, affecting illness whilst in health, and possessing ready means of escape whilst he was complaining of unnecessary restraint — what effect could such statements produce on Lord Bathurst and the other members of the British Ministry, except a disregard to Napoleon's remonstrances, and a rigorous increase of every precaution necessary to prevent his escape?   They had the evidence of one of his most intimate personal attendants to justify them for acting thus; and their own responsibility to Britain, and to Europe, for the safe custody of Napoleon, would have rendered them inexcusable had they acted otherwise.

" It is no concern of mine, however, how the actual truth of the fact stands.   It is sufficient to me to have shown, that I have not laid to General Gourgaud's charge a single expression for which I had not the most indubitable authority.   If I have been guilty of over-credulity in attaching more weight to General Gourgaud's evidence than it deserves, I am well taught not to repeat the error, and the world, too, may profit by the lesson. I am, Sir, your humble servant,   WALTER SCOTT."

To this letter Gourgaud made a fiery rejoinder; but Scott declined to prolong the paper war, simply stating in Ballantyne's print, that " while leaving the question to the decision of the British public, he should have as little hesitation in referring it to the French nation, provided the documents he had produced were allowed to be printed in the French newspapers, *from which hitherto they had been excluded.*"   And he would indeed have been idle had he said more than this, for his cause had been taken up on the instant by every English journal, of whatever politics, and *The Times* thus summed up its very effective demolition of his antagonist :—

" Sir Walter Scott did that which would have occurred to every honest man, whose fair-dealing had violent imputations cast upon it.   He produced his authorities, extracted from the Colonial Office.   To these General Gourgaud's present pamphlet professes to be a reply; but we do conscientiously declare, that with every readiness to acknowledge—and, indeed, with every wish to discover—something like a defence of the character of General Gourgaud, whose good name has alone been implicated —(for that of Sir Walter was abundantly cleared, even had the official documents which he consulted turned out to be as false as they appear to be unquestionable),—the charge against the General stands precisely where it was before this ill-judged attempt at refutation was published; and in no one instance can we make out a satisfactory answer to the plain assertion, that Gourgaud had in repeated instances either betrayed Buonaparte, or sacrificed the truth.   In the General's reply to Sir Walter Scott's statement, there is enough, even to satiety, of declamation against the English Government under Lord Castlereagh, of subterfuge and equivocation with regard to the words on record against himself, and of gross abuse and Billingsgate against the historian who has placarded him; but of direct and successful negative there is not one syllable. The Aide-de-camp of St Helena shows himself to be nothing better than a cross between a blusterer and a sophist."

Sir Walter's family were, of course, relieved from considerable anxiety, when the newspapers ceased to give paragraphs about General Gourgaud; and the blowing over of this alarm was particularly acceptable to his eldest daughter, who had to turn southwards about the beginning of October. He himself certainly cared little or nothing about that (or any similar) affair; and if it had any effect at all upon his spirits, they were pleasurably excited and stimulated. He possessed a pair of pistols taken from Napoleon's carriage at Waterloo, and presented to him, I believe, by the late Hon. Colonel James Stanhope, and he said he designed to make use of them, in case the controversy should end in a rencounter, and his friend Clerk should think as well as he did of their fabric. But this was probably a jest. I may observe that I *once* saw Sir Walter shoot at a mark with pistols, aud he acquitted himself well; so much so as to excite great admiration in some young officers whom he had found practising in his barn on a rainy day. With the rifle, he is said by those who knew him in early life, to have been a very good shot indeed.

Before Gourgaud fell quite asleep, Sir Walter made an excursion to Edinburgh to meet his friends, Mrs Maclean Clephane and Lady Northampton, with whom he had some business to transact; and they, feeling, as all his intimate friends at this time did, that the kindliest thing they could do by him was to keep him as long as possible away from his desk, contrived to seduce him into escorting them as far as Greenock on their way to the Hebrides. He visited on his return his esteemed kinsman, Mr Campbell of Blythswood,* in whose park he saw, with much interest, the Argyle Stone, marking the spot where the celebrated Earl was taken prisoner in 1685. He notes in his Diary, that " the Highland drovers are still apt to break Blythswood's fences to see this Stone;" and then records the capital turtle, &c. of his friend's entertainment, and some good stories told at table, especially this: — " Prayer of the minister of the Cumbrays, two miserable islands in the mouth of the Clyde: ' O Lord, bless and be gracious to the Greater and the Lesser Cumbrays, and in thy mercy do not forget the adjacent islands of

---

* Archibald Campbell, Esq., Lord Lieutenant of Renfrewshire, and often M.P. for Glasgow. This excellent man, whose memory will long be honoured in the district which his munificent benevolence adorned, died in London, September 1838, aged 75.

Great Britain and Ireland.'   This is *nos poma na-tamus* with a vengeance."

Another halt was at the noble seat of his early friend Cranstoun, by the Falls of the Clyde. He says — " Cranstoun and I walked before dinner.   I never saw the Great Fall of Corra Linn from this side before, and I think it the best point perhaps; at all events, it is not that from which it is usually seen; so Lord Corehouse has the sight, and escapes the locusts.   This is a superb place.   Cranstoun has as much feeling about improvement as other things. Like all new improvers, he is at more expense than is necessary, plants too thick, and trenches where trenching is superfluous.   But this is the eagerness of a young artist.   Besides the grand lion, the Fall of Clyde, he has more than one lion's whelp—a fall of a brook in a cleugh called Mill's Gill must be superb in rainy weather.   The old Castle of Core-house, too, is much more castle-like on this than from the other side.   My old friend was very happy when I told him the favourable prospect of my af-fairs.   To be sure, if I come through, it will be wonder to all, and most to myself."

On returning from this trip, Scott found an in-vitation from Lord and Lady Ravensworth to meet the Duke of Wellington at their castle near Durham. The Duke was then making a progress in the north of England, to which additional importance was given by the uncertain state of political arrangements;—the chance of Lord Goderich's being able to maintain himself as Canning's successor seeming very precarious—and the opinion that his Grace must soon be called to a higher station than that of Commander of the Forces, which he had accepted under the new Premier, gaining ground every day. Sir Walter, who felt for the Great Captain the pure and exalted devotion that might have been expected from some honoured soldier of his banners, accepted this invitation, and witnessed a scene of enthusiasm with which its principal object could hardly have been more gratified than he was.

DIARY — " *October* 1.—I set about work for two hours, and finished three pages; then walked for two hours; then home, adjusted sheriff processes, and cleared the table. I am to set off to-morrow for Ravensworth Castle, to meet the Duke of Wellington; a great let-off, I suppose. Yet I would almost rather stay, and see two days more of Lock-hart and my daughter, who will be off before my return. Perhaps—— But there is no end to *perhaps.* We must cut the rope, and let the vessel drive down the tide of destiny.

" *October* 2.—Set out in the morning at seven, and reached Kelso by a little past ten with my own horses.   Then took the Wellington coach to carry me to Wellington—smart that.   Nobody inside but an old lady, who proved a toy-woman in Edinburgh; her head furnished with as substantial ware as her shop, but a good soul, I'se warrant her.   Heard all her debates with her landlord about a new door to the cellar—and the propriety of paying rent on the 15th or 25th of May.   Landlords and tenants will have different opinions on *that* subject.   We dined at Wooler, where an obstreperous horse retarded us for an hour at least, to the great alarm of my friend the toy-woman. — *N. B.*   She would have made a good feather-bed if the carriage had happened to fall, and her undermost.   The heavy roads had retarded us near an hour more, so that I hesitated to go to Ravensworth so late; but my goodwoman's tales of dirty sheets, and certain recollections of a Newcastle inn, induced me to go on.   When I arrived, the family had just retired.   Lord Ravensworth and Mr Liddell came down, however, and both received me as kindly as possible.

" *October* 3.—Rose about eight or later.   My morals begin to be corrupted by travel and fine company.   Went to Durham with Lord Ravensworth betwixt one and two.   Found the gentlemen of Durham county and town assembled to receive the Duke of Wellington.   I saw several old friends, and with

difficulty suited names to faces, and faces to names.
There were Dr Philpotts, Dr Gilly, and his wife,
and a world of acquaintance,—among others, Sir
Thomas Lawrence; whom I asked to come on to
Abbotsford, but he could not. He is, from habit
of coaxing his subjects I suppose, a little too fair-
spoken, otherwise very pleasant. The Duke arrived
very late. There were bells, and cannon, and drums,
trumpets, and banners, besides a fine troop of yeomanry. The address was well expressed, and as
well answered by the Duke. The enthusiasm of the
ladies and the gentry was great—the common people
more lukewarm. The Duke has lost popularity in
accepting political power. He will be more useful
to his country, it may be, than ever, but will scarce
be so gracious in the people's eyes—and he will not
care a curse for what outward show he has lost. But
I must not talk of curses, for we are going to take
our dinner with the Bishop of Durham.—We dined
about one hundred and forty or fifty men, a distinguished company for rank and property. Marshal
Beresford, and Sir John,* amongst others—Marquis
of Lothian, Lord Feversham, Marquis Londonderry
—and I know not who besides—

----

* Admiral Sir John Beresford had some few years before this
commanded on the Leith station — when Sir Walter and he saw
a great deal of each other —" and merry men were they."

> ' Lords and Dukes and noble Princes,
>   All the pride and flower of Spain.'

We dined in the old baronial hall, impressive from
its rude antiquity, and fortunately free from the plaster of former improvement, as I trust it will long be
from the gingerbread taste of modern Gothicizers.
The bright moon streaming in through the old Gothic
windows contrasted strangely with the artificial lights
within; spears, banners, and armour were intermixed
with the pictures of old bishops, and the whole had
a singular mixture of baronial pomp with the grave
and more chastened dignity of prelacy. The conduct
of our reverend entertainer suited the character remarkably well. Amid the welcome of a Count Pala-
tine he did not for an instant forget the gravity of
the Church dignitary. All his toasts were gracefully
given, and his little speeches well made, and the more
affecting that the failing voice sometimes reminded
us that our host laboured under the infirmities of
advanced life. To me personally the Bishop was
very civil."

In writing to me next day, Sir Walter says—" The
dinner was one of the finest things I ever saw; it
was in the old Castle Hall, untouched, for aught I
know, since Anthony Beck feasted Edward Long-
shanks on his way to invade Scotland. *   The moon

---

* The warlike Bishop Beck accompanied Edward I. in his Scotch
expedition, and if we may believe Blind Harry, very narrowly

streamed through the high latticed windows as if she had been curious to see what was going on." I was also favoured with a letter on the subject from Dr Philpotts (now Bishop of Exeter), who said—" I wish you had witnessed this very striking scene. I never saw curiosity and enthusiasm so highly excited, and I may add, as to a great part of the company, so nearly balanced. Sometimes I doubted whether the hero or the poet was fixing most attention — the latter, I need hardly tell you, appeared unconscious that he was regarded differently from the others about him, until the good Bishop rose and proposed his health." Another friend, the Honourable Henry Liddell, enables me to give the words (" *ipsissima verba")* of Sir Walter in acknowledging this toast. He says—" The manner in which Bishop Van Mildert proceeded on this occasion will never be forgotten by those who know how to appreciate scholarship without pedantry, and dignity without ostentation. Sir Walter had been observed throughout the day with extraordinary interest—I should rather say enthusiasm.—The Bishop gave his health with peculiar felicity, remarking that he could reflect upon the labours of a long literary life, with the consciousness that everything he had written tended to the practice

---

missed having the honour to die by the hand of Wallace in a skirmish on the street of Glasgow.

of virtue, and to the improvement of the human race.
Sir Walter replied, ' that upon no occasion of his
life had he ever returned thanks for the honour done
him in drinking his health, with a stronger sense of
obligation to the proposer of it than on the present
—that hereafter he should always reflect with great
pride upon that moment of his existence, when his
health had been given *in such terms*, by the Bishop
of Durham *in his own baronial hall*, surrounded and
supported by the assembled aristocracy of the two
northern counties, and *in the presence of the Duke
of Wellington.*' "

The Diary continues—

" Mrs Van Mildert held a sort of drawing-room
after we rose from table, at which a great many ladies attended. After this we went to the Assembly-
rooms, which were crowded with company. Here I
saw some very pretty girls dancing merrily that old-
fashioned thing called a country-dance, which Old
England has now thrown aside, as she would do her
creed, if there were some foreign frippery offered instead. We got away after midnight, a large party,
and reached Ravensworth Castle — Duke of Wellington, Lord Londonderry, and about twenty besides
—about half-past one. Soda water, and to bed by
two.

" *October* 4.—Slept till nigh ten—fatigued by

our toils of yesterday, and the unwonted late hours. Still too early for this Castle of Indolence, for I found few of last night's party yet appearing. I had an opportunity of some talk with the Duke. He does not consider Foy's book as written by himself, but as a thing *got up* perhaps from notes. Mentioned that Foy, when in Spain, was, like other French officers, very desirous of seeing the English papers, through which alone they could collect any idea of what was going on without their own cantonments, for Napoleon permitted no communication of that kind with France. The Duke growing tired of this, at length told Baron Tripp, whose services he chiefly used in communications with the outposts, that he was not to give them the newspapers. ' What reason shall I allege for withholding them?' said Tripp. ' None,' replied the Duke—' Let *them* allege some reason why they want them.' Foy was not at a loss to assign a reason. He said he had considerable sums of money in the English funds, and wanted to see how stocks fell and rose. The excuse, however, did not go down.—I remember Baron Tripp, a Dutch nobleman, and a dandy of the first water, and yet with an energy in his dandyism which made it respectable. He drove a gig as far as Dunrobin Castle, and back again, *without a whip*. He looked after his own horse, for he had no servant, and after all his little establishment of clothes and necessaries, with all the accuracy of a *petit maître*. He was one of the best-dressed men possible, and his horse was in equally fine condition as if he had had a dozen of grooms. I met him at Lord Somerville's, and liked him much. But there was something exaggerated, as appeared from the conclusion of his life. Baron Tripp shot himself in Italy for no assignable cause.

" What is called great society, of which I have seen a good deal in my day, is now amusing to me, because from age and indifference I have lost the habit of considering myself as a part of it, and have only the feelings of looking on as a spectator of the scene, who can neither play his part well nor ill, instead of being one of the *dramatis personæ ;* so, careless what is thought of myself, I have full time to attend to the motions of others.

" Our party went to-day to Sunderland, when the Duke was brilliantly received by an immense population, chiefly of seamen. The difficulty of getting into the rooms was dreadful—an ebbing and flowing of the crowd, which nearly took me off my legs. The entertainment was handsome; about two hundred dined, and appeared most hearty in the cause which had convened them — some indeed so much so, that, finding themselves so far on the way to perfect happiness, they e'en would go on. After the dinner-party broke up, there was a ball, numerously attended, where there was a prodigious anxiety discovered for shaking of hands. The Duke had enough of it, and I came in for my share; for, though as jackall to the lion, I got some part in whatever was going. We got home about half-past two in the morning, sufficiently tired."

Some months afterwards, Sir Cuthbert Sharp, who had been particularly kind and attentive to Scott when at Sunderland, happened, in writing to him on some matter of business, to say he hoped he had not forgotten his friends in that quarter. Sir Walter's answer to Sir Cuthbert (who had been introduced to him by his old and dear friend Mr Sutrees of Mains-forth) begins thus : —

> " Forget thee? No ! my worthy fere !
> Forget blithe mirth and gallant cheer !
> Death sooner stretch me on my bier !
> > > Forget thee ? No.

> " Forget the universal shout
> When ' canny Sunderland' spoke out —
> A truth which knaves affect to doubt —
> > > Forget thee ? No.

> Forget you? No — though now-a-day
> I've heard your knowing people say,
> Disown the debt you cannot pay,
> You'll find it far the thriftiest way —
> > > But I?—O no. .

" Forget your kindness found for all room,
    In what, though large, seem'd still a small room,
    Forget my *Surtees* in a ball room —
                        Forget you? No.

" Forget your sprightly dumpty-diddles,
    And beauty tripping to the fiddles,
    Forget my lovely friends the *Liddells* —
                        Forget you? No.

" So much for oblivion, my dear Sir C.; and now, having dismounted from my Pegasus, who is rather spavined, I charge a-foot, like an old dragoon as I am," &c. &c.

" DIARY—*October* 5.—A quiet day at Ravensworth Castle, giggling and making giggle among the kind and frankhearted young people. The Castle is modern, excepting always two towers of great antiquity. Lord R. manages his woods admirably well. In the evening plenty of fine music, with heart as well as voice and instrument. Much of this was the spontaneous effusions of Mrs Arkwright (a daughter of Stephen Kemble), who has set Hohenlinden, and other pieces of poetry, to music of a highly-gifted character. The Miss Liddells and Mrs Barrington sang ' The Campbells are coming,' in a tone that might have waked the dead.

" *October* 6.—Left Ravensworth this morning, and travelled as far as Whittingham with Marquis of Lothian. Arrived at Alnwick to dinner, where I was very kindly received. The Duke of Northumberland is a handsome man, who will be corpulent if he does not continue to take hard exercise. The Duchess very pretty and lively, but her liveliness is of that kind which shows at once it is connected with thorough principle, and is not liable to be influenced by fashionable caprice. The habits of the family are early and regular; I conceive they may be termed formal and old-fashioned by such visiters as claim to be the pink of the mode. The Castle is a fine old pile, with various courts and towers, and the entrance is magnificent. It wants, however, the splendid feature of a keep. The inside fitting up is an attempt at Gothic, but the taste is meagre and poor, and done over with too much gilding. It was done half a century ago, when this kind of taste was ill understood. I found here the Bishop of Gloucester,* &c. &c.

" *October* 7.—This morning went to church, and heard an excellent sermon from the Bishop of Gloucester; he has great dignity of manner, and his accent and delivery are forcible. Drove out with the

Dr Bethell, who had been tutor to the Duke of Northumberland, held at this time the See of Gloucester. He was thence translated to Exeter, and latterly to Bangor.—[1839.]

Duke in a phaeton, and saw part of the park, which is a fine one lying along the Alne.   But it has been ill planted.   It was laid out by the celebrated Brown. who substituted clumps of birch and Scottish firs for the beautiful oaks and copse which grow nowhere so freely as in Northumberland.   To complete this the late Duke did not thin, so the wood is in a poor state.   All that the Duke cuts down is so much waste, for the people will not buy it where coals are so cheap.   Had they been oak-coppice, the bark would have fetched its value; had they been grown oaks, the sea-ports wo·ld have found a market; had they been larch, the country demands for ruder purposes would have been unanswerable.   The Duke does the best he can to retrieve his woods, but seems to despond more than a young man ought to do.   It is refreshing to see such a man in his situation give so much of his time and thoughts to the improvement of his estates, and the welfare of the people. He tells me his people in Keeldar were all quite wild the first time his father went up to shoot there.   The women had no other dress than a bed-gown and petticoat.   The men were savage, and could hardly be brought to rise from the heath, either from sullenness or fear.   They sung a wild tune, the burden of which was *orsina, orsina, orsina.* The females sang, the men danced round, and at a certain point of the tune they drew their dirks, which they always wore.

" We came by the remains of an old Carmelite Monastery, which form a very fine object in the park. It was finished by De Vesci. The gateway of Alnwick Abbey, also a fine specimen, is standing about a mile distant. The trees are much finer on the left side of the Alne, where they have been let alone by the capability villain. Visited the *enceinte* of the Castle, and passed into the dungeon. There is also an armoury, but damp, and the arms in indifferent order. One odd petard-looking thing struck me.—Mem. to consult Grose. I had the honour to sit in Hotspur's seat, and to see the Bloody Gap, a place where the external wall must have been breached. The Duchess gave me a book of etchings of the antiquities of Alnwick and Warkworth from her own drawings. I had half a mind to stay to see Warkworth, but Anne is alone. We had prayers in the evening read by the Archdeacon." *

On the 8th Sir Walter reached Abbotsford, and forthwith resumed his Grandfather's Tales, which he composed throughout with the ease and heartiness reflected in this entry :—" This morning was damp, dripping, and unpleasant ; so I even made a work of necessity, and set to the Tales like a dragon. I murdered Maclellan of Bomby at the Thrieve Castle ;

* Mr Archdeacon Singleton.

stabbed the Black Douglas in the town of Stirling ; astonished King James before Roxburgh ; and stifled the Earl of Mar in his bath, in the Canongate. A wild world, my masters, this Scotland of ours must have been. No fear of want of interest ; no lassitude in those days for want of work —

> ' For treason, d'ye see,
>   Was to them a dish of tea,
>   And murder bread and butter.'"

Such was his life in autumn 1827. Before I leave the period, I must note how greatly I admired the manner in which all his dependents appeared to have met the reverse of his fortunes — a reverse which inferred very considerable alteration in the circumstances of every one of them. The butler, instead of being the easy chief of a large establishment, was now doing half the work of the house, at probably half his former wages. Old Peter, who had been for five-and-twenty years a dignified coachman, was now ploughman in ordinary, only putting his horses to the carriage upon high and rare occasions ; and so on with all the rest that remained of the ancient train. And all, to my view, seemed happier than they had ever done before. Their good conduct had given every one of them a new elevation in his own mind — and yet their demeanour had gained, in place of losing, in simple humility of observance. The great loss was that of William Laidlaw, for whom (the estate being all but a fragment in the hands of the trustees and their agent) there was now no occupation here The cottage, which his taste had converted into a loveable retreat, had found a rent-paying tenant; and he was living a dozen miles off on the farm of a relation in the Vale of Yarrow. Every week, however, he came down to have a ramble with Sir Walter over their old haunts — to hear how the pecuniary atmosphere was darkening or brightening; and to read in every face at Abbotsford, that it could never be itself again until circumstances should permit his re-establishment at Kaeside.

All this warm and respectful solicitude must have had a preciously soothing influence on the mind of Scott, who may be said to have lived upon love. No man cared less about popular admiration and applause; but for the least chill on the affection of any near and dear to him he had the sensitiveness of a maiden. I cannot forget, in particular, how his eyes sparkled when he first pointed out to me Peter Mathieson guiding the plough on the haugh: "Egad," said he, "auld *Pepe* (this was the children's name for their good friend)—"auld *Pepe's* whistling at his darg. The honest fellow said, a yoking in a deep field would do baith him and the blackies good.

If things get round with me, easy shall be Pepe's cushion." In general, during that autumn, I thought Sir Walter enjoyed much his usual spirits; and often, no doubt, he did so. His Diary shows (what perhaps many of his intimates doubted during his lifetime) that, in spite of the dignified equanimity which characterised all his conversation with mankind, he had his full share of the delicate sensibilities, the mysterious ups and downs, the wayward melancholy, and fantastic sunbeams of the poetical temperament. It is only with imaginative minds, in truth, that sorrows of the spirit are enduring. Those he had encountered were veiled from the eye of the world, but they lasted with his life. What a picture have we in his entry about the Runic letters he had carved in the day of young passion on the turf among the grave-stones of St Andrews! And again, he wrote neither sonnets, nor elegies, nor monodies, nor even an epitaph on his wife;—but what an epitaph is his Diary throughout the year 1826—ay, and down to the close!

There is one entry of that Diary for the period we are leaving, which paints the man in his tenderness, his fortitude, and his happy wisdom:—" *September* 24. Worked in the morning as usual, and sent off the proofs and copy. Something of the black dog still hanging about me; but I will shake him off. I generally affect good spirits in company of my family, whether I am enjoying them or not. It is too severe to sadden the harmless mirth of others by suffering your own causeless melancholy to be seen; and this species of exertion is, like virtue, its own reward; for the good spirits, which are at first simulated, become at length real."

The first series of Chronicles of the Canongate—(which title supplanted that of " *The Canongate Miscellany, or Traditions of the Sanctuary*")—was published early in the winter. The contents were, the Highland Widow, the Two Drovers, and the Surgeon's Daughter—all in their styles excellent, except that the Indian part of the last does not well harmonize with the rest; and certain preliminary chapters which were generally considered as still better than the stories they introduce. The portraiture of Mrs Murray Keith, under the name of Mrs Bethune Baliol, and that of Chrystal Croftangry throughout, appear to me unsurpassed in Scott's writings. In the former, I am assured he has mixed up various features of his own beloved mother; and in the latter, there can be no doubt that a good deal was taken from nobody but himself. In fact, the choice of the hero's residence, the original title of the book, and a world of minor circumstances, were suggested by the actual condition and prospects of the author's affairs; for it appears from his Diary, though I have not thought it necessary to quote those entries, that from time to time, between December 1826 and November 1827, he had renewed threatenings of severe treatment from Messrs Abud and Co.; and, on at least one occasion, he made every preparation for taking shelter in the Sanctuary of Holyroodhouse. Although these people were well aware that at Christmas 1827 a very large dividend would be paid on the Ballantyne estate, they would not understand that their interest, and that of all the creditors, lay in allowing Scott the free use of his time; that by thwarting and harassing him personally, nothing was likely to be achieved but the throwing up of the trust, and the settlement of the insolvent house's affairs on the usual terms of a sequestration; in which case there could be no doubt that he would, on resigning all his assets, be discharged absolutely, with liberty to devote his future exertions to his own sole benefit. The Abuds would understand nothing, but that the very unanimity of the other creditors as to the propriety of being gentle with him, rendered it extremely probable that their harshness might be rewarded by immediate payment of their whole demand. They fancied that the trustees would clear off any one debt, rather than disturb the arrangements generally adopted; they fancied that, in case they laid Sir Walter Scott in prison, there would be some extraordinary burst of feeling in Edinburgh—

that private friends would interfere—in short, that in one way or another, they should get hold, without farther delay, of their " pound of flesh."—Two or three paragraphs from the Diary will be enough as to this unpleasant subject.

" *October* 31.—Just as I was merrily cutting away among my trees, arrives Mr Gibson with a very melancholy look, and indeed the news he brought was shocking enough. It seems Mr Abud, the same who formerly was disposed to disturb me in London, has given positive orders to take out diligence against me for his debt. This breaks all the measures we had resolved on, and prevents the dividend from taking place, by which many poor persons will be great sufferers. For me the alternative will be more painful to my feelings than prejudicial to my interests. To submit to a sequestration, and allow the creditors to take what they can get, will be the inevitable consequence. This will cut short my labour by several years, which I might spend, and spend in vain, in endeavouring to meet their demands. We shall know more on Saturday, and not sooner.—I went to Bowhill with Sir Adam Fergusson to dinner, and maintained as good a countenance in the midst of my perplexities as a man need desire. It is not bravado; I feel firm and resolute.

" *November* 1.—I waked in the night and lay two hours in feverish meditation. This is a tribute to natural feeling. But the air of a fine frosty morning gave me some elasticity of spirit. It is strange that about a week ago I was more dispirited for nothing at all, than I am now for perplexities which set at defiance my conjectures concerning their issue. I suppose that I, the Chronicler of the Canongate, will have to take up my residence in the Sanctuary, unless I prefer the more airy residence of the Calton Jail, or a trip to the Isle of Man. It is to no purpose being angry with Abud or Ahab, or whatever name he delights in. He is seeking his own, and thinks by these harsh measures to render his road to it more speedy.—Sir Adam Fergusson left Bowhill this morning for Dumfries-shire. I returned to Abbotsford to Anne, and told her this unpleasant news. She stood it remarkably well, poor body.

" *November* 2.—I was a little bilious this night— no wonder. Had sundry letters without any power of giving my mind to answer them—one about Gourgaud with his nonsense. I shall not trouble my head more on that score. Well, it is a hard knock on the elbow: I knew I had a life of labour before me, but I was resolved to work steadily: now they have treated me like a recusant turnspit, and put in a red-hot cinder into the wheel alongst with me. But of what use is philosophy—and I have always pretended to a little of a practical character—if it cannot teach us to do or suffer ?   The day is glorious, yet I have little will to enjoy it ; yet, were a twelvemonth over, I should perhaps smile at what makes me now very serious.   Smile! No—that can never be.   My present feelings cannot be recollected with cheerfulness ; but I may drop a tear of gratitude.

" *November* 3.—Slept ill, and lay one hour longer than usual in the morning.   I gained an hour's quiet by it, that is much.   I feel a little shaken at the result of to-day's post.   I am not able to go out. . My poor workers wonder that I pass them without a word.   I can imagine no alternative but the Sanctuary or the Isle of Man.   Both shocking enough. But in Edinburgh I am always on the scene of action, free from uncertainty, and near my poor daughter ; so I think I shall prefer it, and thus I rest in unrest.   But I will not let this unman me.   Our hope, heavenly and earthly, is pcorly anchored, if the cable parts upon the stream.   I believe in God, who can change evil into good ; and I am confident that what befalls us is always ultimately for the best.

" *November* 4. — Put my papers in some order, and prepared for the journey.   It is in the style of the Emperors of Abyssinia, who proclaim—Cut down the Kantuffa in the four quarters of the world, for I know not where I am going. Yet, were it not for poor Anne's doleful looks, I would feel firm as a piece of granite. Even the poor dogs seem to fawn on me with anxious meaning, as if there were something going on they could not comprehend. They probably notice the packing of the clothes, and other symptoms of a journey.

" Set off at twelve, firmly resolved in body and mind. Dined at Fushie Bridge. Ah! good Mrs Wilson, you know not you are like to lose an old customer ! *

" But when I arrived in Edinburgh at my faithful friend, Mr Gibson's—lo! the scene had again changed, and a new hare is started," &c. &c.

The " new hare" was this. It transpired in the very nick of time, that a suspicion of usury attached to these Israelites without guile, in a transaction with Hurst and Robinson, as to one or more of the bills for which the house of Ballantyne had become responsible This suspicion, upon investigation, assumed a shape

* Mrs Wilson, landlady of the inn at Fushie, one stage from Edinburgh — an old dame of some humour, with whom Sir Walter always had a friendly colloquy in passing. I believe the charm was, that she had passed her childhood among the Gipsies of the Border. But her fiery Radicalism latterly was another source of high merriment.

sufficiently tangible to justify Ballantyne's trustees in carrying the point before the Court of Session; but they failed to establish their allegation.* The amount was then settled—but how and in what manner was long unknown to Scott. Sir William Forbes, whose banking-house was one of Messrs Ballantyne's chief creditors, crowned his generous efforts for Scott's relief by privately paying the whole of Abud's demand (nearly £2000) out of his own pocket—ranking as an ordinary creditor for the amount; and taking care at the same time that his old friend should be allowed to believe that the affair had merged quietly in the general measures of the trustees. In fact it was not until some time after Sir William's death, that Sir Walter learned what he had done on this occasion; and I may as well add here, that he himself died in utter ignorance of some services of a like sort, which he owed to the secret liberality of three of his brethren at the Clerk's table—Hector Macdonald Buchanan, Colin Mackenzie, and Sir Robert Dundas.

I ought not to omit, that as soon as Sir Walter's eldest son heard of the Abud business, he left Ireland

---

* The Editor entirely disclaims giving any opinion of his own respecting these transactions with Messrs Abud & Co. He considers it as his business to represent the views which *Sir Walter* took of the affair from time to time: whether these were or were not uniformly correct, he has no means to decide —and indeed no curiosity to inquire.

for Edinburgh; but before he reached his father, the alarm had blown over.

This vision of the real Canongate has drawn me away from the Chronicles of Mr Croftangry. The scenery of his patrimonial inheritance was sketched from that of Carmichael, the ancient and now deserted mansion of the noble family of Hyndford; but for his strongly Scottish feelings about parting with his *land*, and stern efforts to suppress them, the author had not to go so far a-field. Christie Steele's brief character of Croftangry's ancestry, too, appears to suit well all that we have on record concerning his own more immediate progenitors of the stubborn race of Raeburn:—" They werena ill to the poor folk, sir, and that is aye something; they were just decent bien bodies. Ony poor creature that had face to beg got an awmous, and welcome; they that were shamefaced gaed by, and twice as welcome. But they keepit an honest walk before God and man, the Croftangry's, and as I said before, if they did little good, they did as little ill. They lifted their rents and spent them, called in their kain and eat them; gaed to the kirk`of a Sunday; bowed civilly if folk took aff their bannets as they gaed by, and lookit as black as sin at them that keepit them on." I hope I shall give no offence by adding, that many things in the character and manners of Mr Gideon Gray of Middlemas in the Tale of the Surgeon's Daughter, were considered at the time by Sir Walter's neighbours on Tweedside as copied from Dr Ebenezer Clarkson of Selkirk. " He was," says the Chronicler, " of such reputation in the medical world, that he had been often advised to exchange the village and its meagre circle of practice for Edinburgh. There is no creature in Scotland that works harder, and is more poorly requited than the country doctor, unless perhaps it may be his horse. Yet the horse is, and indeed must be, hardy, active, and indefatigable, in spite of a rough coat and indifferent condition; and so you will often find in his master, under a blunt exterior, professional skill and enthusiasm, intelligence, humanity courage, and science." A true picture—a portrait from the life, of Scott's hard-riding, benevolent, and sagacious old friend, " to all the country dear."

These Chronicles were not received with exceeding favour at the time; and Sir Walter was a good deal discouraged. Indeed he seems to have been with some difficulty persuaded by Cadell and Ballantyne, that it would not do for him to " lie fallow" as a novelist; and then, when he in compliance with their entreaties began a Second Canongate Series, they were both disappointed with his MS., and told him their opinions so plainly, that his good-nature was sharply tried. The Tales which they disapproved of, were those of My Aunt Margaret's Mirror, and The Laird's Jock; he consented to lay them aside.

and began St Valentine's Eve, or the Fair Maid of
Perth, which from the first pleased his critics. It was
in the brief interval occasioned by these misgivings
and debates, that his ever elastic mind threw off another charming paper for the Quarterly Review —
that on Ornamental Gardening, by way of sequel to
the Essay on Planting Waste Lands. Another fruit
of his leisure was a sketch of the life of George Bannatyne, the collector of ancient Scottish poetry, for
the Club which bears his name.

DIARY — " *Edinburgh, November* 6.—Wrought
upon an introduction to the notices which have been
recovered of George Bannatyne, author or rather
transcriber of the famous Repository of Scottish
Poetry, generally known by the name of the Bannatyne MS. They are very jejune these same notices
—a mere record of matters of business, putting forth
and calling in sums of money, and such like. Yet it
is a satisfaction to know that this great benefactor to
the literature of Scotland had a prosperous life, and
enjoyed the pleasures of domestic society, and, in a
time peculiarly perilous, lived unmolested and died in
quiet."

He had taken, for that winter, the house No. 6
Shandwick Place, which he occupied by the month
during the remainder of his servitude as a Clerk of

Session. Very near this house, he was told a few days after he took possession, dwelt the aged mother of his first love—the lady of the *Runic characters*.—and he expressed to his friend Mrs Skene a wish that she should carry him to renew an acquaintance which seems to have been interrupted from the period of his youthful romance. Mrs Skene complied with his desire, and she tells me that a very painful scene ensued, adding—" I think it highly probable that it was on returning from this call that he committed to writing the verses, *To Time*, by his early favourite, which you have printed in your first volume."[*] I believe Mrs Skene will have no doubt on that matter when the following entries from his Diary meet her eye :—

" *November 7.*—Began to settle myself this morning, after the hurry of mind and even of body which I have lately undergone.—I went to make a visit, and fairly softened myself, like an old fool, with recalling old stories, till I was fit for nothing but shedding tears and repeating verses for the whole night. This is sad work. The very grave gives up its dead, and time rolls back thirty years to add to my perplexities. I don't care. I begin to grow case-hardened, and, like a stag turning at bay, my naturally good temper grows fierce and dangerous. Yet what a romance to tell,—and told, I fear, it will one day be. And then my three years of dreaming, and my two years of wakening, will be chronicled, doubtless. But the dead will feel no pain.

" *November* 10.— Wrote out my task and little more. At twelve o'clock I went again to poor Lady —— —— to talk over old stories. I am not clear that it is a right or healthful indulgence to be ripping up old sores, but it seems to give her deep-rooted sorrow words, and that is a mental bloodletting. To me these things are now matter of calm and solemn recollection, never to be forgotten, yet scarce to be remembered with pain.— We go out to Saint Catherine's to-day. I am glad of it, for I would not have these recollections haunt me, and society will put them out of my head."

Sir Walter has this entry on reading the *Gazette* of the battle of Navarino:—" *November* 14. We have thumped the Turks very well. But as to the justice of our interference, I will only suppose some Turkish plenipotentiary, with an immense turban and long loose trousers, comes to dictate to us the mode in which we should deal with our refractory liegemen, the Catholics of Ireland. We hesitate to admit his interference, on which the Moslem runs into Cork Bay, or Bantry Bay, alongside of a British squadron, and sends a boat to tow on a fire-ship. A vessel fires on the boat and sinks it. Is there an aggression on the part of those who fired first, or of those whose manœuvres occasioned the firing ?"

A few days afterwards he received a very agreeable piece of intelligence. The King had not forgotten his promise with respect to the poet's second son; and Lord Dudley, then Secretary of State for the Foreign Department, was a much attached friend from early days — (he had been partly educated at Edinburgh under the roof of Dugald Stewart) — his Lordship had therefore been very well disposed to comply with the royal recommendation. — "*November* 30. The great pleasure of a letter from Lord Dudley, informing me that he has received his Majesty's commands to put down the name of my son Charles for the first vacancy that shall occur in the Foreign Office, and at the same time to acquaint me with his gracious intentions, which were signified in language the most gratifying to me. This makes me really feel light and happy, and most grateful to the kind and gracious sovereign who has always shown, I may say, so much friendship towards me. Would to God *the King's errand might lie in the cadger's gait*, that I might have some better way of showing my feelings than merely by a letter of thanks, or this private memorandum of my gratitude. Public affairs look awkward. The present Ministry are neither Whig nor Tory, and divested of the support of either of the great parties of the state, stand supported by the will of the sovereign alone. This is not constitutional, and though it may be a temporary augmentation of the prince's personal influence, yet it cannot but prove hurtful to the Crown upon the whole, by tending to throw that responsibility on him of which the law has deprived him. I pray to God I may be wrong, but, I think, an attempt to govern *par bascule*, by trimming betwixt the opposite parties, is equally unsafe for the Crown, and detrimental to the country, and cannot do for a long time. That with a neutral Administration, this country, hard ruled at any time, can be long governed, I for one do not believe. God send the good King, to whom I owe so much, as safe and honourable extrication as the circumstances render possible."— The dissolution of the Goderich Cabinet confirmed very soon these shrewd guesses; and Sir Walter anticipated nothing but good from the Premiership of the Duke of Wellington.

The settlement of Charles Scott was rapidly followed by more than one fortunate incident in Sir Walter's literary and pecuniary history. The first Tales of a Grandfather appeared early in December, and their reception was more rapturous than that of any one of his works since Ivanhoe. He had solved for the first time the problem of narrating history, so as at once to excite and gratify the curiosity of youth, and please and instruct the wisest of mature minds.   The popularity of the book has grown with every year that has since elapsed; it is equally prized in the library, the boudoir, the schoolroom, and the nursery; it is adopted as the happiest of manuals, not only in Scotland, but wherever the English tongue is spoken; nay, it is to be seen in the hands of old and young all over the civilized world, and has, I have little doubt, extended the knowledge of Scottish history in quarters where little or no interest had ever before been awakened as to any other parts of that subject, except those immediately connected with Mary Stuart and the Chevalier.   This success effectually rebuked the trepidation of the author's bookseller and printer, and inspired the former with new courage as to a step which he had for some time been meditating, and which had given rise to many a long and anxious discussion between him and Sir Walter.

The question as to the property of the Life of Napoleon and Woodstock having now been settled by the arbiter (Lord Newton) in favour of the author, the relative affairs of Sir Walter and the creditors of Constable were so simplified, that the trustee or that sequestrated estate resolved to bring into the market, with the concurrence of Ballantyne's trustees, and without farther delay, a variety of very valuable copyrights.   This important sale comprised

Scott's novels from Waverley to Quentin Durward inclusive, besides a majority of the shares of the Poetical Works.

Mr Cadell's family and private friends were extremely desirous that he should purchase part at least of these copyrights; and Sir Walter's were not less so that he should seize this last opportunity of recovering a share in the prime fruits of his genius. The relations by this time established between him and Cadell were those of strict confidence and kindness; and both saw well that the property would be comparatively lost, were it not secured, that thenceforth the whole should be managed as one unbroken concern. It was in the success of an uniform edition of the Waverley novels, with prefaces and notes by the author, that both anticipated the means of finally extinguishing the debt of Ballantyne and Co.; and, after some demur, the trustees of that house's creditors were wise enough to adopt their views. . The result was, that the copyrights exposed to sale for behoof of Constable's creditors were purchased, one half for Sir Walter, the other half for Cadell, at the price of £8500—a sum which was considered large at the moment, but which the London competitors soon afterwards convinced themselves they ought to have outbid.

The Diary says:—" *December* 17.—Sent off the

new beginning of the Chronicles to Ballantyne. I
hate cancels—they are a double labour. Mr Cowan,
trustee for Constable's creditors, called in the morning by appointment, and we talked about the sale of
the copyrights of Waverley, &c. It is to be hoped
the high upset price fixed (£5000) will

> ' Fright the fuds
> Of the pock-puds.'

This speculation may be for good or for evil, but it
tends incalculably to increase the value of such copyrights as remain in my own person; and if a handsome and cheap edition of the whole, with notes,
can be instituted in conformity with Cadell's plan, it
must prove a mine of wealth for my creditors. It
is possible, no doubt, that the works may lose their
effect on the public mind; but this must be risked,
and I think the chances are greatly in our favour.
Death (my own, I mean) would improve the property, since an edition with a Life would sell like
wildfire. Perhaps those who read this prophecy may
shake their heads and say—' Poor fellow, he little
thought how he should see the public interest in him
and his extinguished, even during his natural existence.' It may be so, but I will hope better. This I
know, that no literary speculation ever succeeded with
me but where my own works were concerned; and
that, on the other hand, these have rarely failed.

" *December* 20. — Anent the copyrights — the
pock-puds were not frightened by our high price.
They came on briskly, four or five bidders abreast,
and went on till the lot was knocked down to Cadell
at £8500; a very large sum certainly, yet he has
been offered profit on it already. The activity of
the contest serves to show the value of the property.
On the whole, I am greatly pleased with the acqui-
sition."

Well might the " pockpuddings" — the English
booksellers — rue their timidity on this day; but it
was the most lucky one that ever came for Sir Walter Scott's creditors. A dividend of six shillings in
the pound was paid at this Christmas on their whole
claims. The result of their high-hearted debtor's
exertions, between January 1826 and January 1828,
was in all very nearly £40,000. No literary bio-
grapher, in all likelihood, will ever have such another
fact to record. The creditors unanimously passed a
vote of thanks for the indefatigable industry which
had achieved so much for their behoof.

On returning to Abbotsford at Christmas, after
completing these transactions, he says in his Diary:
— " My reflections in entering my own gate to-day
were of a very different and more pleasing cast, than
those with which I left this place about six weeks
ago. I was then in doubt whether I should fly. my
country, or become avowedly bankrupt, and surren-

der up my library and household furniture, with the liferent of my estate, to sale. A man of the world will say I had better done so. No doubt, had I taken this course at once, I might have employed the money I have made since the insolvency of Constable and Robinson's houses in compounding my debts. But I could not have slept sound, as I now can under the comfortable impression of receiving the thanks of my creditors, and the conscious feeling of discharging my duty as a man of honour and honesty. I see before me a long, tedious, and dark path, but it leads to stainless reputation. If I die in the harrows, as is very likely, I shall die with honour; if I achieve my task, I shall have the thanks of all concerned, and the approbation of my own conscience. And so, I think, I can fairly face the return of Christmas-day."

And again, on the 31st December, he says —

" Looking back to the conclusion of 1826, I observe that the last year ended in trouble and sickness, with pressures for the present and gloomy prospects for the future. The sense of a great privation so lately sustained, together with the very doubtful and clouded nature of my private affairs, pressed hard upon my mind. I am now restored in constitution; and though I am still on troubled waters, yet I am rowing with the tide, and less than the continuation of my exertions of 1827 may, with God's blessing, carry me successsfully through 1828, when we may gain a more open sea, if not exactly a safe port. Above all, my children are well. Sophia's situation excites some natural anxiety ; but it is only the accomplishment of the burden imposed on her sex. Walter is happy in the view of his majority, on which matter we have favourable hopes from the Horse-Guards. Anne is well and happy. Charles's entry on life under the highest patronage, and in a line for which, I hope, he is qualified, is about to take place presently.

" For all these great blessings, it becomes me well to be thankful to God, who, in his good time and good pleasure. sends us good as well as evil."

CHAPTER LXXV.

The " Opus Magnum"—" Religious Discourses, by a Layman"—Letters to George Huntly Gordon, Cadell, and Ballantyne—Heath's Keepsake, &c.—Arniston—Dalhousie—Prisons—Dissolution of Yeomanry Cavalry—The Fair Maid of Perth published.

JAN.—APRIL 1828.

WITH the exception of a few weeks occupied by an excursion to London, which business of various sorts had rendered necessary, the year 1828 was spent in the same assiduous labour as 1827. The commercial transaction completed at Christmas cleared the way for two undertakings, which would of themselves have been enough to supply desk-work in abundance; and Sir Walter appears to have scarcely passed a day on which something was not done for them. I allude to Cadell's plan of a new edition of the Poetry,

with biographical prefaces; and the still more extensive one of an uniform reprint of the Novels, each
to be introduced by an account of the hints on which
it had been founded, and illustrated throughout by
historical and antiquarian annotations.   On this last,
commonly mentioned in the Diary as the *Opus Magnum*, Sir Walter bestowed pains commensurate with
its importance;—and in the execution of the very
delicate task which either scheme imposed, he has
certainly displayed such a combination of frankness
and modesty as entitles him to a high place in the
short list of graceful autobiographers.   True dignity
is always simple; and perhaps true genius, of the
highest class at least, is always humble.   These operations took up much time;—yet he laboured hard
this year, both as a novelist and a historian.   He
contributed, moreover, several articles to the Quarterly Review and the Bannatyne Club library; and
to the Journal conducted by Mr Gillies, an excellent
Essay on Molière; this last being again a free gift
to the Editor.

But the first advertisement of 1828 was of a new
order; and the announcement that the Author of
Waverley had *Sermons* in the press, was received
perhaps with as much incredulity in the clerical
world, as could have been excited among them by
that of a romance from the Archbishop of Canterbury.   A thin octavo volume, entitled " Religious

Discourses by a Layman," and having " W. S." at the foot of a short preface, did, however, issue in the course of the spring, and from the shop, that all might be in perfect keeping, of Mr Colburn, a bookseller then known almost exclusively as the standing purveyor of what is called " light reading"— novels of " fashionable life," and the like pretty ephemera. I am afraid that the " Religious Discourses," too, would, but for the author's name, have had a brief existence ; but the history of their composition, besides sufficiently explaining the humility of these tracts in a literary as well as a theological point of view, will, I hope, gratify most of my readers.

It may perhaps be remembered, that Sir Walter's cicerone over Waterloo, in August 1815, was a certain Major Pryse Gordon, then on half-pay and resident at Brussels. The acquaintance, until they met at Sir Frederick Adam's table, had been very slight —nor was it ever carried further; but the Major was exceedingly attentive during Scott's stay, and afterwards took some pains about collecting little reliques of the battle for Abbotsford. One evening the poet supped at his house, and there happened to sit next him the host's eldest son, then a lad of nineteen, whose appearance and situation much interested him. He had been destined for the Church of Scotland, but, as he grew up, a deafness, which had come on him in boyhood, became worse and worse, and at

length his friends feared that it must incapacitate
him for the clerical function. He had gone to spend
the vacation with his father, and Sir Frederick Adam,
understanding how he was situated, offered him a
temporary appointment as a clerk in the Commissariat, which he hoped to convert into a permanent
one, in case the war continued. At the time of
Scott's arrival that prospect was wellnigh gone, and
the young man's infirmity, his embarrassment, and
other things to which his own memorandum makes
no allusion, excited the visiter's sympathy. Though
there were lion-hunters of no small consequence in
the party, he directed most of his talk into the poor
clerk's ear-trumpet; and at parting, begged him not
to forget that he had a friend on Tweedside.

A couple of years elapsed before he heard anything
more of Mr Gordon, who then sent him his father's
little *spolia* of Waterloo, and accompanied them by
a letter explaining his situation, and asking advice,
in a style which renewed and increased Scott's favourable impression. He had been dismissed from
the Commissariat at the general reduction of our
establishments, and was now hesitating whether he
had better take up again his views as to the Kirk,
or turn his eyes towards English orders; and in the
meantime he was anxious to find some way of light-
ening to his parents, by his own industry, the completion of his professional education. There ensued a

copious correspondence between him and Scott, who gave him on all points of his case most paternal advice, and accompanied his counsels with offers of pecuniary assistance, of which the young man rarely availed himself.   At length he resolved on re-entering the Divinity Class at Aberdeen, and in due time was licensed by the Presbytery there as a Preacher of the Gospel; but though with good connexions, for he was " sprung of Scotia's gentler blood," his deafness operated as a serious bar to his obtaining the incumbency of a parish.   The provincial Synod pronounced his deafness an insuperable objection, and the case was referred to the General Assembly.   That tribunal heard Mr Gordon's cause maintained by all the skill and eloquence of Mr Jeffrey, whose good offices had been secured by Scott's intervention, and they overruled the decision of the Presbytery.   But Gordon, in the course of the discussion, gathered the conviction, that a man almost literally stone-deaf could *not* discharge some of the highest duties of a parish-priest in a satisfactory manner, and he with honourable firmness declined to take advantage of the judgment of the Supreme Court.   Meantime he had been employed, from the failure of John Ballantyne's health downwards, as the transcriber of the Waverley MSS. for the press, in which capacity he displayed every quality that could endear an amanuensis to an author; and when the disasters of 1826

rendered it unnecessary for Scott to have his MS.
copied, he exerted himself to procure employment for
his young friend in one of the Government offices in
London.   Being backed by the kindness of the late
Duke of Gordon, his story found favour with the
then Secretary of the Treasury, Mr Lushington —
and Mr Gordon was named assistant private secretary to that gentleman.   The appointment was temporary, but he so pleased his chief that there was
hope of better things by and by.—Such was his situation at Christmas 1827; but that being his first
Christmas in London, it was no wonder that he then
discovered himself to have somewhat miscalculated
about money matters.   In a word, he knew not whi-
ther to look at the moment for extrication, until he
bethought him of the following little incident of his
life at Abbotsford.

He was spending the autumn of 1824 there, daily
copying the MS. of Redgauntlet, and working at
leisure hours on the Catalogue of the Library, when
the family observed him to be labouring under some
extraordinary depression of mind.   It was just then
that he had at length obtained the prospect of a
Living, and Sir Walter was surprised that this
should not have exhilarated him.   Gently sounding
the trumpet, however, he discovered that the agitation of the question about the deafness had shaken
his nerves—his scruples had been roused—his con-

science was sensitive,—and he avowed that, though he thought, on the whole, he ought to go through with the business, he could not command his mind so as to prepare a couple of sermons, which, unless he summarily abandoned his object, must be produced on a certain day—then near at hand—before his Presbytery. Sir Walter reminded him that his exercises when on trial for the Probationership had given satisfaction; but nothing he could say was sufficient to re-brace Mr Gordon's spirits, and he at length exclaimed, with tears, that his pen was powerless,—that he had made fifty attempts, and saw nothing but failure and disgrace before him. Scott answered, " My good young friend, leave this matter to me—do you work away at the Catalogue, and I'll write for you a couple of sermons that shall pass muster well enough at Aberdeen." Gordon assented with a sigh; and next morning Sir Walter gave him the MS. of the " Religious Discourses." On reflection, Mr Gordon considered it quite impossible to produce them as his own, and a letter to be quoted immediately will show, that he by and by had written others for himself in a style creditable to his talents, though, from circumstances above explained, he never delivered them at Aberdeen. But the " Two Discourses" of 1824 had remained in his hands; and it now occurred to him that, if Sir Walter would allow him to dispose of these to some bookseller, they might possibly bring a price that would float him over his little difficulties of Christmas.

Scott consented; and Gordon got more than he had ventured to expect for his MS. But since this matter has been introduced, I must indulge myself with a little retrospect, and give a few specimens of the great author's correspondence with this amiable dependent. The series now before me consists of more than forty letters to Mr Gordon.

"Edinburgh, 5th January 1817.

". . . . . I am very sorry your malady continues to distress you; yet while one's eyes are spared to look on the wisdom of former times, we are the less entitled to regret that we hear less of the folly of the present. The Church always presents a safe and respectable asylum, and has many mansions. But in fact, the great art of life, so far as I have been able to observe, consists in fortitude and perseverance. I have rarely seen, that a man who conscientiously devoted himself to the studies and duties of *any* profession, and did not omit to take fair and honourable opportunities of offering himself to notice when such presented themselves, has not at length got forward. The mischance of those who fall behind, though flung upon fortune, more frequently arises from want of skill and perseverance. Life, my young friend, is like a game at cards — our hands are alternately good or bad, and the whole seems at first glance to depend on mere chance. But it is not so, for in the long run the skill of the player predominates over the casualties of the game. Therefore, do not be discouraged with the prospect before you, but ply your studies hard, and qualify yourself to receive fortune when she comes your way. I shall have pleasure at any time in hearing from you, and more especially in seeing you." . . . .

" 24th July 1818.

" . . . . . . I send you *the Travels of Thiodolf.*[*] Perhaps you might do well to give a glance over Tytler's Principles of Translation, ere you gird up your loins to the undertaking. If the gods have made you poetical, you should imitate, rather than attempt a literal translation of, the verses interspersed; and, in general, I think both the prose and verse might be improved by compression. If you find the versification a difficult or unpleasant task, I must translate for you such parts of the poetry as may be absolutely necessary for carrying on the

* A novel by the Baron de la Motte Fouqué.

story, which will cost an old hack like me very little trouble. I would have you, however, by all means try yourself." . . . .

—————

" 14th October 1818.

" . . . . I am greatly at a loss what could possibly make you think you had given me the slightest offence. If that very erroneous idea arose from my silence and short letters, I must plead both business and laziness, which makes me an indifferent correspondent; but I thought I had explained in my last that which it was needful that you should know. . . . .

" I have said nothing on the delicate confidence you have reposed in me. I have not forgotten that I have been young, and must therefore be sincerely interested in those feelings which the best men entertain with most warmth. At the same time, my experience makes me alike an enemy to premature marriage and to distant engagements. The first adds to our individual cares the responsibility for the beloved and helpless pledges of our affection, and the last are liable to the most cruel disappointments. But, my good young friend, if you have settled your affections upon a worthy object, I can only hope that your progress in life will be such as to make you look forward with prudence to a speedy union." . . . . .

" 12th June 1820.

" . . . . I am very sorry for your illness, and your unpleasant and uncertain situation, for which, unfortunately, I can give no better consolation than in the worn-out and wearying-out word, patience. What you mention of your private feelings on an interesting subject, is indeed distressing; but assure yourself that scarce one person out of twenty marries his first love, and scarce one out of twenty of the remainder has cause to rejoice at having done so. What we love in those early days is generally rather a fanciful creation of our own than a reality. We build statues of snow, and weep when they melt." . . . . . .

" 12th April 1825.

" My Dear Mr Gordon,

" I would have made some additions to your sermon with great pleasure, but it is with even more than great pleasure that I assure you it needs none. It is a most respectable discourse, with good divinity in it, which is always the marrow and bones of a *Concio ad clerum*, and you may pronounce it, *meo periculo*, without the. least danger of failure or of unpleasant comparisons. I am not fond of Mr Irving's

species of eloquence, consisting of *outré* flourishes
and extravagant metaphors. The eloquence of the
pulpit should be of a chaste and dignified character:
earnest, but not high-flown and ecstatic, and consisting as much in close reasoning as in elegant expression. It occurs to me as a good topic for more than
one discourse,—the manner in which the heresies of
the earlier Christian Church are treated in the Acts
and the Epistles. It is remarkable, that while the
arguments by which they are combated are distinct,
clear, and powerful, the inspired writers have not
judged it proper to go beyond general expressions,
respecting the particular heresies which they combated. If you look closely, there is much reason in
this. . . . . In general, I would say, that on entering on the clerical profession, were it my case, I
should be anxious to take much pains with my sermons, and the studies on which they must be founded.
Nothing rewards itself so completely as exercise,
whether of the body or mind. We sleep sound, and
our waking hours are happy, because they are em
ployed ; and a little sense of toil is necessary to the
enjoyment of leisure, even when earned by study and
sanctioned by the discharge of duty. I think most
clergymen diminish their own respectability by falling
into indolent habits, and what players call *walking
through their part.* You, who have to beat up
against an infirmity, and it may be against some un-

reasonable prejudices, arising from that infirmity, should determine to do the thing not only well, but better than others." . . . . . .

"*To G. Huntly Gordon, Esq., Treasury, London.*

"28th December 1827.
" Dear Gordon,

" As I have no money to spare at present, I find it necessary to make a sacrifice of my own scruples, to relieve you from serious difficulties. The enclosed will entitle you to deal with any respectable bookseller. You must tell the history in your own way as shortly as possible. All that is necessary to say is, that the discourses were written to oblige a young friend. It is understood my name is not to be put on the title-page, or blazed at full length in the preface. You may trust that to the newspapers.

" Pray, do not think of returning any thanks about this; it is enough that I know it is likely to serve your purpose. But use the funds arising from this unexpected source with prudence, for such fountains do not spring up at every place of the desert. — I am, in haste, ever yours most truly,

WALTER SCOTT."

The reader will, I believe, forgive this retrospect ; and be pleased to know that the publication of the sermons answered the purpose intended. Mr Gordon now occupies a permanent and respectable situation in her Majesty's Stationery Office ; and he concludes his communication to me with expressing his feeling that his prosperity " is all clearly traceable to the kindness of Sir Walter Scott."

In a letter to me about this affair of the Discourses, Sir Walter says, " Poor Gordon has got my leave to make a *kirk and a mill* of my *Sermons* — heaven save the mark !   Help him, if you can, to the water of Pactolus and a swapping thirlage."   The only entries in the Diary, which relate to the business, are the following : — " *December* 28. Huntly Gordon writes me in despair about £180 of debt which he has incurred. He wishes to publish two sermons which I wrote for him when he was taking orders ; and he would get little money for them without my name. People may exclaim against the undesired and unwelcome zeal of him who stretched his hands to help the ark over, with the best intentions, and cry sacrilege. And yet they will do me gross injustice, for I would, if called upon, die a martyr for the Christian religion, so completely is (in my poor opinion) its divine origin proved by its beneficial effects on the state of society. Were we but to name the abolition of slavery and polygamy, how much has, in these two words, been granted to mankind in the lessons of our Saviour!—*January* 10, 1828. Huntly Gordon has disposed of the two sermons to the bookseller, Colburn, for £250; well sold I think, and to go forth immediately. I would rather the thing had not gone there, and far rather that it had gone nowhere,—yet hang it, if it makes the poor lad easy, what needs I fret about it? After all, there would be little grace in doing a kind thing, if you did not suffer pain or inconvenience upon the score."

The next literary entry is this:—" Mr Charles Heath, the engraver, invites me to take charge of a yearly publication called the Keepsake, of which the plates are beyond comparison beautiful, but the letter-press indifferent enough. He proposes £800 a-year if I would become editor, and £400 if I would contribute from seventy to one hundred pages. I declined both, but told him I might give him some trifling thing or other. To become the stipendiary editor of a New-Year's-Gift Book is not to be thought of, nor could I agree to work regularly, for any quantity of supply, at such a publication. Even the pecuniary view is not flattering, though Mr Heath meant it should be so. One hundred of his close printed pages, for which he offers £400, are nearly equal to one volume of a novel. Each novel of three volumes brings £4000, and I remain proprietor of the mine after the first ore is scooped out." The result of this negotiation with Mr Heath was, that he received, for £500, the liberty of printing in his Keepsake the long forgotten juvenile drama of the House of Aspen, with My Aunt Margaret's Mirror, and two other little tales, which had been omitted, at Ballantyne's entreaty, from the second Chronicles of Croftangry. But Sir Walter regretted having meddled in any way with the toyshop of literature, and would never do so again, though repeatedly offered very large sums—nor even when the motive of private regard was added, upon Mr Allan Cunningham's lending his name to one of these painted bladders.

In the same week that Mr Heath made his proposition, Sir Walter received another, which he thus disposes of in his Diary:— " I have an invitation from Messrs Saunders and Ottley, booksellers, offering me from £1500 to £2000 annually to conduct a journal; but I am their humble servant. I am too indolent to stand to that sort of work, and I must preserve the undisturbed use of my leisure, and possess my soul in quiet. A large income is not my object; I must clear my debts; and that is to be done by writing things of which I can retain the property. Made my excuses accordingly."

In January 1828, reprints both of the Grandfather's Tales and of the Life of Napoleon were called for; and both so suddenly, that the booksellers would fain have distributed the volumes among various printers in order to catch the demand. Ballantyne heard of this with natural alarm; and Scott, in the case of the Napoleon, conceived that his own literary character was trifled with, as well as his old ally's interests. On receiving James's first appeal — that as to the Grandfather's Stories, he wrote thus: — I need scarcely add, with the desired effect.

" *To Robert Cadell, Esq., Edinburgh.*

" Abbotsford, 3d January 1828.

" My Dear Sir,

" I find our friend James Ballantyne is very anxious about printing the new edition of the Tales, which I hope you will allow him to do, unless extreme haste be an extreme object. I need not remind you that we three are like the shipwrecked crew of a vessel, cast upon a desolate island, and fitting up out of the remains of a gallant bark such a cock-boat as may transport us to some more hospitable shore. Therefore, we are bound by the strong tie of common misfortune to help each other, in so far as the claim of self-preservation will permit, and I am happy to think the plank is large enough to float us all.

" Besides my feelings for my own old friend and schoolfellow, with whom I have shared good and bad weather for so many years, I must also remember that, as in your own case, his friends have made great exertions to support him in the printing-office, under an implied hope and trust that these publications would take *in ordinary cases* their usual direction. It is true, no engagement was or could be proposed to this effect; but it was a reasonable expectation. which influenced kind and generous men, and I incline to pay every respect to it in my power.

" Messrs Longman really keep matters a little too quiet for my convenience. The next thing they may tell me is, that Napoleon must go to press instantly to a dozen of printers. I must boot and saddle, off and away at a fortnight's warning. Now this I neither can nor will do. My character as a man of letters is deeply interested in giving a complete revisal of that work, and I wish to have time to do so without being hurried. Yours very truly,   W. S."

The following specimens of his " skirmishes," as he used to call them, with Ballantyne, while the Fair Maid of Perth was in hand, are in keeping with this amiable picture:—

" My Dear James—I return the proofs of Tales, and send some leaves copy of St Valentine's. Pray get on with *this* in case we should fall through again.

When the press does not follow me, I get on slowly and ill, and put myself in mind of Jamie Balfour, who could run when he could not stand still. We *must* go on or stop altogether. Yours," &c. &c.

" I think you are hypercritical in your commentary. I counted the hours with accuracy. In the morning the citizens went to Kinfauns and returned. This puts over the hour of noon, then the dinnerhour. Afterwards, and when the king has had his devotions in private, comes all the scene in the court-yard. The sun sets at half-past five on the 14th February; and if we suppose it to be within an hour of evening, it was surely time for a woman who had a night to put over, to ask where she should sleep. This is the explanation,—apply it as you please to the text; for you who see the doubt can best clear it. Yours truly," &c.

" I cannot afford to be merciful to Master Oliver Proudfoot, although I am heartily glad there is any one of the personages sufficiently interesting to make you care whether he lives or dies. But it would cost my cancelling half a volume, and rather than do so.

I would, like the valiant Baron of Clackmannan, kill the whole characters, the author, and the printer. Besides, *entre nous*, the resurrection of Athelstane was a botch. It struck me when I was reading Ivanhoe over the other day.

" I value your criticism as much as ever; but the worst is, my faults are better known to myself than to you. Tell a young beauty that she wears an unbecoming dress, or an ill-fashioned ornament, or speaks too loud, or commits any other mistake which she can correct, and she will do so, if she has sense, and a good opinion of your taste. But tell a fading beauty, that her hair is getting gray, her wrinkles apparent, her gait heavy, and that she has no business in a ball-room but to be ranged against the wall as an ever-green, and you will afflict the poor old lady, without rendering her any service. She knows all that better than you. I am sure the old lady in question takes pain enough at her toilette, and gives you, her trusty *suivante*, enough of trouble. Yours truly,   W. S."

These notes to the printer appear to have been written at Abbotsford during the holidays. On his way back to Edinburgh, Sir Walter halts for a Saturday and Sunday at Arniston, and the Diary on the second day says—" Went to Borthwick church with the family, and heard a well-composed, well-delivered, sensible discourse from Mr Wright.* After sermon we looked at the old castle, which made me an old man. The castle was not a bit older for the twenty-five years which had passed away, but the ruins of the visiter are very apparent. To climb up ruinous staircases, to creep through vaults and into dungeons, were not the easy labours but the positive sports of my younger years; but I thought it convenient to attempt no more than the access to the large and beautiful hall, in which, as it is somewhere described, an armed horseman might brandish his lance.† This feeling of growing inability is painful to one who boasted, in spite of infirmity, great boldness and dexterity in such feats; the boldness remains, but hand and foot, grip and accuracy of step, have altogether failed me—the spirit is willing, but the flesh is weak; and so I must retreat into the invalided corps, and tell them of my former exploits, which may very likely pass for lies. We then drove to Dalhousie, where the gallant Earl, who has done so much to distinguish the British name in every quarter of the globe, is repairing the castle of his ancestors, which of yore stood a siege against John of Gaunt. I was his companion at school, where he

* The Rev. T. Wright, of Borthwick, is the author of various popular works,—"The Morning and Evening Sacrifice," &c. &c.

† See Scott's account of Borthwick Castle in his Prose Miscellanies, vol. vi.

was as much beloved by his playmates, as he has been ever respected by his companions in arms and the people over whom he had been deputed to exercise the authority of his sovereign. He was always steady, wise, and generous. The old Castle of Dalhousie—*seu potius* Dalwolsey—was mangled by a fellow called, I believe, Douglas, who destroyed, as far as in him lay, its military and baronial character, and roofed it after the fashion of a poor's-house. Burn * is now restoring and repairing in the old taste, and, I think, creditably to his own feeling. God bless the roof-tree!

" We returned home by the side of the South Esk, where I had the pleasure to see that Robert Dundas † is laying out his woods with taste, and managing them with care. His father and uncle took notice of me when I was ' a fellow of no mark nor likelihood,' ‡ and I am always happy in finding myself in the old oak room at Arniston, where I have drank many a merry bottle, and in the fields where I have seen many a hare killed."

At the opening of the Session next day, he misses one of his dear old colleagues of the table, Mr Mac-

* William Burn, Esq , architect, Edinburgh.

† R. Dundas of Arniston, Esq., the worthy representative of an illustrious lineage, died at his paternal seat in June 1838.

‡ *King Henry IV., Act III. Scene* 2.

kenzie, who had long been the official preses in ordinary of the Writers to the Signet. The Diary has a pithy entry here:—" My good friend Colin Mackenzie proposes to retire from indifferent health. A better man never lived—eager to serve every one —a safeguard over all public business which came through his hands. As Deputy-keeper of the Signet he will be much missed. He had a patience in listening to every one, which is of infinite importance in the management of a public body ; for many men care less to gain their point, than they do to play the orator, and be listened to for a certain time. This done, and due quantity of personal consideration being gained, the individual orator is usually satisfied with the reasons of the civil listener, who has suffered him to enjoy his hour of consequence."

The following passages appear (in various ways) too curious and characteristic to be omitted. He is working hard, alas! too hard—at the Fair Maid of Perth.

" *February* 17.—A hard day of work, being, I think, eight pages* before dinner. I cannot, I am sure, tell if it is worth marking down, that yesterday, at dinner-time, I was strangely haunted by what I would call the sense of pre-existence—viz. a con-

* *i. e.* Forty pages of print, or very nearly.

fused idea that nothing that passed was said for the first time—that the same topics had been discussed, and the same persons had stated the same opinions on them. It is true there might have been some ground for recollections, considering that three at least of the company were old friends, and had kept much company together; that is, Justice - Clerk, [Lord] Abercromby, and I. But the sensation was so strong as to resemble what is called a *mirage* in the desert, or a calenture on board of ship, when lakes are seen in the desert, and sylvan landscapes in the sea. It was very distressing yesterday, and brought to my mind the fancies of Bishop Berkeley about an ideal world. There was a vile sense of want of reality in all I did and said. It made me gloomy and out of spirits, though I flatter myself this was not observed. The bodily feeling which most resembles this unpleasing hallucination is the giddy state which follows profuse bleeding, when one feels as if he were walking on feather-beds and could not find a secure footing. I think the stomach has something to do with it. I drank several glasses of wine, but these only augmented the disorder. I did not find the *in vino veritas* of the philosophers. Something of this insane feeling remains to-day, but a trifle only.

"'*February* 20 —Another day of labour, but not

so hard. I worked from eight till three with little intermission, but only accomplished four pages.

" A certain Mr Mackay from Ireland called on me—an active agent, it would seem, about the reform of prisons. He exclaims—justly I doubt not—about the state of our Lock-up House. For myself I have some distrust of the fanaticism even of philanthropy. A good part of it arises in general from mere vanity and love of distinction, gilded over to others and to themselves with some show of benevolent sentiment. The philanthropy of Howard, mingled with his ill-usage of his son, seems to have risen to a pitch of insanity. Yet without such extraordinary men, who call attention to the subject by their own peculiarities, prisons would have remained the same dungeons which they were forty or fifty years ago. I do not, however, see the propriety of making them dandy places of detention. They should be places of punishment, and that can hardly be if men are lodged better, and fed better, than when they are at large. I have never seen a plan for keeping in order these resorts of guilt and misery, without presupposing a superintendence of a kind which might perhaps be exercised, could we turn out upon the watch a guard of angels. But, alas! jailers and turnkeys are rather like angels of a different livery, nor do I see how it is possible to render them otherwise. *Quis custodiet ipsos custodes?* As to reformation, I have no great belief

in it, when the ordinary classes of culprits, who are
vicious from ignorance or habit, are the subjects of
the experiment. ' A shave from a broken loaf' is
thought as little of by the male set of delinquents as
by the fair frail. The state of society now leads to
such accumulations of humanity, that we cannot wonder if it ferment and reek like a compost dunghill.
Nature intended that population should be diffused
over the soil in proportion to its extent. We have
accumulated in huge cities and smothering manufac-
tories the numbers which should be spread over the
face of a country; and what wonder that they should
be corrupted? We have turned healthful and pleasant brooks into morasses and pestiferous lakes,—
what wonder the soil should be unhealthy? A great
deal, I think, might be done by executing the punishment of *death*, without a chance of escape, in all cases
to which it should be found properly applicable; of
course these occasions being diminished to one out of
twenty to which capital punishment is now assigned.
Our ancestors brought the country to order by *kilt-
ing* thieves and banditti with strings. So did the
French when at Naples, and bandits became for the
time unheard of. When once men are taught that a
crime of a certain character is connected inseparably
with death, the moral habits of a population become
altered, and you may in the next age remit the pu-

nishment which in this it has been necessary to inflict with stern severity.

"*February* 21.—Last night after dinner I rested from my work, and read the third series of *Sayings and Doings*, which shows great knowledge of life in a certain sphere, and very considerable powers of wit, which somewhat damages the effect of the tragic parts. But Theodore Hook is an able writer, and so much of his work is well said, that it will carry through what is indifferent. I hope the same good fortune for other folks.

" I am watching and waiting till I hit on some quaint and clever mode of extricating, but do not see a glimpse of any one. James B., too, discourages me a good deal by his silence, waiting, I suppose, to be invited to disgorge a full allowance of his critical bile. But he will wait long enough, for I am discouraged enough. Now here is the advantage of Edinburgh. In the country, if a sense of inability once seizes me, it haunts me from morning to night; but in town the time is so occupied and frittered away by official duties and chance occupations, that you have not leisure to play Master Stephen, and be melancholy and gentlemanlike.* On the other hand,

* See Ben Jonson's '*Every Man in his Humour*,' *Act I. Scene* 3.

you never feel in town those spirit-stirring influences
—those glances of sunshine that make amends for
clouds and mist. The country is said to be the quieter
life; not to me, I am sure. In town the business I
have to do hardly costs me more thought than just
occupies my mind, and I have as much of gossip and
lady-like chat as consumes odd hours pleasantly
enough. In the country I am thrown entirely on my
own resources, and there is no medium betwixt happiness and the reverse.

" *March* 9.—I set about arranging my papers, a
task which I always take up with the greatest possible ill-will, and which makes me cruelly nervous.
I don't know why it should be so, for I have nothing
particularly disagreeable to look at; far from it, I am
better than I was at this time last year, my hopes
firmer, my health stronger, my affairs bettered and
bettering. Yet I feel an inexpressible nervousness
in consequence of this employment. The memory,
though it retains all that has passed, has closed sternly
over it; and this rummaging, like a bucket dropped
suddenly into a well, deranges and confuses the ideas
which slumbered on the mind. I am nervous, and I
am bilious, and, in a word, I am unhappy. This is
wrong, very wrong; and it is reasonably to be apprehended that something of serious misfortune may be
the deserved punishment of this pusillanimous low-

ness of spirits. Strange, that one who in most things may be said to have enough of the ' care na by,' should be subject to such vile weakness!—Drummond Hay, the antiquary and Lyon-herald,* came in. I do not know anything which relieves the mind so much from the sullens as trifling discussions about antiquarian *old womanries.* It is like knitting a stocking, diverting the mind without occupying it; or it is like, by Our Lady, a mill-dam, which leads one's thoughts gently and imperceptibly out of the channel in which they are chafing and boiling. To be sure, it is only conducting them to turn a child's mill: what signifies that?—the diversion is a relief though the object is of little importance. I cannot tell what we talked of.

" *March* 12.—I was sadly worried by the black dog this morning, that vile palpitation of the heart— that *tremor cordis*—that hysterical passion which forces unbidden sighs and tears, and falls upon a contented life like a drop of ink on white paper, which is not the less a stain because it carries no meaning, I wrote three leaves, however, and the story goes on.

" The dissolution of the Yeomanry was the act of the last Ministry. The present did not alter the

---

* W. A. Drummond Hay, Esq. (now consul at Tangier), was at this time the deputy of his cousin the Earl of Kinnoull, hereditary Lord Lyon King at Arms.

measure, on account of the expense saved. I am,
if not the very oldest Yeoman in Scotland, one of
the oldest, and have seen the rise, progress, and now
the fall of this very constitutional part of the national
force. Its efficacy, on occasions of insurrection, was
sufficiently proved in the Radical time. But besides,
it kept up a spirit of harmony between the proprietors of land and the occupiers, and made them known
to and beloved by each other; and it gave to the
young men a sort of military and high-spirited character, which always does honour to a country. The
manufacturers are in great glee on this occasion. I
wish Parliament, as they have turned the Yeomen
adrift somewhat scornfully, may not have occasion to
roar them in again.

> ' The eldrich knight gave up his arms
> With many a sorrowful sigh.' "

Sir Walter finished his novel by the end of March,
and immediately set out for London, where the last
budget of proof-sheets reached him. The Fair Maid
was, and continues to be highly popular, and though
never classed with his performances of the first file,
it has undoubtedly several scenes equal to what the
best of them can show, and is on the whole a work
of brilliant variety and most lively interest. Though

the Introduction of 1830 says a good deal on the most original character, that of Connochar, the reader may not be sorry to have one paragraph on that subject from the Diary:—" *December* 5, 1827. The fellow that swam the Tay, and escaped, would be a good ludicrous character. But I have a mind to try him in the serious line of tragedy. Miss Baillie has made her Ethling a coward by temperament, and a hero when touched by filial affection. Suppose a man's nerves, supported by feelings of honour, or say, by the spur of jealousy, sustaining him against constitutional timidity to a certain point, then suddenly giving way, I think something tragic might be produced. James Ballantyne's criticism is too much moulded upon the general taste of novels to admit (I fear) this species of reasoning. But what can one do? I am hard up as far as imagination is concerned, yet the world calls for novelty. Well, I'll try my brave coward or cowardly brave man. *Valeat quantum.*"

The most careful critic that has handled this Tale, while he picks many holes in the plot, estimates the characters very highly. Of the glee-maiden, he well says —" Louise is a delightful sketch. — Nothing can be more exquisite than the manner in which her story is partly told, and partly hinted, or than the contrast between her natural and her professional character ;" and after discussing at some length

Rothsay, Henbane, Ramorney, &c. &c. he comes to Connochar.

" This character" (says Mr Senior) " is perfectly tragic, neither too bad for sympathy, nor so good as to render his calamity revolting; but its great merit is the boldness with which we are called upon to sympathize with a deficiency which is generally the subject of unmitigated scorn. It is impossible not to feel the deepest commiseration for a youth cursed by nature with extreme sensibility both to shame and to fear, suddenly raised from a life of obscurity and peace, to head a confederacy of warlike savages, and forced immediately afterwards to elect, before the eyes of thousands, between a frightful death and an ignominious escape. The philosophy of courage and cowardice is one of the obscurest parts of human nature: partly because the susceptibility of fear is much affected by physical causes, by habit, and by example; and partly because it is a subject as to which men do not readily state the result of their own experience, and when they do state it, are not always implicitly believed. The subject has been further perplexed, in modern times, by the Scandinavian invention of the point of honour; — a doctrine which represents the manifestation, in most cases, of even well-founded apprehension as fatal to all nobility of character; — an opinion so little admitted by the classical world, that Homer has attributed to Hector, and Virgil to Turnus, certainly without supposing them dishonoured, precisely the same conduct of which Sir Walter makes suicide a consequence, without being an expiation. The result of all this has been, that scarcely any modern writers have made the various degrees of courage a source of much variety and discrimination of character. They have given us indeed plenty of fire-eaters and plenty of poltroons; and Shakspeare has painted in Falstaff constitutional intrepidity unsupported by honour; but by far the most usual modification of character among persons of vivid imagination, that in which a quick feeling of honour combats a quick apprehension of danger, a character which is the precise converse of Falstaff's, has been left almost untouched for Scott."

I alluded, in an early part of these Memoirs (Vol. III. p. 198), to a circumstance in Sir Walter's conduct, which it was painful to mention, and added, that in advanced life he himself spoke of it with a deep feeling of contrition. Talking over this character of Connochar, just before the book appeared, he told me the unhappy fate of his brother Daniel, and how he had declined to be present at his funeral, or wear mourning for him. He added—" My secret motive, in this attempt, was to perform a sort of expiation to my poor brother's manes. I have now learned to have more tolerance and compassion than I had in those days." I said he put me in mind of Samuel Johnson's standing bareheaded, in the last year of his life, on the market-place of Uttoxeter, by way of penance for a piece of juvenile irreverence towards his father. " Well, no matter," said he; " perhaps that's not the worst thing in the Doctor's story."*

* See Croker's *Boswell*, octavo edition, vol. v. p. 268.

CHAPTER LXXVI.

Journey to London — Charlecote-Hall — Holland-House — Chiswick — Kensington Palace — Richmond Park — Gill's-Hill — Boyd — Sotheby — Coleridge — Sir T. Acland — Bishop Copplestone — Mrs Arkwright — Lord Sidmouth — Lord Alvanley — Northcote — Haydon — Chantrey and Cunningham — Anecdotes — Letters to Mr Terry, Mrs Lockhart, and Sir Alexander Wood — Death of Sir William Forbes — Reviews of Hajji Baba in England, and Davy's Salmonia — Anne of Geierstein begun — Second series of the Grandfather's Tales published —

APRIL — DEC. 1828.

SIR WALTER remained at this time six weeks in London. His eldest son's regiment was stationed at Hampton Court; the second had recently taken his desk at the Foreign Office, and was living at his sister's in the Regent's Park; he had thus looked forward to a happy meeting with all his family—but he encountered scenes of sickness and distress, in consequence of which I saw but little of him in general society. I shall cull a few notices from his private volume, which, however, he now opened much less regularly than formerly, and which offers a total blank for the latter half of the year 1828. In coming up to town, he diverged a little for the sake of seeing the interesting subject of the first of these extracts.

" *April* 8.—Learning from Washington Irving's description of Stratford, that the hall of Sir Thomas Lucy, the Justice who rendered Warwickshire too hot for Shakspeare, was still extant, we went in quest of it.

" Charlecote is in high preservation, and inhabited by Mr Lucy, descendant of the worshipful Sir Thomas. The Hall is about three hundred years old—a brick mansion, with a gate-house in advance. It is surrounded by venerable oaks, realizing the imagery which Shakspeare loved to dwell upon; rich verdant pastures extend on every side, and numerous herds of deer were reposing in the shade. All showed that the Lucy family had retained their ' land and beeves.' While we were surveying the antlered old hall, with its painted glass and family pictures, Mr Lucy came to welcome us in person, and to show the house, with the collection of paintings, which seems valuable.

" He told me the park from which Shakspeare stole the buck was not that which surrounds Charlecote, but belonged to a mansion at some distance, where Sir Thomas Lucy resided at the time of the trespass. The tradition went, that they hid the buck in a barn, part of which was standing a few years ago, but now totally decayed. This park no longer belongs to the Lucys. The house bears no marks of decay, but seems the abode of ease and opulence. There were some fine old books, and I was told of many more which were not in order. How odd, if a folio Shakspeare should be found amongst them Our early breakfast did not permit taking advantage of an excellent repast offered by the kindness of Mr and Mrs Lucy, the last a lively Welshwoman. This visit gave me great pleasure; it really brought Justice Shallow freshly before my eyes; — the *luces* ' which do become an old coat well,'* were not more plainly portrayed in his own armorials in the hall window, than was his person in my mind's eye. There is a picture shown as that of the old Sir Thomas, but Mr Lucy conjectures it represents his son. There were three descents of the same name of Thomas. The portrait hath the ' eye severe, and

* *Henry IV. Act III. Scene 2.*

beard of formal cut,' which fill up with judicial aus-
terity the otherwise social physiognomy of the worshipful presence, with his ' fair round belly, with
good capon lined.' *

" *Regent's Park, April* 17.—Made up my jour-
-nal, which had fallen something behind. In this
phantasmagorial place, the objects of the day come
and depart like shadows. Went to Murray's, where
I met Mr Jacob, the great economist. He is proposing a mode of supporting the poor, by compelling
them to labour under a species of military discipline.
I see no objection to it, only it will make a rebellion
to a certainty; and the tribes of Jacob will cut Jacob's
throat. †

" Canning's conversion from popular opinions was
strangely brought round. While he was studying in
the Temple, and rather entertaining revolutionary
opinions, Godwin sent to say that he was coming
to breakfast with him, to speak on a subject of the
highest importance. Canning knew little of him,

* *As You Like It, Act I. Scene* 7.

† Mr Jacob published about this time some tracts concerning
the Poor Colonies instituted by the King of the Netherlands; and
they had marked influence in promoting the scheme of granting
small *allotments* of land, on easy terms to our cottagers; a scheme
which, under the superintendence of Lord Braybroke and other
noblemen and gentlemen in various districts of England, appears
to have been attended with most beneficent results.

but received his visit, and learned to his astonishment, that in expectation of a new order of things, the English Jacobins designed to place him, Canning, at the head of their revolution. He was much struck, and asked time to think what course he should take—and having thought the matter over, he went to Mr Pitt, and made the Anti-Jacobin confession of faith, in which he persevered until ——. Canning himself mentioned this to Sir W. Knighton upon occasion of giving a place in the Charter-house of some ten pounds a-year to Godwin's brother. He could scarce do less for one who had offered him the dictator's curule chair.

" Dined with Rogers with all my own family, and met Sharp, Lord John Russell, Jekyll, and others. The conversation flagged as usual, and jokes were fired like minute-guns, producing an effect not much less melancholy. A wit should always have an atmosphere congenial to him, otherwise he will not shine.

" *April* 18.—Breakfasted at Hampstead with Joanna Baillie, and found that gifted person extremely well, and in the display of all her native knowledge of character and benevolence. I would give as much to have a capital picture of her as for any portrait in the world. Dined with the Dean of Chester, Dr Philpotts—

' Where all above us was a solemn row
Of priests and deacons — so were all below.' *

There were the amiable Bishop of London,† Copplestone, whom I remember the first man at Oxford, now Bishop of Llandaff, and Dean of St Paul's (strongly intelligent), and other dignitaries, of whom I knew less. It was a very pleasant day — the wigs against the wits for a guinea, in point of conversation. Anne looked queer, and much disposed to laugh, at finding herself placed betwixt two prelates in black petticoats.

" *April* 19. — Breakfasted with Sir George Phillips. Had his receipt against the blossoms being injured by frost. It consists in watering them plentifully before sunrise. This is like the mode of thawing beef. We had a pleasant morning, much the better that Morritt was with us. Dined with Sir Robert Inglis, and met Sir Thomas Acland, my old and kind friend. I was happy to see him. He may be considered now as the head of the religious party in the House of Commons — a powerful body, which Wilberforce long commanded. It is a difficult situation; for the adaptation of religious motives to earthly policy is apt — among the infinite delusions of

* Crabbe's Tale of ' the Dumb Orators.'

† Dr Howley, raised in 1828 to the Archbishoprick of Canterbury.

the human heart—to be a snare. But I could con-
fide much in Sir T. Acland's honour and integrity.
Bishop Bloomfield of Chester,* one of the most
learned prelates of the Church, also dined.

"*April* 22.—Sophia left this to take down poor
Johnnie to Brighton. I fear—I fear—but we must
hope the best. Anne went with her sister.

"Lockhart and I dined with Sotheby, where we
met a large party, the orator of which was that extraordinary man Coleridge. After eating a hearty
dinner, during which he spoke not a word, he began
a most learned harangue on the Samothracian Mysteries, which he regards as affording the germ of all
tales about fairies past, present, and to come. He
then diverged to Homer, whose Iliad he considered
as a collection of poems by different authors, at different times, during a century. Morritt, a zealous
worshipper of the old bard, was incensed at a system
which would turn him into a polytheist, gave battle
with keenness, and was joined by Sotheby. Mr Coleridge behaved with the utmost complaisance and temper, but relaxed not from his exertions. ' Zounds,
I was never so bethumped with words.' Morritt's
impatience must have cost him an extra sixpence
worth of snuff.

* Translated to the See of London in 1828.

" *April* 23.—Dined at Lady Davy's with Lord and Lady Lansdowne and several other fine folks— my keys were sent to Bramah's with my desk, so I have not had the means of putting down matters regularly for several days. But who cares for the whipp'd cream of London society?

" *April* 24.—Spent the day in rectifying a road bill which drew a turnpike road through all the Darnicker's cottages, and a good field of my own. I got it put to rights. I was in some apprehension of being obliged to address the Committee. I did not fear them, for I suppose they are no wiser or better in their capacity of legislators than I find them every day at dinner. But I feared for my reputation. They would have expected something better than the occasion demanded, or the individual could produce, and there would have been a failure. We had one or two persons at home in great wretchedness to dinner. I was not able to make any fight, and the evening went off as heavily as any I ever spent in the course of my life.

" *April* 26.—We dined at Richardson's with the two Chief-Barons of England * and Scotland,†—odd enough, the one being a Scotsman and the other an

* Sir William A.exander.   † Sir Samuel Shepherd.

Englishman—far the pleasantest day we have had. I suppose I am partial, but I think the lawyers beat the bishops, and the bishops beat the wits.

" *April* 26.—This morning I went to meet a remarkable man, Mr. Boyd of the house of Boyd, Benfield, & Co., which broke for a very large sum at the beginning of the war. Benfield went to the devil, I believe. Boyd, a man of very different stamp, went over to Paris to look after some large claims which his house had on the French Government. They were such as, it seems, they could not disavow, however they might be disposed to do so. But they used every effort, by foul means and fair, to induce Mr Boyd to depart. He was reduced to poverty; he was thrown into prison; and the most flattering prospects were, on the other hand, held out to him if he would compromise his claims. His answer was uniform. It was the property, he said, of his creditors, and he would die ere he resigned it. His distresses were so great, that a subscription was made amongst his Scottish friends, to which I was a contributor, through the request of poor Will Erskine. After the peace of Paris the money was restored; and, faithful to the last, Boyd laid the whole at his creditors' disposal; stating, at the same time, that he was penniless, unless they consented to allow him a moderate sum in name of per centage, in consideration of twenty years of exile, poverty, and danger, all of which evils he might have escaped by surrendering their rights. Will it be believed that a muckworm was base enough to refuse his consent to this deduction, alleging he had promised to his father, on his deathbed, never to compromise this debt? The wretch, however, was overpowered by the execrations of all around him, and concurred, with others, in setting apart for Mr Boyd a sum of £40,000 or £50,000 out of half a million. This is a man to whom statues should be erected, and pilgrims should go to see him. He is good-looking, but old and infirm. Bright dark eyes and eyebrows contrast with his snowy hair, and all his features mark vigour of principle and resolution.

" *April* 30.—We have Mr Adolphus, and his father,* the celebrated lawyer, to breakfast, and I was greatly delighted with the information of the latter. A barrister of extended practice, if he has any talents at all, is the best companion in the world. Dined with Lord Alvanley, and met Lord Fitzroy Somerset, Marquis and Marchioness of Worcester, &c. Lord Alvanley's wit made this party very pleasant, as well as the kind reception of my friends the Misses Arden.

* The elder Mr Adolphus distinguished himself early in life by his History of the Reign of George III.

" *May* 1.— Breakfasted with Lord and Lady Francis Gower, and enjoyed the splendid treat of hearing Mrs Arkwright sing her own music, which is of the highest order;— no forced vagaries of the voice, no caprices of tone, but all telling upon and increasing the feeling the words require. This is ' marrying music to immortal verse.' * Most people place them on separate maintenance.†

" *May* 2.— I breakfasted with a Mr ——, and narrowly escaped Mr Irving the celebrated preacher. The two ladies of his house seemed devoted to his opinions, and quoted him at every word. Mr —— himself made some apologies for the Millennium. He is a neat antiquary, who thinks he ought to have been a man of letters, and that his genius has been misdi

---

* Milton's *L'Allegro*, v. 137.

† Among other songs Mrs Arkwright (see *ante*, p. 157), delighted Sir Walter with her own set of —

> " Farewell ! farewell !— The voice you hear
> Has left its last soft tone with you ;
> Its next must join the seaward cheer,
> And shout among the shouting crew," &c.

He was sitting by me, at some distance from the lady, and whispered as she closed—" Capital words —whose are they ?—Byron's I suppose, but I don't remember them." He was astonished when I told him that they were his own in the Pirate. He seemed pleased at the moment, but said next minute —" You have distressed me — if memory goes, all is up with me, for that was always my strong point."

rected in turning towards the law. I endeavoured to
combat this idea, which his handsome house and fine
family should have checked. Compare his dwelling,
his comforts, with poor Tom Campbell's.

" *May* 5.—Breakfasted with Haydon, and sat for
my head. I hope this artist is on his legs again.
The King has given him a lift, by buying his clever
picture of the Mock Election in the King's Bench
prison, to which he is adding a second part, representing the chairing of the Member at the moment
it was interrupted by the entry of the guards. Haydon was once a great admirer and companion of the
champions of the Cockney school, and is now disposed
to renounce them and their opinions. To this kind
of conversation I did not give much way. A painter
should have nothing to do with politics. He is certainly a clever fellow, but too enthusiastic, which,
however, distress seems to have cured in some degree.
His wife, a pretty woman, looked happy to see me,
and that is something. Yet it was very little I could
do to help them.*

" *May* 8. — Dined with Mrs Alexander of Bal-

* Sir Walter had shortly before been one of the contributors to
a subscription for Mr Haydon. The imprisonment from which
this subscription relieved the artist produced, I need scarcely say,
the picture mentioned in the Diary.

lochmyle:—Lord and Lady Meath, who were kind to us in Ireland, and a Scottish party, pleasant from having the broad accents and honest thoughts of my native land.   A large circle in the evening.   A gentleman came up to me and asked ' If I had seen the Casket, a curious work, the most beautiful, the most highly ornamented,—and then the editor or editress —a female so interesting,—might he ask a very great favour?' and out he pulled a piece of this pic-nic.   I was really angry, and said, for a subscription he might command me,—for a contributor—No.   This may be misrepresented, but I care not.   Suppose this patron of the Muses gives five guineas to his distressed lady, he will think he does a great deal, yet he takes fifty from me with the calmest air in the world; for the communication is worth that if it be worth anything.   There is no equalizing in the proposal.

" *May* 9.—Grounds of Foote's farce of the Cozeners.   Lady —— ——.   A certain Mrs Phipps audaciously set up in a fashionable quarter of the town as a person through whose influence, properly propitiated, favours and situations of importance might certainly be obtained — always for a consideration.   She cheated many people, and maintained the trick for months.   One trick was to get the equipages of Lord North, and other persons of importance, to halt before her door, as if their owners were within.   With respect to most of them, this was effected by bribing the drivers. But a gentleman who watched her closely, observed that Charles J. Fox actually left his carriage and went into the house, and this more than once. He was then, it must be noticed, in the Ministry. When Mrs Phipps was blown up, this circumstance was recollected as deserving explanation, which Fox readily gave at Brookes's and elsewhere. It seems Mrs Phipps had the art to persuade him that she had the disposal of what was then called a *hyæna*, that is, an heiress—an immense Jamaica heiress, in whom she was willing to give or sell her interest to Charles Fox. Without having perfect confidence in the obliging proposal, the great statesman thought the thing worth looking after, and became so earnest in it, that Mrs Phipps was desirous to back out for fear of discovery. With this view she made confesssion one fine morning, with many professions of the deepest feelings, that the hyæna had proved a frail monster, and given birth to a girl or boy—no matter which. Even this did not make Charles quit chase of the hyæna. He intimated that if the cash was plenty and certain, the circumstance might be overlooked. Mrs Phipps had nothing for it but to double the disgusting dose. ' The poor child,' she said, ' was unfortunately of a mixed colour, somewhat tinged with the blood of Africa; no doubt Mr Fox was himself very dark, and the circumstance might not draw attention,' &c. &c. This singular anecdote was touched upon by Foote, and is the cause of introducing the negress into the Cozeners, though no express allusion to Charles Fox was admitted. Lady —— tells me that, in her youth, the laugh was universal so soon as the black woman appeared. It is one of the numerous hits that will be lost to posterity.

" This day, at the request of Sir William Knighton, I sat to Northcote, who is to introduce himself in the same piece in the act of painting me, like some pictures of the Venetian school. The artist is an old man, low in stature, and bent with years—fourscore at least. But the eye is quick and the countenance noble. A pleasant companion, familiar with recollections of Sir Joshua, Samuel Johnson, Burke, Goldsmith, &c. His account of the last confirms all that we have heard of his oddities.

" *May* 11.—Another long sitting to the old Wizard Northcote. He really resembles an animated mummy. Dined with his Majesty in a very private party, five or six only being present. I was received most kindly, as usual. It is impossible to conceive a more friendly manner than that his Majesty used towards me. I spoke to Sir William Knighton about the dedication of the collected novels, and he says it will be highly well taken.*

* The *Magnum Opus* was dedicated to King George IV.

" *May* 17.—A day of busy idleness. Richardson came and breakfasted with me, like a good fellow. Then I went to Mr Chantrey.*   Thereafter about 12 o'clock, I went to breakfast the second at Lady Shelley's, where there was a great morning party. A young lady† begged a lock of my hair, which was not worth refusing.   I stipulated for a kiss, which I was permitted to take.   From this I went to the Duke of Wellington, who gave me some hints or rather details.   Afterwards I drove out to Chiswick, where I had never been before.   A numerous and gay party were assembled to walk and enjoy the beauties of that Palladian dome.   The place and highly ornamented gardens belonging to it resemble a picture of Watteau.   There is some affectation in the picture, but in the *ensemble* the original looked very well.   The Duke of Devonshire received every one with the best possible manners.   The scene was dignified by the presence of an immense elephant, who, under charge of a groom, wandered up and down, giving an air of Asiatic pageantry to the entertainment.   I was never before sensible of the dignity which largeness of size and freedom of movement give to this otherwise very ugly animal.   As I was to dine at Holland House, I

---

* Sir F. Chantrey was at this time executing his *second* bust of Sir Walter — that ordered by Sir Robert Peel, and which is now at Draycote.   The reader will find more of this in a subsequent page.

† Miss Shelley—now the Honourable Mrs George Edgecumbe.

did not partake in the magnificent repast which was offered to us, and took myself off about five o'clock. I contrived to make a demi-toilette at Holland House, rather than drive all the way to London. Rogers came to the dinner, which was very entertaining. Lady Holland pressed us to stay all night, which we did accordingly.

" *May* 18.— The freshness of the air, the singing of the birds, the beautiful aspect of nature, the size of the venerable trees, gave me altogether a delightful feeling this morning. It seemed there was pleasure even in living and breathing without anything else. We (*i. e.* Rogers and I) wandered into a green lane, bordered with fine trees, which might have been twenty miles from a town. It will be a great pity when this ancient house must come down and give way to rows and crescents. It is not that Holland House is fine as a building,—on the contrary it has a tumble-down look ; and although decorated with the bastard Gothic of James I.'s time, the front is heavy. But it resembles many respectable matrons, who having been absolutely ugly during youth, acquire by age an air of dignity. But one is chiefly affected by the air of deep seclusion which is spread around the domain.

" *May* 19.—Dined by command with the Duchess of Kent. I was very kindly recognised by Prince

Leopold—and presented to the little Princess Victoria—I hope they will change her name—the heir-apparent to the crown as things now stand. How strange that so large and fine a family as that of his late Majesty should have died off, or decayed into old age, with so few descendants. Prince George of Cumberland is, they say, a fine boy about nine years old—a bit of a Pickle. This little lady is educating with much care, and watched so closely that no busy maid has a moment to whisper, ' You are heir of England.' I suspect, if we could dissect the little heart, we should find that some pigeon or other bird of the air had carried the matter. She is fair, like the Royal family—the Duchess herself very pleasing and affable in her manners. I sat by Mr Spring Rice, a very agreeable man. There were also Charles Wynn and his lady—and the evening, for a court evening, went agreeably off. I am commanded for two days by Prince Leopold, but will send excuses.

" *May* 24.— This day dined at Richmond Park with Lord Sidmouth. Before dinner his Lordship showed me letters which passed between his father, Dr Addington, and the great Lord Chatham. There was much of that familiar friendship which arises, and must arise between an invalid, the head of an invalid family, and their medical adviser, supposing the last to be a wise and well-bred man. The cha racter of Lord Chatham's handwriting is strong and bold, and his expressions short and manly. There are intimations of his partiality for William, whose health seems to have been precarious during boyhood. He talks of William imitating him in all he did, and calling for ale because his father was recommended to drink it. ' If I should smoke,' he said, ' William would instantly call for a pipe;' and, he wisely infers, ' I must take care what I do.' The letters of the late William Pitt are of great curiosity; but as, like all 'real letters of business, they only *allude* to matters with which his correspondent is well acquainted, and do not enter into details, they would require an ample commentary. I hope Lord Sidmouth will supply this, and have urged it as much as I can. I think, though I hate letters, and abominate interference, I will write to him on this subject. Here I met my old and much esteemed friend, Lord Stowell, looking very frail and even comatose. *Quantum mutatus!* He was one of the pleasantest men I ever knew.[*]

" Respecting the letters, I picked up from those of Pitt that he was always extremely desirous of peace with France, and even reckoned upon it at a moment when he ought to have despaired. I suspect this false view of the state of France (for such it was) which induced the British Minister to look for

[*] Sir William Scott, Lord Stowell, died 28th January 1836, aged 90.

peace when there was no chance of it, damped his ardour in maintaining the war. He wanted the lofty ideas of his father — you read it in his handwriting, great statesman as he was. I saw a letter or two of Burke's, in which there is an *epanchement de cœur* not visible in those of Pitt, who writes like a Premier to his colleague. Burke was under the strange hallucination that his son, who predeceased him, was a man of greater talents than himself. On the contrary, he had little talent, and no nerve. On moving some resolutions in favour of the Catholics, which were ill-received by the House of Commons, young Burke actually ran away, which an Orangeman compared to a cross-reading in the newspapers. ' Yesterday the Catholic resolutions were moved, &c. — but the pistol missing fire, the villains ran off ! ! !'

" *May* 25. — After a morning of letter-writing, leave-taking, papers destroying, and God knows what trumpery, Sophia and I set out for Hampton Court, carrying with us the following lions and lionesses — Samuel Rogers, Tom Moore, Wordsworth, with wife and daughter. We were very kindly and properly received by Walter and his wife, and had a very pleasant day. At parting, Rogers gave me a gold-mounted pair of glasses, which I will not part with in a hurry. I really like S. R., and have always found him most friendly."

This is the last London entry; but I must mention two circumstances that occurred during that
visit. Breakfasting one morning with Allan Cunningham, and commending one of his publications,
he looked round the table, and said—" what are you
going to make of all these boys, Allan?" " I ask
that question often at my own heart," said Allan,
" and I cannot answer it." " What does the eldest
point to?" " The callant would fain be a soldier,
Sir Walter—and I have a half promise of a commission in the king's army for him; but I wish
rather he could go to India, for there the pay is a
maintenance, and one does not need interest at every
step to get on." Scott dropped the subject, but went
an hour afterwards to Lord Melville (who was now
President of the Board of Control), and begged a
cadetship for young Cunningham. Lord Melville
promised to enquire if he had one at his disposal, in
which case he would gladly serve the son of honest
Allan; but the point being thus left doubtful, Scott,
meeting Mr John Loch, one of the East-India Di-
rectors, at dinner the same evening, at Lord Stafford's, applied to him, and received an immediate
assent. On reaching home at night, he found a note
from Lord Melville, intimating that he had enquired,
and was happy in complying with his request. Next

morning, Sir Walter appeared at Sir F. Chantrey's breakfast-table, and greeted the sculptor (who is a brother of the angle) with — " I suppose it has sometimes happened to you to catch one trout (which was all you thought of) with the fly, and another with the bobber. I have done so, and I think I shall land them both. Don't you think Cunningham would like very well to have cadetships for two of those fine lads ?" " To be sure he would," said Chantrey, " and if you'll secure the commissions, I'll make the outfit easy." Great was the joy in Allan's household on this double good news; but I should add, that before the thing was done he had to thank another benefactor. Lord Melville, after all, went out of the Board of Control before he had been able to fulfil his promise; but his successor, Lord Ellenborough, on hearing the circumstances of the case, desired Cunningham to set his mind at rest; and both his young men are now prospering in the India service.

Another friend's private affairs occupied more unpleasantly much of Scott's attention during this residence in London. He learned, shortly after his arrival, that misfortunes (as foreseen by himself in May 1825) had gathered over the management of the Adelphi Theatre.* The following letter has been selected from among several on the same painful subject.

* See *ante*, Vol. VII. p. 368.

" *To Daniel Terry, Esq., Boulogne-sur-Mer.*

" London, Lockhart's, April 15, 1828.

" My Dear Terry,

" I received with sincere distress your most melancholy letter. Certainly want of candour with one's friends is blameable, and procrastination in circumstances of embarrassment is highly unwise. But they bring such a fearful chastisement on the party who commits them, that he may justly expect, not the reproaches, but the sympathy and compassion of his friends ; at least of all such whose conscience charges them with errors of their own. For my part, I feel as little title, as God knows I have wish, to make any reflections on the matter, more than are connected with the most sincere regret on your own account. The sum at which I stand noted in the schedule is of no consequence in the now more favourable condition of my affairs, and the loss to me personally is the less, that I always considered £200 of the same as belonging to my godson ; but he is young, and may not miss the loss when he comes to be fitted out for the voyage of life ; we must hope the best. I told your solicitor that I desired he would consider me as a friend of yours, desirous to take as a creditor the measures which seemed best to forward your interest. It might be inconvenient to me were í called upon to make up such instalments of the price of the theatre as are unpaid; but of this, I suppose, there can be no great danger. Pray let me know as soon as you can, how this stands. I think you are quite right to stand to the worst, and that your retiring was an injudicious measure which cannot be too soon retraced, *coute qui coute.* I am at present in London with Lockhart, who, as well as my daughter, are in deep sorrow for what has happened, as they, as well as I on their account, consider themselves as deeply obliged to Mrs Terry's kindness, as well as from regard to you. These hard times must seem still harder while you are in a foreign country. I am not, you know, so wealthy as I have been, but £20 or £30 are heartily at your service if you will let me know how the remittance can reach you. It does not seem to me that an arrangement with your creditors will be difficult; but for God's sake do not temporize and undertake burdens which you cannot discharge, and which will only lead to new difficulties.

" As to your views about an engagement at Edinburgh I doubt much, though an occasional visit would probably succeed. My countrymen, taken in their general capacity, are not people to have recourse to in adverse circumstances. John Bull is a better beast in misfortune. Your objections to an American trip are quite satisfactory, unless the success of your solicitor's measures should in part remove them, when it may be considered as a *pis-aller*. As to Walter, there can be no difficulty in procuring his admission to the Edinburgh Academy, and if he could be settled with his grandfather, or under his eye, as to domestic accommodation, I would willingly take care of his schooling, and look after him when I am in town. I shall be anxious, indeed, till I hear that you are once more restored to the unrestrained use of your talents; for I am sensible how dreadfully annoying must be your present situation, which leaves so much time for melancholy retrospection without any opportunity of exertion. Yet this state, like others, must be endured with patience: the furiously impatient horse only plunges himself deeper in the slough, as our old hunting excursions may have taught us. In general, the human mind is strong in proportion to the internal energy which it possesses. Evil fortune is as transient as good, and if the endangered ship is still manned by a sturdy and willing crew, why then

> ' Up and rig a jury foremast,
>   She rights, she rights, boys; wear off shore.

This was the system I argued upon in my late distresses; and, therefore, I strongly recommend it to you. I beg my kindest compliments to Mrs Terry, and I hope better days may come. I shall be here till the beginning of May; therefore we may meet; believe me very truly yours, WALTER SCOTT."

On the afternoon of the 28th of May, Sir Walter started for the north, but could not resist going out of his way to see the spot where " Mr William Weare, who dwelt in Lyon's Inn," was murdered. His Diary says :—

" Our elegant researches carried us out of the highroad and through a labyrinth of intricate lanes, which seem made on purpose to afford strangers the full benefit of a dark night and a drunk driver, in order to visit Gill's Hill, in Hertfordshire, famous for the murder of Mr Weare. The place has the strongest title to the description of Wordsworth—

> ' A merry spot, 'tis said, in days of yore;
> But something ails it now — the place is curst.'

The principal part of the house has been destroyed, and only the kitchen remains standing. The garden has been dismantled, though a few laurels and flowering-shrubs, run wild, continue to mark the spot. The fatal pond is now only a green swamp, but so near the house that one cannot conceive how it was ever chosen as a place of temporary concealment for the murdered body. Indeed the whole history of the murder, and the scenes which ensued, are strange pictures of desperate and short-sighted wickedness.

The feasting—the singing—the murderer, with his hands still bloody, hanging round the neck of one of the females the watch-chain of the murdered man—argue the utmost apathy. Even Probart, the most frightened of the party, fled no farther for relief than to the brandy bottle, and is found in the very lane, nay, at the very spot of the murder, seeking for the weapon, and exposing himself to the view of the passengers. Another singular mark of stupid audacity was their venturing to wear the clothes of their victim. There was a want of foresight in the whole arrangements of the deed, and the attempts to conceal it, which a professed robber would not have exhibited. There was just one shade of redeeming character about a business so brutal, perpetrated by men above the very lowest rank of life : it was the mixture of revenge, which afforded some relief to the circumstances of treachery and premeditation. But Weare was a cheat,* and had no doubt pillaged Thurtell, who therefore deemed he might take greater liberties with him than with others. The dirt of the present habitation equalled its wretched desolation, and a truculent-looking hag, who showed us the place, and received half-a-crown, looked not unlike the natural inmate of such a mansion. She hinted as much

---

* Weare, Thurtell, and all the rest, were professed gamblers. See *ante*, Vol. VIII. p. 381.

herself, saying the landlord had dismantled the place, because no respectable person would live there. She seems to live entirely alone, and fears no ghosts, she says. One thing about this tragedy was never explained. It is said that Weare, as is the habit of such men, always carried about his person, and between his flannel waistcoat and shirt, a sum of ready money, equal to £1500 or £2000. No such money was ever recovered, and as the sum divided by Thurtell among his accomplices was only about £20, he must in slang phrase, have *bucketed his palls.*

" *May* 29.—We travelled from Alconbury Hill to Ferry Bridge, upwards of a hundred miles, amid all the beauties of flourish and verdure which spring awakens at her first approach in the midland counties of England, but without any variety, save those of the season's making. I do believe this great north road is the dullest in the world, as well as the most convenient for the travellers. The skeleton at Barnby Moor has deserted his gibbet, and that is the only change I recollect.

" *Rokeby, May* 30.—We left Ferry Bridge at seven, and reached this place at past three. A mile from the house we met Morritt, looking for us. I had great pleasure in finding myself at Rokeby, and recollecting a hundred passages of past time. Morritt looks well and easy in his mind, which I am delighted to see. He is now one of my oldest, and, I believe, one of my most sincere friends;—a man unequalled in the mixture of sound good sense, high literary cultivation, and the kindest and sweetest temper that ever graced a human bosom. His nieces are much attached to him, and are deserving and elegant, as well as beautiful young women. What there is in our partiality to female beauty that commands a species of temperate homage from the aged, as well as ecstatic admiration from the young, I cannot conceive; but it is.certain that a very large portion of some other amiable quality is too little to counterbalance the absolute want of this advantage. I, to whom beauty is, and shall henceforward be, a picture, still look upon it with the quiet devotion of an old worshipper, who no longer offers incense on the shrine, but peaceably presents his inch of taper, taking special care in doing so not to burn his own fingers. Nothing in life can be more ludicrous or contemptible than an old man aping the passions of his youth.

"Talking of youth, there was a certain professor at Cambridge, who used to keep sketches of all the lads who, from their conduct at college, seemed to bid fair for distinction in life. He showed them one day to an old shrewd sarcastic master of arts, who looked over the collection, and then observed—' A promising nest of eggs : what a pity the great part will turn out addle!' And so they do:—looking round amongst the young men, one sees to all appearances fine flourish—but it ripens not.

" *May* 31.—I have finished Napier's War in the Peninsula.* It is written in the spirit of a Liberal, but the narrative is distinct and clear. He has, however, given a bad sample of accuracy in the case of Lord Strangford, where his pointed affirmation has been as pointedly repelled. It is evident he would require probing. His defence of Moore is spirited and well argued, though it is evident he defends the statesman as much as the general. As a *Liberal* and a military man, Napier finds it difficult to steer his course. The former character calls on him to plead for the insurgent Spaniards; the latter induces him to palliate the cruelties of the French. Good-even to him until next volume, which I shall long to see. This was a day of pleasure, and nothing else."

Next night Sir Walter rested at Carlisle. " A sad place," says the Diary, "in my domestic remembrances, since here I married my poor Charlotte. She is gone, and I am following—faster, perhaps, than I wot of. It is something to have lived and loved; and our poor children are so hopeful and affectionate, that it chas

* The first volume of Colonel Napier's work had recently been published.

tens the sadness attending the thoughts of our separation. . . . My books being finished, I lighted on an odd volume of the Gentleman's Magazine, a work in which, as in a pawnbroker's shop, much of real curiosity and value are stowed away amid the frippery and trumpery of those reverend old gentlewomen who were the regular correspondents of Mr Urban."

His companion wrote thus a day or two afterwards to her sister :*—" Early in the morning before we started, papa took me with him to the Cathedral. This he had often done before; but he said he must stand once more on the spot where he married poor mamma. After that we went to the Castle, where a new showman went through the old trick of pointing out Fergus MacIvor's *very* dungeon. Peveril said—' Indeed ?—are you quite sure, sir ?' And on being told there could be no doubt, was troubled with a fit of coughing, which ended in a laugh. The man seemed exceeding indignant: so when papa moved on, I whispered who it was. I wish you had seen the man's start, and how he stared and bowed as he parted from us; and then rammed his keys into his pocket, and went

* I copy from a letter which has no date, so that I cannot be quite sure of this being the halt at Carlisle it refers to. I once witnessed a scene almost exactly the same at Stirling Castle, where an old soldier called Sir Walter's attention to the " very dungeon" of Roderick Dhu.

off at a hand-gallop to warn the rest of the garrison But the carriage was ready, and we escaped a row."

They reached Abbotsford that night, and a day or two afterwards Edinburgh; where Sir Walter was greeted with the satisfactory intelligence, that his plans as to the " *opus magnum*" had been considered at a meeting of his trustees, and finally approved *in toto*. As the scheme inferred a large outlay on drawings and engravings, and otherwise, this decision had been looked for with much anxiety by him and Mr Cadell. He says—" I trust it will answer; yet who can warrant the continuance of popularity? Old Nattali Corri, who entered into many projects, and could never set the sails of a windmill to catch the *aura popularis*, used to say he believed that, were he to turn baker, it would put bread out of fashion. I have had the better luck to dress my sails to every wind; and so blow on, good wind, and spin round, whirligig." The *Corri* here alluded to was an unfortunate adventurer, who, among many other wild schemes, tried to set up an Italian Opera at Edinburgh.

The Diary for the next month records the usual meeting at Blair-Adam, but nothing worth quoting, that was done or said, except, perhaps, these two scraps—

" *Salutation of two old Scottish Lairds—*' Ye're

maist obedient hummil servant, Tannachy-Tulloch.
—' Your nain man, Kilspindie.'

" *Hereditary descent in the Highlands.*—A cler-
gyman showed John Thomson the island of Inchma-
chome, on the Port of Monteith, and pointed out the
boatman as a remarkable person, the representative
of the hereditary gardeners of the Earls of Monteith,
while these Earls existed. His son, a puggish boy,
follows up the theme—' Feyther, when Donald Mac-
Corkindale dees, will not the family be extinct?'—
Father—' No; I believe there is a man in Bal-
quhidder who takes up the *succession.*'"

During the remainder of this year, as I already
mentioned, Sir Walter never opened his " locked
book." Whether in Edinburgh or the country, his
life was such, that he describes himself, in several
letters, as having become " a writing automaton." He
had completed, by Christmas, the Second Series of
Tales on Scottish History, and made considerable
progress in another novel—Anne of Geierstein: he
had also drawn up for the Quarterly Review his article
on Mr Morier's Hajji Baba in England; and that
delightful one on Sir Humphrey Davy's *Salmonia*—
which, like those on Planting and Gardening, abounds
in sweet episodes of personal reminiscence: And,
whenever he had not proof-sheets to press him, his
hours were bestowed on the *opus magnum.*

A few extracts from his correspondence may supply

in part this blank in the Diary. Several of them touch on the affairs of Mr Terry, whose *stamina* were not sufficient to resist the stroke of misfortune. He had a paralytic seizure, very shortly after the ruin of his theatre was made public. One, addressed to a dear and early friend, Sir Alexander Wood, was written on the death of his brother-in-law, Sir William Forbes of Pitsligo—the same modest, gentle, and high-spirited man with whose history Sir Walter's had (as the Diary of 1826 tells) been very remarkably intertwined.

" *To John Lockhart, Esq., Regent's Park.*

" Abbotsford, July 14, 1828.

" My Dear L.

" I wrote myself blind and sick last week about * * * * † God forgive me for having thought it possible that a schoolmaster should be out and out a rational being. I have a letter from Terry—but written by his poor wife—his former one was sadly scrawled. I hope he may yet get better—but I suspect the shot has gone near the heart.

† These letters, chiefly addressed to Sir Walter's excellent friend, James Heywood Markland, Esq. (Editor of the Chester Mysteries), were on a delicate subject connected with the incipient arrangements of King's College, London.

> ' O what a world of worlds were it,
>   Would sorrow, pain, and sickness spare it,
>   And aye a rowth roast-beef and claret ,
>   Syne wha would starve?

" If it be true that Longman and Co. have offered £1000 for a history of Ireland, Scotland must stand at fifty per cent. discount, for they lately offered me £500 for one of the latter country, which of course I declined. I have also had Murray's request to do some biography for his new undertaking.* But I really can't think of any Life I could easily do, excepting Queen Mary's; and that I decidedly would not do, because my opinion, in point of fact, is contrary both to the popular feeling and to my own. I see, by the by, that your Life of Burns is going to press again, and therefore send you a few letters which may be of use to you. In one of them (to that singular old curmudgeon, Lady Winifred Constable) you will see he plays high Jacobite, and, on that account, it is curious; though I imagine his Jacobitism, like my own, belonged to the fancy rather than the reason. He was, however, a great Pittite down to a certain period. There were some passing stupid verses in the papers, attacking and defending his satire on a certain preacher, whom he termed ' an unco calf.' In

* Mr Murray of Albemarle Street was at this time projecting his *Family Library,* one of the many imitations of Constable's last scheme.

one of them occurred these lines in vituperation of the adversary—

'A Whig, I guess. But Rab's a Tory,
An gies us mony a funny story.'

" This was in 1787.—Ever yours,

WALTER SCOTT."

" *To Robert Cadell, Esq., Edinburgh.*

" Abbotsford, 4th October 1828.

" My Dear Sir,

" We were equally gratified and surprised by the arrival of the superb time-piece with which you have ornamented our halls. There are grand discussions where it is to be put, and we are only agreed upon one point, that it is one of the handsomest things of the kind we ever saw, and that we are under great obligations to the kind donor. On my part, I shall never look on it without recollecting that the employment of my time is a matter of consequence to you, as well as myself.*

" I send you two letters, of which copies will be requisite for the *magnum opus.* They must be

* The allusion is to a clock in the style of Louis Quatorze, now in the drawing-room at Abbotsford.

copied separately. I wish you would learn from Mr Walter Dickson, with my best respects, the maiden name of Mrs Goldie, and the proper way in which she ought to be designated. Another point of information I wish to have is, concerning the establishment of the King's beadsmen or blue-gowns. Such should occur in any account of the Chapel-Royal, to which they were an appendage, but I have looked into Arnott and Maitland, without being able to find anything. My friend, Dr Lee, will know at once where this is to be sought for.

" Here is a question. Burns in his poetry repeatedly states the idea of his becoming a beggar— these passages I have. But there is a remarkable one in some of his *prose*, stating with much spirit the qualifications he possessed for the character. I have looked till I am sick, through all the letters of his which I have seen, and cannot find this. Do you know any amateur of the Ayrshire Bard who can point it out? It will save time, which is precious to me.*

" J. B. has given me such a dash of criticism, that I have laid by the Maid of the Mist for a few days. But I am working hard, meanwhile, at the illustrations; so no time is lost.—Yours very truly,

WALTER SCOTT."

* These queries all point to the annotation of *The Antiquary.*

"*To Mrs Lockhart, Brighton.*

"Abbotsford, 24th October 1828.

" My Dear Sophia,

" I write to you rather than to the poor Terrys, on the subject of their plans, which appear to me to require reconsideration, as I have not leisure so to modify my expressions as to avoid grating upon feelings which may be sore enough already. But if I advise I must be plain. The plan of a cottage in this neighbourhood is quite visionary. London or its vicinity is the best place for a limited income, because you can get everything you want without taking a pennyweight more of it than you have occasion for. In the country (with us at least) if you want a basin of milk every day, you must keep a cow—if you want a bunch of straw, you must have a farm. But what is still worse, it seems to me that such a plan would remove Terry out of his natural sphere of action. It is no easy matter, at any rate, to retreat from the practice of an art to the investigation of its theory; but common sense says, that if there is one branch of literature which has a chance of success for our friend, it must be that relating to the drama. Dramatic works, whether designed for the stage or the closet,—dramatic biography (an article in which the public is always interested)—dramatic criticism—these can all be conducted with best advantage in London,—or, rather, they can be conducted nowhere else. In coming down to Scotland, therefore, Terry would be leaving a position in which, should he prove able to exert himself and find the public favourable, he might possibly do as much for his family as he could by his profession. But then he will require to be in book-shops and publishing-houses, and living among those up to the current of public opinion. And although poor Terry's spirits might not at first be up to this exertion, he should remember that the power of doing things easily is only to be acquired by resolution and habit, and if he really could give heart and mind to literature in any considerable degree, I can't see how, amidst so many Bijoux, and Albums, and Souvenirs —not to mention daily papers, critics, censors, and so forth—I cannot see how he could fail to make £200 or £300 a-year. In Edinburgh there is nothing of this kind going forwards, positively nothing. Since Constable's fall, all exertion is ended in the Gude Town in the publishing business, excepting what I may not long be able to carry on.

" We have had little Walter Terry with us. He is a nice boy. I have got him sent to the New Academy in Edinburgh, and hope he will do well. Indeed, I have good hopes as to them all; but the prospect of success must remain, first, with the restoration of Terry to the power of thought and labour, a matter which is in God's hand; and, secondly, on the choice he shall make of a new sphere of occupation. On these events no mortal can have influence, unless so far as Mrs Terry may be able to exert over him that degree of power which mind certainly possesses over body.

" Our worthy old aunt, Lady Raeburn, is gone, and I am now the eldest living person of my father's family. My old friend, Sir William Forbes, is extremely ill,—dying, I fear; and the winter seems to approach with more than usual gloom. We are well here, however, and send love to Lockhart and the babies. I want to see L. much, and hope he may make a run down at Christmas.

" You will take notice, that all the advice I venture to offer to the Terrys is according as matters now stand.* Indeed, I think he is better now, than when struggling against a losing concern, turning worse every day. With health I have little doubt he may do well yet, and without it what can any one do? Poor Rose,—he too seems to be very badly; and so

* Mr Terry died in London on the 22d June 1829. His widow, to whom these Memoirs have owed many of their materials, is now (1837) married to Mr Charles Richardson of Tulse Hill, the author of the well-known Dictionary of the English Language, &c.

end, if I lose him, wit, talent, frolic beyond the bounds
of sobriety, all united with an admirable heart and
feelings.

"Besides all other objections to Terry's plan, the
poor invalid would be most uncomfortable here. As
my guest, it was another thing; but without power
to entertain the better sort of folk, and liable from
his profession to the prejudices of our middling people, without means too of moving about, he must,
while we are not at Abbotsford, be an absolute hermit. Besides, health may be restored so as to let
him act again—regimen and quiet living do much
in such cases—and he should not rashly throw up
professional connexions. If they be bent on settling
in Scotland, a small house in Edinburgh would be
much better than the idea of residing here.

"I have been delighted with your views of coming
back to Chiefswood next summer,—but had you not
better defer that for another year? Here is plenty
of room for you all—plenty of beef and mutton—
plenty of books for L., and he should have the little
parlour (the monkey-room, as Morritt has christened
it) inviolate—and he and I move on easily without
interrupting each other. Pray think of all this, and
believe that, separated as I am so much from you
both and the grandchildren, the more I can see of
you all while I have eyes left to see you with, the
greater will be my pleasure. I am turning a terrible

fixture with rheumatism, and go about little but in the carriage, and round the doors. A change of market-days,—but seams will slit, and elbows will out. My general health is excellent.—I am always, dearest Sophia, your affectionate father,

WALTER SCOTT."

" *To Sir Alexander Wood, &c. &c. &c., Colinton House, Edinburgh.*

" Abbotsford, Oct. 28, 1828.

" My Dear Sir Alexander,

" Your letter brought me the afflicting intelligence of the death of our early and beloved friend Sir William. I had little else to expect, from the state of health in which he was when I last saw him, but that circumstance does not diminish the pain with which I now reflect that I shall never see him more. He was a man who, from his habits, could not be intimately known to many, although everything which he did partook of that high feeling and generosity which belongs perhaps to a better age than that we live in. In him I feel I have sustained a loss which no after years of my life can fill up to me. Our early friendship none knew better than you; and you also well know that if I look back to the gay and happy hours of youth, they must be filled with recollections of our departed friend. In the whole course of life

our friendship has been uninterrupted as his kindness
has been unwearied. Even the last time I saw him
(so changed from what I knew him) he came to town
when he was fitter to have kept his room, merely because he could be of service to some affairs of mine.
It is most melancholy to reflect that the life of a man
whose principles were so excellent, and his heart so
affectionate, should have, in the midst of external
prosperity, been darkened, and I fear, I may say,
shortened, by domestic affliction. But ' those whom
He loveth, he chasteneth;'* and the o'er-seeing Pro-
vidence, whose ways are as just and kind as they are
inscrutable, has given us, in the fate of our dear friend,
an example that we must look to a better world for
the reward of sound religion, active patriotism, and
extended benevolence. I need not write more to you
on this subject; you must feel the loss more keenly
than any one. But there is another and a better
world, in which, I trust in God, those who have
loved each other in this transitory scene, may meet
and recognise the friends of youth, and companions
of more advanced years.

" I beg my kindest compliments and sincere expressions of sympathy to Lady Wood, and to any of
the sorrowing family who may be gratified by the interest of one of their father's oldest friends and most
afflicted survivors.

* Hebrews, xii. 6.

" God bless you, my dear Wood! and I am sure you will believe me

Yours in sorrow as in gladness,

WALTER SCOTT."

" *To J. G. Lockhart, Esq., Brighton.*

" October 30, 1828.

" Dear John,

" I have a sad affliction in the death of poor Sir William Forbes. You loved him well, I know, but it is impossible that you should enter into all my feelings on this occasion. My heart bleeds for his children. God help all!

" Your scruples about doing an epitome of the Life of Boney, for the Family Library that is to be, are a great deal over delicate. My book in nine thick volumes can never fill the place which our friend Murray wants you to fill, and which, if you don't, some one else will, right soon. Moreover, you took much pains in helping me when I was beginning my task, which I afterwards greatly regretted that Constable had no means of remunerating, as no doubt he intended, when you were giving him so much good advice in laying down his grand plans about the Miscellany. By all means do what the Emperor asks. He is what Emperor Nap. was not, much a gentleman, and, knowing our footing in all things, would not have proposed anything that ought to have excited scruples on your side. Alas, poor Crafty! Do you remember his exultation when my Boney affair was first proposed? Good God! I see him as he then was at this moment—how he swelled and rolled and reddened, and outblarneyed all blarney! Well, so be it.   I hope

' After life's fitful fever he sleeps well.' *

But he has cost me many a toilsome dreary day, and drearier night, and will cost me more yet.

" I am getting very unlocomotive—something like an old cabinet that looks well enough in its own corner, but will scarce bear wheeling about even to be dusted. But my work has been advancing gaily, or at least rapidly nevertheless, all this harvest. Master Littlejohn will soon have three more tomes in his hand, and the Swiss story too will be ready early in the year.   I shall send you Vol. I. with wee Johnnie's affair.   Fat James, as usual, has bored and bothered me with his criticisms, many of which, however, may have turned to good.   At first my not having been in Switzerland was a devil of a poser for him—but had I not the honour of an intimate personal acquaintance with every pass in the Highlands; and if that were not enough, had I not seen pictures and

* Macbeth.

prints *galore?* I told him I supposed he was becoming a geologist, and afraid of my misrepresenting
the *strata* of some rock on which I had to perch my
Maid of the Mist, but that he should be too good a
Christian to join those humbugging sages, confound
them, who are all tarred with the same stick as Mr
Whiston—

> ' Who proved as sure as God's in Glo'ster,
>   That Moses was a grand impostor; ' *

and that at any rate I had no mind to rival the accuracy of the traveller, I forget who, that begins
his chapter on Athens with a disquisition on the
formation of the Acropolis Rock. Mademoiselle de
Geierstein, is now, however, in a fair way—I mean
of being married and a' the lave o't, and I of having
her ladyship off my hands. I have also twined off
a world of not bad balaam in the way of notes, &c.
for my Magnum, which if we could but manage the
artists decently, might soon be afloat, and will, I do
think, do wonders for my extrication. I have no
other news to trouble you with. It is possible the
Quarterly may be quite right to take the Anti-Catholic line so strongly; but I greatly doubt the prudence of the thing, for I am convinced the question
must and will be carried very soon, whoever may or

* Swift

may not be Minister; and as to the Duke of Wellington, my faith is constant, that there is no other man living who can work out the salvation of this country. I take some credit to myself for having foreseen his greatness, before many would believe him to be anything out of the ordinary line of clever officers. He is such a man as Europe has not seen since Julius Cæsar; and if Spain had had the brains to make him king, that country might have been one of the first of the world before his death.—Ever affectionately yours,   WALTER SCOTT."

Of the same date was the following letter, addressed to the projector of a work, entitled, " The Courser's Manual."*   He had asked Sir Walter for

* This work, though ultimately published under the name of another editor, was projected and arranged by the late Rev. Mr Barnard of Brantinghamthorpe in Yorkshire; whose undertaking had no doubt been introduced to Sir Walter's notice by his father-in-law, Mr Archdeacon Wrangham. That elegant scholar had visited Abbotsford with some of his family about this period. He has since embalmed in pathetic verse the memory of Barnard, whose skill in rural sports by no means interfered with his graceful devotion to literature, or his pious assiduity in the labours of his profession. The reader will find his virtues and accomplishments affectionately recorded in the learned and interesting preface (p. 30) to a Translation of Arrian's Cynegeticus " by a Graduate of Medicine:" London, quarto, 1831.

a contribution; and received the ancient Scottish ditty of " *Auld Heck :*"—

' Dear Sir,

"I have loved the sport of coursing so well, and pursued it so keenly for several years, that I would with pleasure have done anything in my power to add to your collection on the subject; but I have long laid aside the amusement, and still longer renounced the poetical pen, which ought to have celebrated it; and I could only send you the laments of an old man, and the enumeration of the number of horses and dogs which have been long laid under the sod. I cannot, indeed, complain with the old huntsman, that—

> '———— No one now,
> Dwells in the hall of Ivor;
> Men, dogs, and horses, all are dead,
> And I the sole survivor;' *

but I have exchanged my whip for a walking-stick, my smart hack has dwindled into a Zetland shelty, and my two brace of greyhounds into a pair of terriers. Instead of entering on such melancholy topics, I judge it better to send you an Elegy on ' Bonny Heck,' an old Scottish poem, of very considerable merit in the eyes of those who understand the dialect.

* Wordsworth.

"The elegy itself turns upon a circumstance which, when I kept greyhounds, I felt a considerable alloy to the sport; I mean, the necessity of despatching the instruments and partakers of our amusement, when they begin to make up, by cunning, for the deficiency of youthful vigour. A greyhound is often termed an inferior species of the canine race, in point of sagacity; and in the eyes of an accomplished sportsman it is desirable they should be so, since they are valued for their spirit, not their address. Accordingly, they are seldom admitted to the rank of personal favourites. I have had such greyhounds, however, and they possessed as large a share of intelligence, attachment, and sagacity, as any other species of dog that I ever saw. In such cases, it becomes difficult or impossible to execute the doom upon the antiquated greyhound, so coolly recommended by Dame Juliana Berners :—

> ' And when he comes to that yere,
>   Have him to the tannere,
>   For the best whelp ever bitch had
>   At nine years is full bad.'

Modern sportsmen anticipate the doom by three years at least.

"I cannot help adding to the ' Last Words of Bonny Heck,' a sporting anecdote, said to have happened in Fife, and not far from the residence of that famous greyhound, which may serve to show in what regard the rules of fair play between hound and hare are held by Scottish sportsmen. There was a coursing club, once upon a time, which met at Balchristy, in the Province, or, as it is popularly called, the Kingdom of Fife. The members were elderly social men, whom a very moderate allowance of sport served as an introduction to a hearty dinner and jolly evening. Now, there had her seat on the ground where they usually met, a certain large stout hare, who seemed made on purpose to entertain these moderate sportsmen. She usually gave the amusement of three or four turns, as soon as she was put up,—a sure sign of a strong hare, when practised by any beyond the age of a leveret,—then stretched out in great style, and after affording the gentlemen an easy canter of a mile or two, threw out the dogs by passing through a particular gap in an inclosure. This sport the same hare gave to the same party for one or two seasons, and it was just enough to afford the worthy members of the club a sufficient reason to be alleged to their wives, or others whom it might concern, for passing the day in the public-house. At length, a fellow who attended the hunt nefariously thrust his plaid, or great coat, into the gap I mentioned, and poor puss, her retreat being thus cut off, was, in the language of the dying Desdemona, ' basely—basely murdered.'   The sport of the Balchristy club seemed to end with this famous hare.   They either found no hares, or such as afforded only a halloo and a squeak, or such, finally, as gave them farther runs than they had pleasure of following.   The spirit of the meeting died away, and at length it was altogether given up.

" The publican was, of course, the party most especially affected by the discontinuance of the club, and regarded, it may be supposed, with no complacency, the person who had prevented the hare from escaping, and even his memory.   One day, a gentleman asked him what was become of such a one, naming the obnoxious individual.   ' He is dead, sir,' answered mine host, with an angry scowl, ' and his soul kens this day whether the hare of Balchristy got fair play or not.'   WALTER SCOTT "

Resuming his journal at the close of the year, he says—" Having omitted to carry on my Diary for two or three days, I lost heart to make it up, and left it unfilled for many a month and day.   During this period nothing has happened worth particular notice:—the same occupations,—the same amusements,—the same occasional alternations of spirits, gay or depressed,—the same absence, for the most part, of all sensible or rational cause for the one or the other. I half grieve to take up my pen, and doubt if it is worth my while to record such an infinite quantity of nothing."

CHAPTER LXXVII.

Visit to Clydesdale — John Greenshields, sculptor — Letter to Lord Elgin — The Westport Murders — Execution of Burke — Letter to Miss Edgeworth — Ballantyne's Hypochondria — Roman Catholic Emancipation carried — Edinburgh Petition, &c. — Deaths of Lord Buchan, Mr Terry, and Mr Shortrede — Rev. Edward Irving — Anne of Geierstein published — Issue of the " Opus Magnum" begun — Its success — Nervous attack — Hæmorrhages — Reviewals on Ancient Scottish History, and Pitcairn's Trials — Third Series of Tales of a Grandfather, and first volume of the Scottish History in Lardner's Cyclopædia, published — Death and Epitaph of Thomas Purdie.

1829.

SIR WALTER having expressed a wish to consult me about some of his affairs, I went down to Abbotsford at Christmas, and found him apparently well in health (except that he suffered from rheumatism), and enjoying the society as usual of the Fergussons, with the welcome addition of Mr Morritt and Sir James Stuart of Allanbank — a gentleman whose masterly pencil had often been employed on subjects from his poetry and novels, and whose conversation on art (like that of Sir George Beaumont and Mr Scrope), being devoid of professional pedantries and jealousies, was always particularly delightful to him. One snowy morning, he gave us sheets of Anne of Geierstein, extending to, I think, about a volume and a half; and we read them together in the library, while he worked in the adjoining room, and occasionally dropt in upon us to hear how we were pleased. All were highly gratified with those vivid and picturesque pages, and both Morritt and Stuart, being familiar with the scenery of Switzerland, could not sufficiently express their astonishment at the felicity with which he had divined its peculiar character, and outdone, by the force of imagination, all the efforts of a thousand actual tourists. Such approbation was of course very acceptable. I had seldom seen him more gently and tranquilly happy.

Among other topics connected with his favourite studies, Sir James Stuart had much to say on the merits and prospects of a remarkable man (well known to myself), who had recently occupied general

attention in the North.   I allude to the late John
Greenshields, a stonemason, who at the age of twenty-
eight began to attempt the art of sculpture, and after
a few years of solitary devotion to this new pursuit,
had produced a statue of the Duke of York, which
formed at this time a popular exhibition in Edinburgh.
Greenshields was the son of a small farmer, who
managed also a ferry-boat, on my elder brother's estate in Lanarkshire; and I could increase the interest
with which both Sir James and Sir Walter had examined the statue, by bearing testimony to the purity
and modesty of his character and manners.   Another
eminent lover of art, who had been especially gratified
by Greenshields' work, was the Earl of Elgin.   Just
at this time, as it happened, the sculptor had been
invited to spend a day or two at his Lordship's seat
in Fife; but learning that Sir Walter was about to
visit Clydesdale, Greenshields would not lose the
chance of being presented to him on his native spot,
and left Broomhall without having finished the in-
spection of Lord Elgin's marbles.   His Lordship
addressed a long and interesting letter to Sir Walter,
in which he mentioned this circumstance, and be -
sought him, after having talked with the aspirant,
and ascertained his own private views and feelings,
to communicate his opinion as to the course which
might most advantageously be pursued for the encouragement and developement of his abilities.

Sir Walter went in the middle of January to Milton-Lockhart; there saw the sculptor in the paternal cottage, and was delighted with him and some of the works he had on hand, particularly a statue of George IV. Greenshields then walked with us for several hours by the river side, and among the woods. His conversation was easy and manly, and many sagacious remarks on life, as well as art, lost nothing to the poet's ear by being delivered in an accent almost as broad and unsophisticated as Tom Purdie's. John had a keen sense of humour, and his enjoyment of Sir Walter's lectures on planting, and jokes on everything, was rich. He had exactly that way of drawing his lips into a grim involuntary whistle, when a sly thing occurred, which the author of Rob Roy assigns to Andrew Fairservice. After he left us, Scott said— " There is much about that man that reminds me of Burns." On reaching Edinburgh, he wrote as follows :—

" To the Right Hon. the Earl of Elgin, &c. &c.
Broomhall, Fife.

Edinburgh, 20th January 1829

" My Dear Lord,

" I wish I were able to pay in better value the debt which I have contracted with your Lordship, by being the unconscious means of depriving you of Mr

Greenshields sooner than had been meant. It is a complicated obligation, since I owe a much greater debt to Greenshields for depriving him of an invaluable opportunity of receiving the advice, and profiting by the opinions of one whose taste for the arts is strong by nature, and has been so highly cultivated. If it were not that he may again have an opportunity to make up for that which he has lost, I would call the loss irreparable.

" My own acquaintance with art is so very small, that I almost hesitate to obey your Lordship in giving an opinion. But I think I never saw a more successful exertion of a young artist than the King's statue, which, though the sculptor had only an indifferent print to work by, seems to me a very happy likeness. The position (as if in act of receiving some person whom his Majesty delighted to honour) has equal ease and felicity, and conveys an idea of grace and courtesy, and even kindness, mixed with dignity, which, as he never saw the original, I was surprised to find mingled in such judicious proportions. The difficulties of a modern military or court dress are manfully combated; and I think the whole thing purely conceived. In a word, it is a work of great promise.

" I may speak with more confidence of the artist than of the figure. Mr Greenshields seems to me to be one of those remarkable men who must be distinguished in one way or other. He showed during my conversation with him sound sense on all subjects, and considerable information on such as occupied his mind. His habits, I understand, are perfectly steady and regular. His manners are modest and plain. without being clownish or rude; and he has all the good-breeding which nature can teach. Above all, I had occasion to remark that he had a generous and manly disposition — above feeling little slights, or acts of illiberality. Having to mention some very reasonable request of his which had been refused by an individual, he immediately, as if to obliterate the unfavourable impression, hastened to mention several previous instances of kindness which the same individual had shown to him. His mind seems to be too much bent upon fame, to have room for love of money, and his passion for the arts seems to be unfeignedly sincere.

" The important question of how he is to direct his efforts, must depend on the advice of his friends, and I know no one so capable of directing him as your Lordship. At the same time, I obey your commands, by throwing together in haste the observations which follow.

" Like all heaven-born geniuses, he is ignorant of the rules which have been adopted by artists before him, and has never seen the *chefs-d'œuvre* of classical time. Such men having done so much without education, are sometimes apt either to despise it, or to feel so much mortification at seeing how far short their efforts fall of excellence, that they resign their art in despair. I do think and hope, however, that the sanguine and the modest are so well mixed in this man's temper, that he will study the best models with the hope of improvement, and will be bold, as Spencer says, without being too bold. But opportunity of such study is wanting, and that can only be had in London. To London, therefore, he should be sent if possible. In addition to the above, I must remark, that Mr G. is not master of the art of tempering his clay, and other mechanical matters relating to his profession. These he should apply to without delay, and it would probably be best, having little time to lose, that he should for a while lay the chisel aside, and employ himself in making models almost exclusively. The transference of the figure from the clay to the marble is, I am informed by Chantrey, a mere mechanical art, excepting that some finishing touches are required. Now it follows that Greenshields may model, I dare say, six figures while he could only cut one in stone, and in the former practice must make a proportional progress in the principles of his art. The knowledge of his art is only to be gained in the studio of some sculptor of eminence.

" The task which Mr G. is full of at present seems to be chosen on a false principle, chiefly adopted from a want of acquaintance with the genuine and proper object of art. The public of Edinburgh have been deservedly amused and delighted with two figures in the character of Tam O'Shanter and his drunken companion Souter Johnny. The figures were much and justly applauded, and the exhibition being of a kind adapted to every taste, is daily filled. I rather think it is the success of this piece by a man much in his own circumstances, which has inclined Mr Greenshields to propose cutting a group of grotesque figures from the Beggar's Cantata of the same poet. Now, in the first place, I suspect six figures will form too many for a sculptor to group to advantage. But besides, I deprecate the attempt at such a subject. I do not consider caricature as a proper style for sculpture at all. We have Pan and his Satyrs in ancient sculpture, but the place of these characters in the classic mythology gives them a certain degree of dignity. Besides this, " the gambol has been shown." Mr Thom has produced a group of this particular kind, and instead of comparing what Greenshields might do in this way with higher models, the public would certainly regard him as the rival of Mr Thom, and give Mr Thom the preference, on the same principle that the Spaniard says when one man walks first, all the rest must be his followers. At the same time I highly approved of one figure in the group, I mean that of Burns himself. Burns (taking his

.ore contemplative moments) would indeed be a noble study, and I am convinced Mr G. would do it nobly—as, for example, when Coila describes him as gazing on a snow-storm,—

> ' I saw grim Nature's visage hoar,
>   Strike thy young eye.' *

I suppose it possible to represent rocks with icicles in sculpture.

" Upon the moment I did not like to mention to Mr G. my objections against a scheme which was obviously a favourite one, but I felt as I did when my poor friend John Kemble threatened to play Falstaff. In short, the perdurable character of sculpture, the grimly and stern severity of its productions, their size too, and their consequence, confine the art to what is either dignified and noble, or beautiful and graceful: it is, I think, inapplicable to situations of broad humour. A painting of Teniers is very well —it is of a moderate size, and only looked at when we choose; but a group of his drunken boors dancing in stone, as large as life, to a grinning fiddler at the bottom of a drawing-room, would, I think, be soon found intolerable bad company.

" I think, therefore, since Mr Greenshields has a decided call to the higher and nobler department of

* Burns's *Vision.*

his art, he should not be desirous of procuring immediate attention by attempting a less legitimate object. I desired Mr Lockhart of Milton to state to Mr G. what I felt on the above subject, and I repeat it to you, that, if I am so fortunate as to agree in opinion with your Lordship, you may exert your powerful influence on the occasion.

" I have only to add, that I am quite willing to contribute my mite to put Mr Greenshields in the way of the best instruction, which seems to me the best thing which can be done for him. I think your Lordship will hardly claim another epistolary debt from me, since I have given it like a tether, which, Heaven knows, is no usual error of mine. I am always, with respect, my dear Lord, your Lordship's most faithful and obedient servant,

WALTER SCOTT.

" P. S.—I ought to mention, that I saw a good deal of Mr Greenshields, for he walked with us, while we went over the grounds at Milton to look out a situation for a new house."

Mr Greenshields saw Sir Walter again in Clydesdale in 1831, and profited so well by these scanty opportunities, as to produce a statue of the poet, in a sitting posture, which, all the circumstances considered, must be allowed to be a very wonderful performance.   He subsequently executed various other works, each surpassing the promise of the other; but I fear his enthusiastic zeal had led him to unwise exertions. His health gave way, and he died in April 1835, at the age of forty, in the humble cottage of his parents. Celebrity had in no degree changed his manners or his virtues. The most flattering compliment he ever received was a message from Sir Francis Chantrey, inviting him to come to London, and offering to take him into his house, and give him all the benefits of his advice, instruction, and example. This kindness filled his eyes with tears — but the hand of fate was already upon him.

Scott's Diary for the day on which he wrote to Lord Elgin says — " We strolled about Milton on as fine a day as could consist with snow on the ground, in company with John Greenshields, the new sculptor, a sensible, strong-minded man. The situation is eminently beautiful; a fine promontory round which the Clyde makes a magnificent bend. We fixed on a situation for William's new house where the sitting rooms will command the upper valley; and, with an ornamental garden, I think it may be made the prettiest place in Scotland. Next day, on our way to Edinburgh, we stopped at Allanton to see a tree transplanted, which was performed with great ease. Sir Henry Stewart is lifted beyond the solid earth by the effect of his book's success; — but the book well deserves it.[*] He is in practice particularly anxious to keep the roots of the trees near the surface, and only covers them with about a foot of earth.—*Note.* Lime rubbish dug in among the roots of ivy encourages it much.—The operation delayed us three nours, so it was seven before we reached our dinner and a good fire in Shandwick Place, and we were well-nigh frozen to death. During the excursion I walked very ill—with more pain in fact than I ever remember to have felt—and, even leaning on John Lockhart, could hardly get on.—Well, the day of return to Edinburgh is come. I don't know why, but I am more happy at the change than usual. I am not working hard, and it is what I ought to do and must do. Every hour of laziness cries fie upon me. But there is a perplexing sinking of the heart which one cannot always overcome. At such times I have wished myself a clerk, quill-driving for two-pence per page. You have at least application, and that is all that is necessary, whereas, unless your lively faculties are awake and propitious, your application will do you as little good as if you strained your sinews to lift Arthur's Seat."

On the 23d he says —" The Solicitor[†] came to

---

[*] See Sir Walter's article on Ornamental Gardening — *Miscellaneous Prose Works*, vol. xxi. Sir H. Stewart, Bart. died in March 1836.

[†] John Hope, Esq., Solicitor-General — now Dean of the Faculty of Advocates.

dine with me—we drank a bottle of champaign, and two bottles of claret, which, in former days, I should have thought a very sober allowance, since, Lockhart included, there were three persons to drink it. But I felt I had drunk too much, and was uncomfortable. The young men stood it like young men.—Skene and his wife and daughter looked in in the evening. I suppose I am turning to my second childhood, for not only am I filled drunk, or made stupid at least, with one bottle of wine, but I am disabled from writing by chilblains on my fingers—a most babyish complaint."

At this time the chief topic of discourse in Edinburgh was the atrocious series of murders perpetrated by a gang of Irish desperadoes, Burke, Hare, &c., in a house or cellar of the West Port, to which they seduced poor old wayfaring people, beggar women, idiots, and so forth, and then filled them drunk, and smothered or strangled them, for the mere purpose of having bodies to sell to the anatomists. Sir Walter writes, on the 28th —" Burke the murderer, hanged this morning. The mob, which was immense, demanded Knox and Hare, but though greedy for more victims, received with shouts the solitary wretch who found his way to the gallows out of five or six who seem not less guilty than he. But the story begins to be stale, insomuch that I believe a doggrel ballad upon it would be popular, how brutal soever the wit. This is the progress of human passion. We ejaculate, exclaim, hold up to heaven our hand, like the rustic Phidyle *—next morning the mood changes, and we dance a jig to the tune which moved us to tears."

A few days later he discusses the West Port tragedy in this striking letter. It was written in answer to one announcing Miss Fanny Edgeworth's marriage with Mr Lestock Wilson:—

" *To Miss Edgeworth, Edgeworthstown.*

" Edinburgh, Feb. 4, 1829.

My Dear Miss Edgeworth,

" I have had your letter several days, and only answer just now—not, you may believe, from want of interest in the contents, but from the odd circumstance of being so much afflicted with chilblains in the fingers, that my pen scrambles every way but the right one. Assuredly I should receive the character of the most crabbed fellow from those modern sages who judge of a man from his handwriting. But as an old man becomes a child, I must expect, I sup-

* Cœlo supinas si tuleris manus
Nascente lunâ, rustica Phidyle, &c.
Hor. Lib. iii. Od. 23.

pose, measles and small-pox. I only wish I could
get a fresh set of teeth. To tell you the truth, I feel
the advance of age more than I like, though my
general health is excellent; but I am not able to walk
as I did, and I fear I could not now visit St Kevin's
Bed. This is a great affliction to one who has been
so active as I have been, in spite of all disadvantages.
I must now have a friendly arm, instead of relying
on my own exertions; and it is sad to think I shall
be worse before I am . better. However, the mild
weather may help me in some degree, and the worst
is a quiet pony (I used to detest a quiet pony), or
perhaps a garden-chair. All this does not prevent
my sincere sympathy in the increase of happiness,
which I hope Miss Fanny's marriage will afford to
herself, and you, and all who love her. I have not
had the same opportunity to know her merits as those
of my friends Mrs Butler and Mrs Fox; but I saw
enough of her (being your sister) when at Dublin,
to feel most sincerely interested in a young person
whose exterior is so amiable. In Mr Wilson you
describe the national character of John Bull, who is
not the worst of the three nations, though he has not
the quick feeling and rich humour of your countrymen, nor the shrewd sagacity, or the romantic spirit
of thinking and adventuring which the Scotch often
conceal under their apparent coldness, and which you
have so well painted in the M'Leod of your Ennui.

Depend upon it, I shall find Russell Square when I go to London, were I to have a voyage of discovery to make it out; and it will be Mr Wilson's fault if we do not make an intimate acquaintance.

" I had the pleasure of receiving, last autumn, your American friend Miss Douglas,* who seems a most ingenuous person; and I hope I succeeded in making her happy during her short visit at Abbotsford; for I was compelled to leave her to pay suit and service at the Circuit. The mention of the Circuit brings me to the horrors which you have so well described, and which resemble nothing so much as a wild dream Certainly I thought, like you, that the public alarm was but an exaggeration of vulgar rumour; but the tragedy is too true, and I look in vain for a remedy of the evils, in which it is easy to see this black and unnatural business has found its origin. The principal source certainly lies in the feelings of attachment which the Scotch have for their deceased friends. They are curious in the choice of their sepulchre, and a common shepherd is often, at whatever ruinous expense to his family, transported many miles to some favourite place of burial which has been occupied by his fathers. It follows, of course, that any interference with these remains is considered with

* Now married to Henry D. Cruger, Esq. of New York.—
[1839.]

most utter horror and indignation. To such of their
superiors as they love from clanship or habits of de-
pendance, they attach the same feeling. I experienced
it when I had a great domestic loss; for I learned
afterwards that the cemetery was guarded, out of good
will, by the servants and dependants who had been
attached to her during life; and were I to be laid
beside my lost companion just now, I have no doubt
it would be long before my humble friends would dis-
continue the same watch over my remains, and that
it would incur mortal risk to approach them with the
purpose of violation. This is a kind and virtuous
principle, in which every one so far partakes, that,
although an unprejudiced person would have no objection to the idea of his own remains undergoing
dissection, if their being exposed to scientific research
could be of the least service to humanity, yet we all
shudder at the notion of any who had been dear to
us, especially a wife or sister, being subjected to a
scalpel among a gazing and unfeeling crowd of stu-
dents. One would fight and die to prevent it. This
current of feeling is encouraged by the law which, as
distinguishing murderers and other atrocious crimi-
nals, orders that their bodies shall be given for public
dissection. This makes it almost impossible to con-
sign the bodies of those who die in the public hos-
pitals to the same fate; for it would be inflicting on
poverty the penalty which, wisely or unwisely, the

law of the country has denounced against guilt of the highest degree; and it would assuredly deprive all who have a remaining spark of feeling or shame, of the benefit of those consolations of charity of which they are the best objects. If the prejudice be not very liberal, it is surely natural, and so deeply-seated that many of the best feelings must be destroyed ere it can be eradicated. What then remains? The only chance I see is to permit importation from other countries. If a subject can be had in Paris for ten or twenty francs, it will surely pay the importer who brings it to Scotland. Something must be done, for there is an end of the *Cantabit vacuus,** the last prerogative of beggary, which entitled him to laugh at the risk of robbery. The veriest wretch in the highway may be better booty than a person of consideration, since the last may have but a few shillings in his pocket, and the beggar, being once dead, is worth ten pounds to his murderer.

" The great number of the lower Irish which have come over here since the peace, is, like all important occurrences, attended with its own share of good and evil. It must relieve Ireland in part of the excess of population, which is one of its greatest evils, and it accommodates Scotland with a race of hardy and indefatigable labourers, without which it would be im-

* Cantabit vacuus coram latrone viator. — *Juvenal,*

possible to carry on the very expensive improvements which have been executed. Our canals, our rail-roads, and our various public works, are all wrought by Irish. I have often employed them myself at burning clay, and similar operations, and have found them as labourers quiet and tractable, light-spirited, too, and happy to a degree beyond belief, and in no degree quarrelsome, keep whisky from them and them from whisky. But most unhappily for all parties they work at far too low a rate—at a rate, in short, which can but just procure salt and potatoes; they become reckless, of course, of all the comforts and decencies of life, which they have no means of procuring. Extreme poverty brings ignorance and vice, and these are the mothers of crime. If Ireland were to submit to some kind of poor-rate—I do not mean that of England, but something that should secure to the indigent their natural share of the fruits of the earth, and enable them at least to feed while others are feasting—it would, I cannot doubt, raise the character of the lower orders, and deprive them of that recklessness of futurity which leads them to think only of the present. Indeed, where intoxication of the lower ranks is mentioned as a vice, we must allow the temptation is well-nigh inevitable; meat, clothes, fire, all that men can and do want, are supplied by a drop of whisky, and no one should be surprised that the relief (too often the only one within the wretches' power) is eagerly grasped at.

" We pay back, I suspect, the inconveniences we receive from the character of our Irish importation, by sending you a set of half-educated, cold-hearted Scotchmen, to be agents and middle-men. Among them, too, there are good and excellent characters, yet I can conceive they often mislead their employers. I am no great believer in the extreme degree of improvement to be derived from the advancement of science; for every study of that nature tends, when pushed to a certain extent, to harden the heart, and render the philosopher reckless of everything save the objects of his own pursuit; all equilibrium in the character is destroyed, and the visual force of the understanding is perverted by being fixed on one object exclusively. Thus we see theological sects (although inculcating the moral doctrines) are eternally placing man's zeal in opposition to them; and even in the practice of the bar, it is astonishing how we become callous to right and wrong, when the question is to gain or lose a cause. I have myself often wondered how I became so indifferent to the horrors of a criminal trial, if it involved a point of law. In like manner, the pursuit of physiology inflicts tortures on the lower animals of creation, and at length comes to rub shoulders against the West Port. The state of high civilization to which we have arrived, is perhaps scarcely a national blessing, since, while the *few* are improved to the highest point, the *many* are in proportion tantalized and degraded, and the same nation displays at the same time the very highest and the very lowest state in which the human race can exist in point of intellect. *Here* is a doctor who is able to take down the whole clock-work of the human frame, and may in time find some way of repairing and putting it together again; and *there* is Burke with the body of his murdered countrywoman on his back, and her blood on his hands, asking his price from the learned carcass-butcher. After all, the golden age was the period for general happiness, when the earth gave its stores without labour, and the people existed only in the numbers which it could easily subsist; but this was too good to last. As our numbers grew, our wants multiplied—and here we are, contending with increasing difficulties by the force of repeated inventions. Whether we shall at last eat each other, as of yore, or whether the earth will get a flap with a comet's tail first, who but the reverend Mr Irving will venture to pronounce?

" Now here is a fearful long letter, and the next thing is to send it under Lord Francis Gower's omnipotent frank.[*]   Anne sends best compliments; she says she had the honour to despatch her congratula-

---

[*] Lord F. G. (now Lord F. Egerton) was Secretary for Ireland, under the Duke of Wellington's Ministry.

tions to you already. Walter and his little wife are at Nice; he is now major of his regiment, which is rapid advancement, and so has gone abroad to see the world. Lockhart has been here for a week or two, but is now gone for England. I suspect he is at this moment stopped by the snow-storm, and solacing himself with a cigar somewhere in Northumberland; that is all the news that can interest you. Dr and Mrs Brewster are rather getting over their heavy loss, but it is still too visible on their brows, and that broad river lying daily before them is a sad remembrancer. I saw a brother of yours on a visit at Allerley;* he dined with us one day, and promised to come and see us next summer, which I hope he will make good.—My pen has been declaring itself independent this last half hour, which is the more unnatural, as it is engaged in writing to its former mistress.†

Ever yours affectionately,

W. Scott."

Sir Walter's operations appear to have been interrupted ever and anon, during January and February

---

* Allerley is the seat of Sir David Brewster, opposite Melrose. A fine boy, one of Sir David's sons, had been drowned a year before in the Tweed.

† Miss Edgeworth had given Sir Walter a bronze inkstand (said to have belonged to Ariosto), with appurtenances.

1829, in consequence of severe distress in the household of his printer; whose warm affections were not, as in his own case, subjected to the authority of a stoical will. On the 14th of February the Diary says —" The letters I received were numerous, and craved answers, yet the 3d vol. is getting on *hooly and fairly.* I am twenty leaves before the printer, but Ballantyne's wife is ill, and it is his nature to indulge apprehensions of the worst, which incapacitates him for labour. I cannot help regarding this amiable weakness of the mind with something too nearly allied to contempt." On the 17th—" I received the melancholy news that James Ballantyne has lost his wife. With his domestic habits the blow is irretrievable. What can he do, poor fellow, at the head of such a family of children? I should not be surprised if he were to give way to despair." James was not able to appear at his wife's funeral; and this Scott viewed with something more than pity. Next morning, however, says the Diary:—" Ballantyne came in, to my surprise, about twelve o'clock. He was very serious, and spoke as if he had some idea of sudden and speedy death. He mentioned that he had named Cadell, Cowan, young Hughes, and his brother, to be his trustees, with myself. He has settled to go to the country, poor fellow!"

Ballantyne retired accordingly to some sequestered place near Jedburgh, and there indulged his grief in solitude. Scott regarded this as weakness, and in part at leas. as wilful weakness, and addressed to him several letters of strong remonstrance and rebuke. I have read them, but do not possess them; nor perhaps would it have been proper for me to print them. In writing of the case to myself, he says — " I have a sore grievance in poor Ballantyne's increasing lowness of heart, and I fear he is sinking rapidly into the condition of a religious dreamer. His retirement from Edinburgh was the worst advised scheme in the world. I in vain reminded him, that when our Saviour himself was to be led into temptation, the first thing the Devil thought of was to get him into the wilderness." Ballantyne, after a few weeks, resumed his place in the printing office; but he addicted himself more and more to what his friend considered as erroneous and extravagant notions of religious doctrine; and I regret to say that in this difference originated a certain alienation, not of affection, but of confidence, which was visible to every near observer of their subsequent intercourse. Towards the last, indeed, they saw but little of each other. I suppose, however, it is needless to add that, down to the very last, Scott watched over Ballantyne's interests with undiminished attention.

I must give a few more extracts from the Diary, for the Spring Session, during which Anne of Geierstein was finished, and the Prospectus of the Opus

Magnum issued. — Several entries refer to the final carrying of the Roman Catholic Question. When the Duke of Wellington and Sir Robert Peel. announced their intention of conceding those claims, on which the reader has already seen Scott's opinion, there were meetings and petitions enough in Edinburgh as elsewhere; and though he felt considerable repugnance to acting in any such matter with Whigs and Radicals, in opposition to a great section of the Tories, he ultimately resolved not to shrink from doing his part in support of the Duke's government on that critical experiment. He wrote, I believe, several articles in favour of the measure for the Weekly Journal; he spoke, though shortly, at the principal meeting, and proposed one of its resolutions; and when the consequent petition was read in the House of Commons, his name among the subscribers was received with such enthusiasm, that Sir Robert Peel thought fit to address to him a special. and very cordial letter of thanks on that occasion.

DIARY—" *February* 23.—Anne and I dined at Skene's, where we met Mr and Mrs George Forbes, Colonel and Mrs Blair, George Bell, &c. The party was a pleasant one. Colonel Blair told us that at the commencement of the battle of Waterloo, there was some trouble to prevent the men from breaking their ranks. He expostulated with one man—' Why, my good fellow, you cannot propose to beat the French alone? You had better keep your ranks.' The man, who was one of the 71st, returned to his place, saying, ' I believe you are right, sir, but I am a man of a very *hot temper.'* There was much *bon-hommie* in the reply.

" *February* 24.—Snowy miserable morning. I corrected my proofs, and then went to breakfast with Mr Drummond Hay, where we again met Colonel and Mrs Blair, with Thomas Thomson. We looked over some most beautiful drawings which Mrs Blair had made in different parts of India, exhibiting a species of architecture so gorgeous, and on a scale so extensive, as to put to shame the magnificence of Europe;* and yet, in most cases, as little is known of the people who wrought these wonders as of the kings who built the Pyramids. Fame depends on literature, not on architecture. We are more eager to see a broken column of Cicero's villa, than all these mighty labours of barbaric power. Mrs Blair is full of enthusiasm. She told me, that when she worked with her pencil she was glad to have some one to read to her as a sort of sedative, otherwise her excitement made her tremble, and burst out a-

* Some of these fine drawings have been engraved for Colonel Tod's Travels in Western India. London, 4to, 1839.

crying. I can understand this very well. On returning home, I wrought, but not much — rather dawdled and took to reading Chambers's Beauties of Scotland, which would be admirable if they were accurate. He is a clever young fellow, but hurts himself by too much haste. I am not making too much myself I know — and I know, too, it is time I were making it — unhappily there is such a thing as more haste and less speed. I can very seldom think to purpose by lying perfectly idle, but when I take an idle book, or a walk, my mind strays back to its task, out of contradiction as it were; the things I read become mingled with those I have been writing, and something is concocted. I cannot compare this process of the mind to anything save that of a woman to whom the mechanical operation of spinning serves as a running bass to the songs she sings, or the course of ideas she pursues. The phrase *Hoc age.* so often quoted by my father, does not jump with my humour. I cannot nail my mind to one subject of contemplation, and it is by nourishing two trains of ideas that I can bring one into order.

" *February* 28. — Finished my proofs this morning; and read part of a curious work, called Memoirs of Vidocq; a fellow who was at the head of Buonaparte's police. It is a *picaresque* tale; in other words, a romance of roguery. The whole seems much exaggerated, and got up; but I suppose there is truth *au fond*. I came home about two o'clock, and wrought hard and fast till now — night. I cannot get myself to feel at all anxious about the Catholic question. I cannot see the use of fighting about the platter, when you have let them snatch the meat off it. I hold Popery to be such a mean and depraving superstition, that I am not sure I could have found myself liberal enough for voting the repeal of the penal laws as they existed before 1780. They must, and would, in course of time, have smothered Popery; and, I confess, I should have seen the old lady of Babylon's mouth stopped with pleasure. But now, that you have taken the plaster off her mouth, and given her free respiration, I cannot see the sense of keeping up the irritation about the claim to sit in Parliament. Unopposed, the Catholic superstition may sink into dust, with all its absurd ritual and solemnities. Still it is an awful risk. The world is, in fact, as silly as ever, and a good competence of nonsense will always find believers. Animal magnetism, phrenology, &c. &c., have all had their believers, and why not Popery? Ecod! if they should begin to make Smithfield broils, I do not know where many an honest Protestant could find courage enough to be carbonadoed? I should shrink from the thoughts of tar-barrels and gibbets, I am afraid, and make a very pusillanimous martyr. So I hope the Duke of

Wellington will keep the horned beast well in hand, and not let her get her leg over the harrows.

" *March* 4. — At four o'clock arrives Mr Cadell, with his horn charged with good news. The prospectus of the Magnum, although issued only a week. has produced such a demand among the trade, that he thinks he must add a large number of copies, that the present edition of 7000 may be increased to meet the demand; he talks of raising it to 10 or 12,000. If so, I shall have a powerful and constant income to bear on my unfortunate debts for several years to come, and may fairly hope to put every claim in a secure way of payment. Laidlaw dined with me, and, poor fellow, was as much elated with the news as I am, for it is not of a nature to be kept secret. I hope I shall have him once more at Kaeside to debate, as we used to do, on religion and politics.

" *March* 5. — I am admitted a member of the Maitland Club of Glasgow, a Society on the principle of the Roxburgh and Bannatyne. What a tail of the alphabet I should draw after me were I to sign with the indications of the different societies I belong to, beginning with President of the Royal Society of Edinburgh, and ending with Umpire of the Six-feet-high Club.*

* This was a sportive association of young athletes. Hogg, I think, was their Poet Laureate

" *March* 6.—Made some considerable additions to the Appendix to General Preface. I am in the sentiments towards the public that the buffoon player expresses towards his patron—

> ' Go tell my good Lord, said this modest young man,
>   If he will but invite me to dinner,
> I'll be as diverting as ever I can —
>   I will, on the faith of a sinner.'

I will multiply the notes, therefore, when there is a chance of giving pleasure and variety. There is a stronger gleam of hope on my affairs than has yet touched on them; it is not steady or certain, but it is bright and conspicuous. Ten years may last with me, though I have but little chance of it.

" *March* 7.—Sent away proofs. This extrication of my affairs, though only a Pisgah prospect, occupies my mind more than is fitting; but without some such hopes I must have felt like one of the victims of the wretch Burke, struggling against a smothering weight on my bosom, till nature could endure it no longer.

" *March* 8.—Ballantyne, by a letter of this morning, totally condemns Anne of Geierstein. Third volume nearly finished—a pretty thing, truly, for I shall be expected to do all over again. Great dishonour in this, as Trinculo says, besides an infinite

loss. Sent for Cadell to attend me to-morrow morning, that we may consult about this business.——Peel
has made his motion on the Catholic question with a
speech of three hours. It is almost a complete sur-
render to the Catholics; and so it should be, for half
measures do but linger out the feud. This will, or
rather ought to satisfy all men who sincerely love
peace, and, therefore, all men of property. But will
this satisfy Pat, who, with all his virtues, is certainly
not the most sensible person in the world? Perhaps
not; and if not, it is but fighting them at last. I
smoked away, and thought of ticklish politics and
bad novels.

" *March* 9.—Cadell came to breakfast. We resolved in privy council to refer the question whether
Anne of G——n be sea-worthy or not, to further
consideration, which, as the book cannot be published,
at any rate, during the full rage of the Catholic question, may be easily managed. After breakfast I went
to Sir William Arbuthnot's,* and met there a select
party of Tories, to decide whether we should act

* This gentleman was a favourite with Sir Walter — a special
point of communion being the Antiquities of the British Drama.
He was Provost of Edinburgh in 1816-17, and again in 1822,
and the King gracefully surprised him by proposing his health, at
the civic Banquet in the Parliament House (see *ante*, Vol. VII
p. 67), as " Sir William Arbuthnot, Baronet."

with the Whigs, by adopting their petition in favour of the Catholics. I was not free from apprehension that the petition might be put into such language as I, at least, should be unwilling to homologate by my subscription. The Solicitor was voucher that they would keep the terms quite general; whereupon we subscribed the requisition for a meeting, with a slight alteration, affirming that it was our desire not to have intermeddled, had not the anti-Catholics pursued that course; and so the Whigs and we are embarked in the same boat—*vogue la galère.*

" Went about one o'clock to the Castle, where we saw the auld murderess Mons Meg* brought up in solemn procession to re-occupy her ancient place on the Argyle battery. The day was cold, but serene, and I think the ladies must have been cold enough, not to mention the Celts who turned out upon the occasion, under the leading of Cluny Macpherson, a fine spirited lad. Mons Meg is a monument of our pride and poverty. The size is enormous, but six smaller guns would have been made at the same expense, and done six times as much execution as she could have done. There was immense interest taken in the show by the people of the town, and the numbers who crowded the Castle-hill had a magnificent appearance. About thirty of our Celts attended in costume: and as there was a Highland regiment

* See *ante*, Vol. VII. p. 86.

for duty, with dragoons and artillerymen, the whole made a splendid show. The style in which the last manned and wrought the windlass which raised Old Meg, weighing seven or eight tons, from her temporary carriage to that which has been her basis for many years, was singularly beautiful as a combined exhibition of skill and strength. My daughter had what might have proved a frightful accident. Some rockets were let off, one of which lighted upon her head, and set her bonnet on fire. She neither screamed nor ran, but quietly permitted Charles Sharpe to extinguish the fire, which he did with great coolness and dexterity. All who saw her, especially the friendly Celts, gave her merit for her steadiness, and said she came of good blood. My own courage was not tried, for being at some distance escorting the beautiful and lively Countess of Hopetoun, I did not hear of the accident till it was over.

" We lunched with the regiment (73d) now in the castle. The little entertainment gave me an opportunity of observing what I have often before remarked—the improvement in the character of the young and subaltern officers in the army, which in the course of a long and bloody war had been, in point of rank and manners, something deteriorated. The number of persons applying for commissions (3000 being now on the lists) gives an opportunity of selection; and officers should certainly be *gentlemen*, with a complete opening to all who can rise by merit. The style in which duty and the knowledge of their profession are now enforced, prevents *faineants* from remaining long in the profession.

" In the evening I presided at the annual festival of the Celtic Club. I like this Society, and willingly give myself to be excited by the sight of handsome young men with plaids and claymores, and all the alertness and spirit of Highlanders in their native garb. There was the usual degree of excitation— excellent dancing, capital songs, a general inclination to please and to be pleased. A severe cold caught on the battlements of the Castle prevented me from playing first fiddle so well as on former occasions, but what I could do was received with the usual partiality of the Celts. I got home fatigued and *vino gravatus* about eleven o'clock. We had many guests, some of whom, English officers, seemed both amused and surprised at our wild ways, especially at the dancing without ladies, and the mode of drinking favourite toasts, by springing up with one foot on the bench and one on the table, and the peculiar shriek of applause, so unlike English cheering.

" *Abbotsford, March* 18.—I like the hermit life indifferent well, nor would, I sometimes think, break my heart, were I to be in that magic mountain where food was regularly supplied by ministering genii, and plenty of books were accessible without the least interruption of human society. But this is thinking like a fool. Solitude is only agreeable when the power of having society is removed to a short space, and can be commanded at pleasure. ' It is not good for man to be alone.'* It blunts our faculties and freezes our active virtues. And now, my watch pointing to noon, I think after four hours' work I may indulge myself with a walk. The dogs see me about to shut my desk, and intimate their happiness by caresses and whining. By your leave, Messrs Genii of the Mountain, if I come to your retreat I'll bring my dogs with me.

" The day was showery, but not unpleasant—soft dropping rains, attended by a mild atmosphere, that spoke of flowers in their seasons, and a chirping of birds, that had a touch of spring in it. I had the patience to get fully wet, and the grace to be thankful for it.

" Come, a little flourish on the trumpet. Let us rouse the Genius of this same red mountain — so called, because it is all the year covered with roses. There can be no difficulty in finding it, for it lies towards the Caspian, and is quoted in the Persian Tales. Well, I open my ephemerides, form my scheme under the suitable planet, and the Genius

* Genesis. ii. 18.

obeys the invitation, and appears. The Gnome is a misshapen dwarf, with a huge jolter-head like that of Boerhaave on the Bridge,* his limbs and body monstrously shrunk and disproportioned. —' Sir Dwarf,' said I, undauntedly, ' thy head is very large, and thy feet and limbs somewhat small in proportion.' ' I have crammed my head, even to the overflowing, with knowledge; and I have starved my limbs by disuse of exercise and denial of sustenance!'—' Can I acquire wisdom in thy solitary library?' ' Thou mayest!'—' On what condition?' ' Renounce all gross and fleshly pleasures, eat pulse and drink water, converse with none but the wise and learned, alive and dead.'—' Why, this were to die in the cause of wisdom!' ' If you desire to draw from our library only the advantage of seeming wise, you may have it consistent with all your favourite enjoyments.'—' How much sleep?' ' A Lapland night—eight months out of the twelve.'—' Enough for a dormouse, most generous Genius —a bottle of wine?' ' Two, if you please; but you must not seem to care for them— cigars in loads, whisky in lushings—only they must be taken with an air of contempt, a *flocci-pauci-*

* This head may still be seen over a laboratory at No. 100 of the South Bridge, Edinburgh. — *N. B.* There is a tradition that the venerable busto in question was once dislodged by " Colonel Grogg " and some of his companions, and waggishly planted in a very inappropriate position.

nihili-piti-fication of all that can gratify the outward man.'—' I am about to ask you a serious question—when one has stuffed his stomach, drunk his bottle, and smoked his cigar, how is he to keep himself awake?' ' Either by cephalic snuff or castle-building.' —' Do you approve of castle-building as a frequent exercise?'—*Genius.* ' Life were not life without it—

> " Give me the joy that sickens not the heart,
> Give me the wealth that has no wings to fly."

Author. ' I reckon myself one of the best aërial architects now living, and *Nil me pœnitet.'—Genius.* ' *Nec est cur te pœniteat.*   Most of your novels had previously been subjects for airy castles.'—*Author.* ' You have me—and moreover a man derives experience from such fanciful visions.   There are few situations I have not in fancy figured, and there are few, of course, which I am not previously prepared to take some part in.' — *Genius.* ' True; but I am afraid your having fancied yourself victorious in many a fight, would be of little use were you suddenly called to the field, and your personal infirmities and nervous agitations both rushing upon you and incapacitating you.'—*Author.* ' My nervous agitations! down with them!—

> ' Down, down to limbo and the burning lake!
> False fiend, avoid!—
> So there ends the tale, with a hoy, with a hoy,

So there ends the tale with a ho.
There's a moral — if you fail
To seize it by the tail,
Its import will exhale, you must know.

" *March* 19.—The above was written yesterday before dinner, though appearances are to the contrary. I only meant that the studious solitude I have sometimes dreamed of, unless practised with rare stoicism, might perchance degenerate into secret indulgences of coarser appetites, which, when the cares and restraints of social life are removed, are apt to make us think, with Dr Johnson, our dinner the most important event of the day. So much in the way of explanation, a humour which I love not. Go to. I fagged at my Review on Ancient Scottish History, both before and after breakfast. I walked from one o'clock till near three. I make it out rather better than of late I have been able to do in the streets of Edinburgh, where I am ashamed to walk so slow as would suit me. Indeed nothing but a certain suspicion, that once drawn up on the beach, I would soon break up, prevents my renouncing pedestrian exercises altogether, for it is positive suffering, and of an acute kind too.

" *March* 26.—Sent off ten pages of the Maid of the Mist this morning with a murrain:— But how to get my catastrophe packed into the compass allotted for it ?

> ' It sticks like a pistol half out of its holster,
>   Or rather indeed like an obstinate bolster,
>   Which I think I have seen you attempting, my dear,
>   In vain to cram into a small pillow-beer.'

There is no help for it—I must make a *tour de force*, and annihilate both time and space.

" *March* 28.—In spite of the temptation of a fine morning, I toiled manfully at the Review till two o'clock, commencing at seven. I fear it will be uninteresting, but I like the muddling work of antiquities, and, besides, wish to record my sentiments with regard to the Gothic question. No one that has not laboured as I have done on imaginary topics can judge of the comfort afforded by walking on all fours, and being grave and dull. I daresay, when the clown of the pantomime escapes from his nightly task of vivacity, it is his especially to smoke a pipe and be prosy with some good-natured fellow, the dullest of his acquaintance. I have seen such a tendency in Sir Adam Fergusson, the gayest man I ever knew; and poor Tom Sheridan has complained to me on the fatigue of supporting the character of an agreeable companion.

" *April* 3.—Both Sir James Mackintosh and Lord Haddington have spoken very handsomely in Parliament of my accession to the Catholic petition, and I think it has done some good; yet I am not confiden that the measure will disarm the Catholic spleen— nor am I entirely easy at finding myself allied to the Whigs even in the instance where I agree with them. This is witless prejudice, however.

" *April* 8.—We have the news of the Catholic question being carried in the House of Lords, by a majority of 105 upon the second reading. This is decisive, and the balsam of Fierabras must be swallowed.

" *April* 9.—I have bad news of James Ballantyne. Hypochondria, I am afraid, and religiously distressed in mind.

" *April* 18.—Corrected proofs. I find J. B. has not returned to his business, though I wrote to say how necessary it was. My pity begins to give way tc anger. Must he sit there and squander his thoughts and senses upon dowdy metaphysics and abstruse theology, till he addles his brains entirely, and ruins his business?—I have written to him again, letter third, and, I am determined, last.

April 20.—Lord Buchan is dead, a person whose immense vanity, bordering upon insanity, obscured, or rather eclipsed, very considerable talents. His imagination was so fertile, that he seemed really to believe the extraordinary fictions which he delighted in telling. His economy, most laudable in the early part of his life, when it enabled him, from a small income, to pay his father's debts, became a miserable habit, and led him to do mean things. He had a desire to be a great man and a Mecænas—*a bon marché*. The two celebrated lawyers, his brothers, were not more gifted by nature than I think he was, but the restraints of a profession kept the eccentricity of the family in order. Henry Erskine was the best-natured man I ever knew, thoroughly a gentleman, and with but one fault—He could not say *no*, and thus sometimes misled those who trusted him. Tom Erskine was positively mad. I have heard him tell a cock-and-a-bull story of having seen the ghost of his father's servant, John Burnet, with as much gravity as if he believed every word he was saying. Both Henry and Thomas were saving men, yet both died very poor. The latter at one time possessed £200,000; the other had a considerable fortune. The Earl alone has died wealthy. It is saving, not getting, that is the mother of riches. They all had wit. The Earl's was crack-brained, and sometimes caustic; Henry's was of the very kindest, best-humoured, and gayest sort that ever cheered society; that of Lord Erskine was moody and muddish. But I never saw him in his best days.

" *April* 25.— After writing a heap of letters, it was time to set out for Lord Buchan's funeral at Dryburgh Abbey. The letters were signed by Mr David Erskine, his Lordship's natural son; and his nephew, the young Earl, was present; but neither of them took the head of the coffin. His Lordship's burial took place in a chapel amongst the ruins. His body was in the grave with its feet pointing westward. My cousin, Maxpopple,* was for taking notice of it, but I assured him that a man who had been wrong in the head all his life would scarce become right-headed after death. I felt something at parting with this old man, though but a trumpery body. He gave me the first approbation I ever obtained from a stranger. His caprice had led him to examine Dr Adam's class when I, a boy of twelve years old, and then in disgrace for some aggravated case of negligence, was called up from a low bench, and recited my lesson with some spirit and appearance of feeling the poetry—(it was the apparition of Hector's ghost in the Æneid)—which called forth the noble Earl's applause. I was very proud of this at the time. I was sad from another account—it was the first time

---

* William Scott, Esq. — the present Laird of Raeburn — was commonly thus designated from a minor possession, during his father's lifetime. Whatever, in things of this sort, used to be practised among the French noblesse, might be traced, till very lately, in the customs of the Scottish provincial gentry.

I had been among those ruins since I left a very valued pledge there. My next visit may be involuntary.
Even God's will be done — at least I have not the
mortification of thinking what a deal of patronage
and fuss Lord Buchan would bestow on my funeral.[*]
Maxpopple dined and slept here with four of his family, much amused with what they heard and saw.
By good fortune, a ventriloquist and parcel juggler
came in, and we had him in the library after dinner.
He was a half-starved wretched-looking creature,
who seemed to have eat more fire than bread. So
I caused him to be well stuffed, and gave him a
guinea — rather to his poverty than to his skill —
and now to finish Anne of Geierstein."

Anne of Geierstein was finished before breakfast
on the 29th of April; and his Diary mentions that
immediately after breakfast he began his Compendium
of Scottish History for Dr Lardner's Cyclopædia. We
have seen, that when the proprietors of that work,
in July 1828, offered him £500 for an abstract of
Scottish History in one volume, he declined the proposal. They subsequently offered £700, and this was
accepted; but though he began the task under the
impression that he should find it a heavy one, he soon
warmed to the subject, and pursued it with cordial

* *See ante,* Vol. VI. p. 90.

zeal and satisfaction.   One volume, it by and by appeared, would never do—in his own phrase, " he must have elbow-room".—and I believe it was finally settled that he should have £1500 for the book in two volumes; of which the first was published before the end of this year.

Anne Geierstein came out about the middle of May; and this, which may be almost called the last work of his imaginative genius, was received at least as well—(out of Scotland, that is)—as the Fair Maid of Perth had been, or indeed as any novel of his after the Crusaders.   I partake very strongly, I am aware, in the feeling which most of my own countrymen have little shame in avowing, that no novel of his, where neither scenery nor character is Scottish, belongs to the same pre-eminent class with those in which he paints and peoples his native landscape. I have confessed that I cannot rank even his best English romances with such creations as Waverley and Old Mortality; far less can I believe that posterity will attach similar value to this Maid of the Mist.   Its pages, however, display in undiminished perfection all the skill and grace of the mere artist, with occasional outbreaks of the old poetic spirit, more than sufficient to remove the work to an immeasurable distance from any of its order produced in this country in our own age.   Indeed, the various play of fancy in the combination of persons and events,

and the airy liveliness of both imagery and diction,
may well justify us in applying to the author what
he beautifully says of his King René—

> " A mirthful man he was ; the snows of age
>   Fell, but they did not chill him.   Gaiety,
>   Even in life's closing, touch'd his teeming brain
>   With such wild visions as the setting sun
>   Raises in front of some hoar glacier,
>   Painting the bleak ice with a thousand hues."

It is a common saying that there is nothing so
distinctive of *genius* as the retention, in advanced
years, of the capacity to depict the feelings of youth
with all their original glow and purity. But I apprehend this blessed distinction belongs to, and is the
just reward of, virtuous genius only.   In the case of
extraordinary force of imagination, combined with
the habitual indulgence of a selfish mood—not combined, that is to say, with the genial temper of mind
and thought which God and Nature design to be kept
alive in man by those domestic charities out of which
the other social virtues so easily spring, and with
which they find such endless links of interdependence ;—in this unhappy case, which none who has
studied the biography of genius can pronounce to be
a rare one, the very power which heaven bestowed
seems to become, as old age darkens, the sternest
avenger of its own misapplication.   The retrospect
of life is converted by its energy into one wide black-

ness of desolate regret; and whether this breaks out in the shape of a rueful contemptuousness, or a sarcastic mockery of tone, the least drop of the poison is enough to paralyze all attempts at awakening sympathy by fanciful delineations of love and friendship. Perhaps Scott has nowhere painted such feelings more deliciously than in those very scenes of Anne of Geierstein, which offer every now and then, in some incidental circumstance or reflection, the best evidence that they are drawn by a grey-headed man. The whole of his own life was too present to his wonderful memory to permit of his brooding with exclusive partiality, whether painfully or pleasurably, on any one portion or phasis of it; and besides, he was always living over again in his children, young at heart whenever he looked on them, and the world that was opening on them and their friends. But above all, he had a firm belief in the future re-union of those whom death has parted.

He lost two more of his old intimates about this time;—Mr. Terry in June, and Mr Shortreed in the beginning of July. The Diary says:—" *July* 9. Heard of the death of poor Bob Shortreed, the companion of many a long ride among the hills in quest of old ballads. He was a merry companion, a good singer and mimic, and full of Scottish drollery. In his company, and under his guidance, I was able to see much of rural society in the mountains, which

I could not otherwise have attained, and which I have made my use of.   He was, in addition, a man of worth and character.   I always burdened his hospitality while at Jedburgh on the circuit, and have been useful to some of his family.   Poor fellow! So glide our friends from us.*   Many recollections die with him and with poor Terry."

His Diary has few more entries for this twelvemonth.   Besides the volume of History for Dr Lardner's collection, he had ready for publication by December the last of the *Scottish* Series of Tales of a Grandfather; and had made great progress in the prefaces and notes for Cadell's *Opus Magnum*. He had also overcome various difficulties which for a time interrupted the twin scheme of an illustrated edition of his Poems: and one of these in a manner so agreeable to him, and honourable to the other party, that I must make room for the two following letters :—

---

* Some little time before his death, the worthy Sheriff-substitute of Roxburghshire received a set of his friend's works, with this inscription : —" To Robert Shortreed, Esq., the friend of the author from youth to age, and his guide and companion upon many an expedition among the Border hills, in quest of the materials of legendary lore which have at length filled so many volumes, this collection of the results of their former rambles is presented by his sincere friend, *Walter Scott*."

" *To J. G. Lockhart, Esq., Regent's Park.*

" Shandwick Place, 4th June 1829.

" My Dear Lockhart,

" I have a commission for you to execute for me, which I shall deliver in a few words. I am now in possession of my own copyrights of every kind, excepting a few things in Longman's hands, and which I am offered on very fair terms — and a fourth share of Marmion, which is in the possession of our friend Murray. Now, I should consider it a great favour if Mr Murray would part with it at what he may consider as a fair rate, and would be most happy to show my sense of obligation by assisting his views and speculations as far as lies in my power. I wish you could learn as soon as you can Mr Murray's sentiments on this subject, as they would weigh with me in what I am about to arrange as to the collected edition. The Waverley Novels are doing very well indeed. — I put you to a shilling's expense, as I wish a speedy answer to the above query. I am always, with love to Sophia, affectionately yours,   WALTER SCOTT."

" *To Sir Walter Scott, Bart., Edinburgh.*

" Albemarle Street, June 8, 1829.

" My Dear Sir,

" Mr Lockhart has this moment communicated

your letter respecting my fourth share of the copy-
right of Marmion. I have already been applied to by
Messrs Constable and by Messrs Longman, to know
what sum I would sell this share for—but so highly
do I estimate the honour of being, even in so small
a degree, the publisher of the author of the poem—
that no pecuniary consideration whatever can induce
me to part with it.

" But there is a consideration of another kind,
which until now I was not aware of, which would
make it painful to me if I were to retain it a moment
longer. I mean the knowledge of its being required
by the author, into whose hands it was spontaneously
resigned in the same instant that I read his request.

" This share has been profitable to me fifty-fold
beyond what either publisher or author could have
anticipated, and, therefore, my returning it on such
an occasion you will, I trust, do me the favour to
consider in no other light than as a mere act of grateful acknowledgment for benefits already received by,
my dear Sir, your obliged and faithful servant,

JOHN MURRAY "

The success of the collective novels was far beyond
what either Sir Walter or Mr Cadell had ventured
to anticipate. Before the close of 1829, eight volumes had been issued; and the monthly sale had
reached as high as 35,000. Should this go on, there

was, indeed, every reason to hope that, coming in aid of undiminished industry in the preparation of new works, it would wipe off all his load of debt in the course of a very few years. And during the autumn (which I spent near him) it was most agreeable to observe the effects of the prosperous intelligence, which every succeeding month brought, upon his spirits.

This was the more needed, that at this time his eldest son, who had gone to the south of France on account of some unpleasant symptoms in his health, did not at first seem to profit rapidly by the change of climate. He feared that the young man was not quite so attentive to the advice of his physicians as he ought to have been; and in one of many letters on this subject, after mentioning some of Cadell's good news as to the great affair, he says—" I have wrought hard, and so far successfully. But I tell you plainly, my dear boy, that if you permit your health to decline from want of attention, I have not strength of mind enough to exert myself in these matters as I have hitherto been doing." Happily Major Scott was, ere long, restored to his usual state of health and activity.

Sir Walter himself, too, besides the usual allowance of rheumatism, and other lesser ailments, had an attack that season of a nature which gave his family great alarm, and which for some days he himself regarded with the darkest prognostications. After some weeks, during which he complained of headach and nervous irritation, certain hæmorrhages indicated the sort of relief required, and he obtained it from copious cupping. He says, in his Diary for June 3d—" The ugly symptom still continues. Dr Ross does not make much of it; and I think he is apt to look grave. Either way I am firmly resolved. I wrote in the morning. The Court kept me till near two, and then home comes I. Afternoon and evening were spent as usual. In the evening Dr Ross ordered me to be cupped, an operation which I only knew from its being practised by those eminent medical practitioners the barbers of Bagdad. It is not painful; and, I think, resembles a giant twisting about your flesh between his finger and thumb." After this he felt better, he said, than he had done for years before; but there can be little doubt that the natural evacuation was a very serious symptom. It was, in fact, the precursor of apoplexy. In telling the Major of his recovery, he says—" The sale of the Novels is pro—di—gi—ous. If it last but a few years, it will clear my feet of old incumbrances, nay, perhaps, enable me to talk a word to our friend Nicol Milne.

'But old ships must expect to get out of commission,
    Nor again to weigh anchor with *yo heave ho!* '

However that may be, I should be happy to die a

free man; and I am sure you will all be kind to poor Anne, who will miss me most. I don't intend to die a minute sooner than I can help for all this; but when a man takes to making blood instead of water, he is tempted to think on the possibility of his soon making earth."

One of the last entries in this year's Diary gives a sketch of the celebrated Edward Irving, who was about this time deposed from the ministry of the Church of Scotland on account of his wild heresies.* Sir Walter, describing a large dinner party, says— " I met to-day the celebrated divine and *soi-disant* prophet, Irving. He is a fine-looking man (bating a diabolical squint), with talent on his brow and madness in his eye. His dress, and the arrangement of his hair, indicated that. I could hardly keep my eyes off him while we were at table. He put me in mind of the devil disguised as an angel of light, so ill did that horrible obliquity of vision harmonize with the dark tranquil features of his face, resembling that of .our Saviour in Italian pictures, with the hair carefully arranged in the same manner. There was much real or affected simplicity in the manner in which he spoke. He rather *made play*, spoke much, and seemed to be good-humoured. But he spoke with that kind of unction which is nearly allied to *cajo lerie*. He boasted much of the tens of thousands

* Mr Irving died on 6th December 1834, aged 42.

that attended his ministry at the town of Annan, his native place, till he well-nigh provoked me to say he was a distinguished exception to the rule that a prophet was not esteemed in his own country. But time and place were not fitting."

Among a few other friends from a distance, Sir Walter received this autumn a short visit from Mr Hallam, and made in his company several of the little excursions which had in former days been of constant recurrence. Mr Hallam had with him his son, Arthur, a young gentleman of extraordinary abilities, and as modest as able, who not long afterwards was cut off in the very bloom of opening life and genius. In a little volume of " Remains," which his father has since printed for private friends — with this motto —

> " Vattene in pace alma beata e bella,"—

there occurs a memorial of Abbotsford and Melrose, which I have pleasure in being allowed to quote :—

" STANZAS — AUGUST 1829.

" I lived an hour in fair Melrose;
    It was not when " the pale moonlight "
Its magnifying charm bestows;
    Yet deem I that I " viewed it right."
The wind-swept shadows fast careered,
Like living things that joyed or feared,
Adown the sunny Eildon Hill,
And the sweet winding Tweed the distance crowned well.

" I inly laughed to see that scene
 Wear such a countenance of youth,
Though many an age those hills were green,
 And yonder river glided smooth,
Ere in these now disjointed walls
The Mother Church held festivals,
And full-voiced anthemings the while
Swelled from the choir, and lingered down the echoing aisle.

" I coveted that Abbey's doom;
 For if, I thought, the early flowers
Of our affection may not bloom,
 Like those green hills, through countless hours,
Grant me at least a tardy waning,
Some pleasure still in age's paining;
Though lines and forms must fade away,
Still may old Beauty share the empire of Decay!

" But looking toward the grassy mound
 Where calm the Douglas chieftains lie,
Who, living, quiet never found,
 I straightway learnt a lesson high:
For there an old man sat serene,
And well I knew that thoughtful mien
Of him whose early lyre had thrown
Over these mouldering walls the magic of its tone.

" Then ceased I from my envying state,
 And knew that aweless intellect
Hath power upon the ways of fate,
 And works through time and space uncheck'd.
That minstrel of old chivalry,
In the cold grave must come to be,
But his transmitted thoughts have part
In the collective mind, and never shall depart.

" It was a comfort too to see
    Those dogs that from him ne'er would rove,
  And always eyed him reverently,
    With glances of depending love.
  They know not of that eminence
  Which marks him to my reasoning sense;
  They know but that he is a man,
  And still to them is kind, and glads them all he can.

" And, hence, their quiet looks confiding,
    Hence grateful instincts seated deep,
  By whose strong bond, were ill betiding,
    They'd risk their own his life to keep.
  What joy to watch in lower creature
  Such dawning of a moral nature,
  And how (the rule all things obey)
  They look to a higher mind to be their law and stay '"

———————

The close of the autumn was embittered by a sudden and most unexpected deprivation. Apparently in the fullest enjoyment of health and vigour, Thomas Purdie leaned his head one evening on the table, and dropped asleep. This was nothing uncommon in a hard-working man; and his family went and came about him for several hours, without taking any notice. When supper came, they tried to awaken him, and found that life had been for some time extinct. Far different from other years, Sir Walter seemed impatient to get away from Abbotsford to Edinburgh. " I have lost," he writes (4th November) to Cadell,

" my old and faithful servant—my factotum—and am so much shocked, that I really wish to be quit of the country and safe in town. I have this day laid him in the grave. This has prevented my answering your letters."

The grave, close to the Abbey at Melrose, is surmounted by a modest monument, having on two sides these inscriptions :—

IN GRATEFUL REMEMBRANCE

OF

THE FAITHFUL AND ATTACHED SERVICES

OF

TWENTY-TWO YEARS,

AND IN SORROW

FOR THE LOSS OF A HUMBLE BUT SINCERE FRIEND;

THIS STONE WAS ERECTED

BY

SIR WALTER SCOTT, BART.,

OF ABBOTSFORD.

———

HERE LIES THE BODY

OF

THOMAS PURDIE,

WOOD-FORESTER AT ABBOTSFORD,

WHO DIED 29th OCTOBER 1829.

AGED SIXTY-TWO YEARS.

———

" Thou hast been faithful
over a few things,
I will make thee ruler
over many things."

St Matthew, chap. xxv. ver. 21st.

CHAPTER LXXVIII.

Auchindrane, or the Ayrshire Tragedy—Second Volume of the History of Scotland—Paralytic seizure—Letters on Demonology, and Tales on the History of France begun—Poetry, with Prefaces, published—Reviewal of Southey's Life of Bunyan—Excursions to Culross and Preston pans—Resignation of the Clerkship of Session—Commission on the Stuart Papers—Offers of a Pension, and of the rank of Privy-Councillor, declined—Death of George IV.—General Election—Speech at Jedburgh—Second paralytic attack—Demonology, and French History, published—Arrival of King Charles X. at Holyrood House—Letter to Lady Louisa Stuart.

1830.

Sir Walter's reviewal of the early parts of Mr Pitcairn's Ancient Criminal Trials had, of course

much gratified the editor, who sent him, on his arrival in Edinburgh, the proof-sheets of the Number
then in hand, and directed his attention particularly
to its details on the extraordinary case of Mure of
Auchindrane, A.D. 1611. Scott was so much interested with these documents, that he resolved to
found a dramatic sketch on their terrible story; and
the result was a composition far superior to any of
his previous attempts of that nature. Indeed there
are several passages in his " Ayrshire Tragedy"—
especially that where the murdered corpse floats
upright in the wake of the assassin's bark—(an
incident suggested by a lamentable chapter in Lord
Nelson's history)—which may bear comparison with
anything but Shakspeare. Yet I doubt whether the
prose narrative of the preface be not, on the whole,
more dramatic than the versified scenes. It contains, by the way, some very striking allusions to the
recent atrocities of Gill's Hill and the West Port.
This piece was published in a thin octavo early in
the year; and the beautiful Essays on Ballad Poetry,
composed with a view to a collective edition of all his
Poetical Works in small cheap volumes, were about
the same time attached to the octavo edition then on
sale; the state of stock not as yet permitting the new
issue to be begun.

Sir Walter was now to pay the penalty of his un-
paralleled toils. On the 15th of February, about

two o'clock in the afternoon, he returned from the
Parliament House apparently in his usual state, and
found an old acquaintance, Miss Young of Hawick,
waiting to show him some MS. memoirs of her father
(a dissenting minister of great worth and talents),
which he had undertaken to revise and correct for
the press.   The old lady sat by him for half an hour
while he seemed to be occupied with her papers; at
length he rose, as if to dismiss her, but sunk down
again—a slight convulsion agitating his features.
After a few minutes he got up and staggered to the
drawing-room, where Anne Scott and my sister
Violet Lockhart were sitting.   They rushed to meet
him, but he fell at all his length on the floor ere
they could reach him.   He remained speechless for
about ten minutes, by which time a surgeon had arrived and bled him.   He was cupped again in the
evening, and gradually recovered possession of speech,
and of all his faculties, in so far that, the occurrence
being kept quiet, when he appeared abroad again
after a short interval, people in general observed
no serious change.   He submitted to the utmost
severity of regimen, tasting nothing but pulse and
water for some weeks, and the alarm of his family
and intimate friends subsided.   By and by he again
mingled in society much as usual, and seems to have
almost persuaded himself that the attack had proceeded merely from the stomach, though his let-

ters continued ever and anon to drop hints that the symptoms resembled apoplexy or paralysis. When we recollect that both his father and his elder brother died of paralysis, and consider the terrible violences of agitation and exertion to which Sir Walter had been subjected during the four preceding years, the only wonder is that this blow (which had, I suspect, several indistinct harbingers) was deferred so long ; there can be none that it was soon followed by others of the same description.

He struggled manfully, however, against his malady, and during 1830 covered almost as many sheets with his MS. as in 1829. About March I find, from his correspondence with Ballantyne, that he was working regularly at his Letters on Demonology and Witchcraft for Murray's Family Library, and also on a Fourth Series of the Tales of a Grandfather — the subject being French history. Both of these books were published by the end of the year; and the former contains many passages worthy of his best day — little snatches of picturesque narrative and the like — in fact, transcripts of his own familiar fireside stories. The shrewdness with which evidence is sifted on legal cases attests, too, that the main reasoning faculty remained unshaken. But, on the whole, these works can hardly be submitted to a strict ordeal of criticism. There is in both a cloudiness both of words and arrangement. Nor can I speak differently of

the second volume of his Scottish History for Lardner's Cyclopædia, which was published in May.   His
very pretty reviewal of Mr Southey's Life and Edition of Bunyan was done in August—about which
time his recovery seems to have reached its *acmé*.

In the course of the Spring Session, circumstances
rendered it highly probable that Sir Walter's resignation of his place as Clerk of Session might be acceptable to the Government—and it is not surprising
that he should have, on the whole, been pleased to
avail himself of this opportunity.

His Diary was resumed in May, and continued
at irregular intervals for the rest of the year; but
its contents are commonly too medical for quotation.
Now and then, however, occur entries which I cannot
think of omitting.   For example:—

" *Abbotsford, May* 23, 1830.— About a year ago
I took the pet at my Diary, chiefly because I thought
it made me abominably selfish; and that by record-
ing my gloomy fits, I encouraged their recurrence,
whereas out of sight, out of mind, is the best way to
get rid of them; and now I hardly know why I take
it up again—but here goes.   I came here to attend
Raeburn's funeral.   I am near of his kin, my great-
grandfather, Walter Scott, being the second son, or
first cadet of this small family.   My late kinsman was
also married to my aunt, a most amiable old lady.

He was never kind to me, and at last utterly ungracious. Of course I never liked him, and we kept
no terms. He had forgot, though, an infantine cause
of quarrel, which I always remembered. When I
was four or five years old, I was staying at Lessudden
Place, an old mansion, the abode of this Raeburn.
A large pigeon-house was almost destroyed with
starlings, then a common bird, though now seldom
seen. They were seized in their nests and put in a
bag, and I think drowned, or thrashed to death, or
put to some such end. The servants gave one to
me, which I in some degree tamed, and the laird
seized and wrung its neck. I flew at his throat like
a wild-cat, and was torn from him with no little
difficulty. Long afterwards I did him the mortal
offence to recall some superiority which my father
had lent to the laird to make up a qualification, which
he meant to exercise by voting for Lord Minto's
interest against the Duke of Buccleuch's. This
made a total breach between two relations who had
never been friends; and though I was afterwards
of considerable service to his family, he kept his ill
humour, alleging, justly enough, that I did these
kind actions for the sake of his wife and name, not
for his benefit. I now saw him at the age of eighty-
two or three deposited in the ancestral grave; dined
with my cousins, and returned to Abbotsford about
eight o'clock.

"*Edinburgh, May* 26.—Wrought with proofs, &c. at the Demonology, which is a cursed business to do neatly. I must finish it though. I went to the Court, from that came home, and scrambled on with half writing, half reading, half idleness, till evening. I have laid aside smoking much; and now, unless tempted by company, rarely take a cigar. I was frightened by a species of fit which I had in March [February], which took from me my power of speaking. I am told it is from the stomach. It looked woundy like palsy or apoplexy. Well, be what it will, I can stand it.

"*May* 27.—Court as usual. I am agitating a proposed retirement from the Court. As they are only to have four instead of six Clerks of Session in Scotland, it will be their interest to let me retire on a superannuation. Probably I shall make a bad bargain, and get only two-thirds of the salary, instead of three-fourths. This would be hard, but I could save between two or three hundred pounds by giving up town residence. At any rate, *jacta est alea*— Sir Robert Peel and the Advocate acquiesce in the arrangement, and Sir Robert Dundas retires alongst with me. I think the difference will be infinite in point of health and happiness. Yet I do not know It is perhaps a violent change in the end of life to quit the walk one has trod so long, and the cursed

splenetic temper which besets all men makes you value opportunities and circumstances when one enjoys
them no longer. Well—'Things must be as they
may,' as says that great philosopher Corporal Nym.

" *June* 3.—I finished my proofs, and sent them
off with copy. I saw Mr Dickinson * on Tuesday;
a right plain sensible man. He is so confident in
my matters, that being a large creditor himself, he
offers to come down, with the support of all the
London creditors, to carry through any measure that
can be devised for my behoof. Mr Cadell showed
him that we were four years forward in matter
prepared for the press. Got Heath's Illustrations,
which I daresay are finely engraved, but common-
place enough in point of art.

" *June* 17.—Went last night to Theatre, and saw
Miss Fanny Kemble's Isabella, which was a most
creditable performance. It has much of the genius
of Mrs Siddons her aunt. She wants her beautiful
countenance, her fine form, and her matchless dignity
of step and manner. On the other hand, Miss Fanny
Kemble has very expressive, though not regular features, and what is worth it all, great energy mingled
with and chastised by correct taste. I suffered by

* Mr John Dickinson of Nash-mill, Herts, the eminent paper-
maker.

the heat, lights, and exertion, and will not go back to-night, for it has purchased me a sore headach this theatrical excursion. Besides, the play is Mrs Beverley, and I hate to be made miserable about domestic distress; so I keep my gracious presence at home to-night, though I love and respect Miss Kemble for giving her active support to her father in his need, and preventing Covent Garden from coming down about their ears. I corrected proofs before breakfast, attended Court, but was idle in **the** forenoon, the headach annoying me much.

" *Blair-Adam, June* 18.— Our meeting cordial, but our numbers diminished; the good and very clever Lord Chief-Baron [Shepherd] is returned to his own country with more regrets than in Scotland usually attend a stranger. Will Clerk has a bad cold, Tom Thomson is detained, but the Chief Commissioner, Admiral Adam, Sir Adam, John Thomson and I, make an excellent concert.

" *June* 19.— Arose and expected to work a little, but a friend's house is not favourable; you are sure to want the book you have not brought, and are, in short, out of sorts, like the minister who could not preach out of his own pulpit. There is something fanciful in this, and something real too. After breakfast to Culross, where the veteran, Sir Robert Preston, showed us his curiosities. Life has done as much for him as most people. In his ninety-second year, he has an ample fortune, a sound understanding, not the least decay of eyes, ears, or taste, is as big as two men, and eats like three. Yet he too experiences the " *singula prædantur,*" and has lost something since I last saw him.* If his appearance renders old age tolerable, it does not make it desirable. But I fear, when death comes, we shall be unwilling for all that to part with our bundle of sticks. Sir Robert amuses himself with repairing the old House of Culross, built by the Lord Bruce. What it is destined for is not very evident. It is too near his own mansion of Valleyfield to be useful as a residence, if indeed it could be formed into a comfortable modern house. But it is rather like a banqueting-house. Well, he follows his own fancy. We had a sumptuous cold dinner. Sir Adam grieves it was not hot, so little can war and want break a man to circumstances. The beauty of Culross consists in magnificent terraces rising on the sea beach, and commanding the opposite shore of Lothian; the house is repairing in the style of James VI. There are some fine relics of the Old Monastery, with large Saxon arches. At Anstruther I saw with pleasure the painting, by Raeburn, of my old friend Adam Rolland, Esq., who

* Sir R. Preston, Bart. died in May 1834, aged 95.

was in the external circumstances, but not in frolic
or fancy, my prototype for Paul Pleydell.

" *June* 9.——Dined with the Bannatyne, where we
had a lively party. Touching the songs, an old *roué*
must own an improvement in the times, when all
paw-paw words are omitted;——and yet, when the
naughty innuendoes are gazers, one is apt to say——

> 'Swear me, Kate, like a lady as thou art,
>   A good mouth-filling oath! and leave In sooth,
>   And such protests of pepper gingerbread.' *

I think there is more affectation than improvement
in the new mode."

Not knowing how poor Maida had been replaced,
Miss Edgeworth at this time offered Sir Walter a fine
Irish staghound.   He replies thus:——

" *To Miss Edgeworth, Edgeworthstown,*

" Edinburgh, 23d June 1830
" My Dear Miss Edgeworth,
    " Nothing would be so valuable to me as the
mark of kindness which you offer, and yet my kennel
is so much changed since I had the pleasure of seeing

* Hotspur — 1st *King Henry IV. Act III. Scene* 1.

you, that I must not accept of what I wished so sincerely to possess. I am the happy owner of two of the noble breed, each of gigantic size, and the gift of that sort of Highlander whom we call a High Chief, so I would hardly be justified in parting with them even to make room for your kind present, and I should have great doubts whether the mountaineers would receive the Irish stranger with due hospitality. One of them I had from poor Glengarry, who, with all wild and fierce points of his character, had a kind, honest, and warm heart. The other from a young friend, whom Highlanders call MacVourigh, and Lowlanders MacPherson of Cluny. He is a fine spirited boy, fond of his people and kind to them, and the best dancer of a Highland reel now living. I fear I must not add a third to Nimrod and Bran, having little use for them except being pleasant companions. As to labouring in their vocation, we have only one wolf which I know of, kept in a friend's menagerie near me, and no wild deer. Walter has some roebucks indeed, but Lochore is far off, and I begin to feel myself distressed at running down these innocent and beautiful creatures, perhaps because I cannot gallop so fast after them as to drown sense of the pain we are inflicting. And yet I suspect I am like the sick fox; and if my strength and twenty year could come back, I would become again a copy of my namesake, remembered by the sobriquet of

Walter *ill to hauld* (to hold, that is.) ' But age has clawed me in its clutch,'* and there is no remedy for increasing disability except dying, which is an awkward score.

" There is some chance of my retiring from my official situation upon the changes in the Court of Session. They cannot reduce my office, though they do not wish to fill it up with a new occupant. I shall be therefore *de trop ;* and in these days of economy they will be better pleased to let me retire on three parts of my salary than to keep me a Clerk of Session on the whole; and small grief at our parting, as the old horse said to the broken cart. And yet, though I thought such a proposal when first made was like a Pisgah peep of Paradise, I cannot help being a little afraid of changing the habits of a long life all of a sudden and for ever. You ladies have always your work-basket and stocking-knitting to wreak an hour of tediousness upon. The routine of business serves, I suspect, for the same purpose to us male wretches ; it is seldom a burden to the mind, but a something which must be done, and is done almost mechanically; and though dull judges and duller clerks, the routine of law proceedings, and law forms, are very unlike the plumed troops and the tug of war, yet the result is the same. The occupation's gone.† The morning,

---

* *Hamlet, Act V. Sc. 1.*   † *Othello, Act III. Sc. 3.*

that the day's news must all be gathered from other sources—that the jokes which the principal Clerks of Session have laughed at weekly for a century, and which would not move a muscle of any other person's face, must be laid up to perish like those of Sancho in the Sierra Morena—I don't above half like forgetting all these moderate habits; and yet

> ' Ah, freedom is a noble thing ! '

as says the old Scottish poet.* So I will cease my regrets, or lay them by to be taken up and used as arguments of comfort, in case I do not slip my cable after all, which is highly possible. Lockhart and Sophia have taken up their old residence at Chiefswood. They are very fond of the place; and I am glad also my grandchildren will be bred near the heather, for certain qualities which I think are best taught there.

" Let me enquire about all my friends, Mrs Fox, Mr and Mrs Butler, Mrs Edgeworth, the hospitable squire, and plan of education, and all and sundry of the household of Edgeworthstown. I shall long remember our delightful days — especially those under the roof of Protestant Frank.†

" Have you forsworn merry England, to say

* Barbour's *Bruce.*

† I believe the ancestor who built the House at Edgeworthstown was distinguished by this appellation.

nothing of our northern regions?   This meditated
retreat will make me more certain of being at Abbotsford the whole year; and I am now watching
the ripening of those plans which I schemed five
years, ten years, twenty years ago.   Anne is still the
Beatrix you saw her; Walter, now major, predominating with his hussars at Nottingham and Sheffield;
but happily there has been no call to try Sir Toby's
experiment of drawing three souls out of the body of
one weaver.   Ireland seems to be thriving.   A friend
of mine laid out £40,000 or £50,000 on an estate
there, for which he gets seven per cent.; so you are
looking up.   Old England is distressed enough;—
we are well enough here — but we never feel the
storm till it has passed over our neighbours.   I ought
to get a frank for this, but our Members are all up
mending the stops of the great fiddle.   The termination of the King's illness is considered as inevitable,
and expected with great apprehension and anxiety.
Believe me always with the greatest regard, yours.

WALTER SCOTT."

On the 26th of June, Sir Walter heard of the
death of King George IV. with the regret of a devoted and obliged subject.   He had received almost
immediately before two marks of his Majesty's kind
attention.   Understanding that his retirement from
the Court of Session was at hand, Sir William

Knighton suggested to the King that Sir Walter might henceforth be more frequently in London, and that he might very fitly be placed at the head of a new commission for examining and editing the MSS. collections of the exiled Princes of the House of Stuart, which had come into the King's hands on the death of the Cardinal of York. This Sir Walter gladly accepted, and contemplated with pleasure spending the ensuing winter in London. But another proposition, that of elevating him to the rank of Privy Councillor, was unhesitatingly declined. He felt that any increase of rank under the circumstances of diminished fortune and failing health would be idle and unsuitable, and desired his friend, the Lord Chief Commissioner, whom the King had desired to ascertain his feelings on the subject, to convey his grateful thanks, with his humble apology.

He heard of the King's death, on what was otherwise a pleasant day. The Diary says— " *June* 27. Yesterday morning I worked as usual at proofs and copy of my infernal Demonology, a task to which my poverty and not my will consents. About twelve o'clock, I went to the country to take a day's relaxation. We (*i. e.* Mr Cadell, James Ballantyne, and I) went to Prestonpans, and getting there about one, surveyed the little village, where my aunt and I were lodgers for the sake of sea-bathing, in 1778, I believe. I knew the house of Mr Warroch, where we lived, a poor cottage, of which the owners and their family are extinct. I recollected my juvenile ideas of dignity attendant on the large gate, a black arch which lets out upon the sea. I saw the church where I yawned under the inflictions of a Dr M'Cormick, a name in which dulness seems to have been heredi-tary. I saw the links where I arranged my shells upon the turf, and swam my little skiff in the pools. Many comparisons between the man and the boy — many recollections of my kind aunt — of old George Constable, who, I think, dangled after her — of Dal-getty, a virtuous half-pay lieutenant, who swaggered his solitary walk on the parade, as he called a little open space before the same port. We went to Pres-ton, and took refuge from a thunder-plump in the old tower. I remembered the little garden where I was crammed with gooseberries, and the fear I had of Blind Harry's Spectre of Fawdon showing his headless trunk at one of the windows. I remembered also a very good-natured pretty girl (my Mary Duff) whom I laughed and romped with, and loved as chil-dren love. She was a Miss Dalrymple, daughter of Lord Westhall, a Lord of Session ; was afterwards married to Anderson of Winterfield, and her daugh ter is now the spouse of my colleague, Robert Ha-milton. So strangely are our cards shuffled. I was a mere child, and could feel none of the passion which Byron alleges, yet the recollection of this good-humoured companion of my childhood is like that of a morning dream, nor should I greatly like to dispel it by seeing the original, who must now be sufficiently time-honoured.

" Well, we walked over the field of battle; saw the Prince's Park, Cope's Road, marked by slaughter in his disastrous retreat, the thorn-tree which marks the centre of the battle, and all besides that was to be seen or supposed. We saw two broadswords, found on the field of battle, one a Highlander's, an Andrew Ferrara, another the Dragoon's sword of that day.* Lastly, we came to Cockenzie, where Mr Francis Cadell, my publisher's brother, gave us a kind reception. I was especially glad to see the mother of the family, a fine old lady, who was civil to my aunt and me, and, I recollect well, used to have us to tea at Cockenzie. Curious that I should long afterwards have an opportunity to pay back this attention to her son Robert. Once more, what a kind of shuffling of the hand dealt us at our nativity. There was Mrs F. Cadell and one or two young ladies, and some fine fat children. I should be. " a Bastard to the Time" did I not tell our fare: we had a tiled whiting, a dish unknown elsewhere, so there is a bone for the gastronomers to pick. Honest John Wood, my old friend, dined with us; I only regret

* The Laird of Cockenzie kindly sent these swords next day to the armoury of Abbotsford.

I cannot understand him, as he has a very powerful memory, and much curious information.* The whole day of pleasure was damped by the news of the King's death; it was fully expected, indeed, as the termination of his long illness; but he was very good to me personally, and a kind sovereign. The common people and gentry join in their sorrows. Much is owing to kindly recollections of his visit to this country, which gave all men an interest in him."

When the term ended in July, the affair of Sir Walter's retirement was all but settled; and soon afterwards he was informed that he had ceased to be a Clerk of Session, and should thenceforth have, in lieu of his salary, &c. (£1300) an allowance of £800 per annum. This was accompanied by an intimation from the Home Secretary, that the Ministers were quite ready to grant him a pension covering the reduction in his income. Considering himself as the bond-slave of his creditors, he made known to them this proposition, and stated that it would be extremely painful to him to accept of it; and with the delicacy and generosity which throughout characte-

---

* Mr Wood published a History of the Parish of Cramond, in 1794 — an enlarged edition of Sir Robert Douglas's Peerage of Scotland, 2 vols. folio, in 1813—and a Life of the celebrated John Law, of Lauriston, in 1824. In the preface to the Cramond History he describes himself as *scopulis surdior Icari.* [Mr Wood died 25th October 1838, in his 74th year.]

rised their conduct towards him, they, without hesitation, entreated him on no account to do injury
to his own feelings in such a matter as this. Few
things gave him more pleasure than this handsome
communication.

Just after he had taken leave of Edinburgh, as he
seems to have thought for ever, he received a communication of another sort, as inopportune as any
that ever reached him. His Diary for the 13th July
says briefly —" I have a letter from a certain young
gentleman, announcing that his sister had so far mistaken the intentions of a lame baronet nigh sixty
years old, as to suppose him only prevented by modesty from stating certain wishes and hopes, &c.
The party is a woman of rank, so my vanity may be
satisfied. But I excused myself, with little picking
upon the terms."

During the rest of the summer and autumn his
daughter and I were at Chiefswood, and saw him of
course daily. Laidlaw, too, had been restored to the
cottage at Kaeside; and though Tom Purdie made a
dismal blank, old habits went on, and the course of
life seemed little altered from what it had used to be.
He looked jaded and worn before evening set in, yet
very seldom departed from the strict regimen of his
doctors, and often brightened up to all his former
glee, though passing the bottle, and sipping toast and
water. His grandchildren especially saw no change.

However languid, his spirits revived at the sight of them, and the greatest pleasure he had was in pacing Douce Davie through the green lanes among his woods, with them clustered about him on ponies and donkeys, while Laidlaw, the ladies, and myself, walked by, and obeyed his directions about pruning and marking trees. After the immediate alarms of the spring, it might have been even agreeable to witness this placid twilight scene, but for our knowledge that nothing could keep him from toiling many hours daily at his desk, and alas! that he was no longer sustained by the daily commendations of his printer. It was obvious, as the season advanced, that the manner in which Ballantyne communicated with him was sinking into his spirits, and Laidlaw foresaw, as well as myself, that some trying crisis of discussion could not be much longer deferred. A nervous twitching about the muscles of the mouth was always more or less discernible from the date of the attack in February; but we could easily tell, by the aggravation of that symptom, when he had received a packet from the Canongate. It was distressing indeed to think that he might, one of these days, sustain a second seizure, and be left still more helpless, yet with the same undiminished appetite for literary labour. And then, if he felt his printer's complaints so keenly, what was to be expected in the case of a plain and undeniable manifestation of disappointment on the part of the public, and consequently of the bookseller?

All this was for the inner circle. Country neighbours went and came, without, I believe, observing almost anything of what grieved the family. Nay, this autumn he was far more troubled with the invasions of strangers, than he had ever been since his calamities of 1826. The astonishing success of the new editions was, as usual, doubled or trebled by rumour. The notion that he had already all but cleared off his incumbrances seems to have been widely prevalent, and no doubt his refusal of a pension tended to confirm it. Abbotsford was, for some weeks at least, besieged much as it had used to be in the golden days of 1823 and 1824; and if sometimes his guests brought animation and pleasure with them, even then the result was a legacy of redoubled lassitude. The Diary, among a very few and far-separated entries, has th :—

" *September* 5. — In spite of Resolution, I have left my Diary for some weeks, I cannot well tell why We have had abundance of travelling Counts and Countesses, Yankees male and female, and a Yankee-Doodle-*Dandy* into the bargain — a smart young Virginia-man. But we have had friends of our own also—the Miss Ardens, young Mrs Morritt and Anne Morritt, most agreeable visiters. Cadell came out

nere yesterday with his horn filled with good news.
He calculates that in October the debt will be reduced
to the sum of £60,000, half of its original amount.
This makes me care less about the terms I retire upon.
The efforts by which we have advanced thus far are
new in literature, and what is gained is secure."

Mr Cadell's great hope, when he offered this visit,
had been that the good news of the *Magnum* might
induce Sir Walter to content himself with working
at notes and prefaces for its coming volumes, without
straining at more difficult tasks. He found his friend,
however, by no means disposed to adopt such views;
and suggested very kindly, and ingeniously too, by
way of *mezzo-termine*, that before entering upon
any new novel, he should draw up a sort of *catalogue
raisonnée* of the most curious articles in his library
and museum. Sir Walter grasped at this, and began
next morning to dictate to Laidlaw what he designed
to publish in the usual novel shape, under the title of
" Reliquiæ Trottcosienses, or the Gabions of Jona-
than Oldbuck."   Nothing, as it seemed to all about
him, could have suited the time better; but after a
few days he said he found this was not sufficient —
that he should proceed in it during *horæ subcesivæ.*
but must bend himself to the composition of a romance, founded on a story which he had more than
once told cursorily already, and for which he had

been revolving the various titles of Robert of the Isle — Count Robert de L'Isle — and Count Robert of Paris. There was nothing to be said in reply to the decisive announcement of this purpose. The usual agreements were drawn out; and the Tale was begun.

But before I come to the results of this experiment, I must relieve the reader by Mr Adolphus's account of some more agreeable things. The death of George IV. occasioned a general election; and the Revolution of France in July, with its rapid imitation in the Netherlands, had been succeeded by such a quickening of hope among the British Liberals, as to render this in general a scene of high excitement and desperate struggling of parties. In Teviotdale, however, all was as yet quiescent. Mr Adolphus says —

" One day, during my visit of 1830, I accompanied Sir Walter to Jedburgh, when the eldest son of Mr Scott of Harden (now Lord Polwarth) was for the third time elected member for Roxburghshire. There was no contest; an opposition had been talked of, but was adjourned to some future day. The meeting in the Court-house, where the election took place, was not a very crowded or stirring scene; but among those present, as electors or spectators, were many gentlemen of the most ancient and honourable names in Roxburghshire and the adjoining counties. Sir

Walter seconded the nomination. It was the first time I had heard him speak in public, and I was a little disappointed. His manner was very quiet and natural, but seemed to me too humble, and wanting in animation. His air was sagacious and reverend; his posture somewhat stooping; he rested, or rather pressed, the palm of one hand on the head of his stick, and used a very little gesticulation with the other. As he went on, his delivery acquired warmth, but it never became glowing. His points, however, were very well chosen, and his speech, perhaps, upon the whole, was such as a sensible country gentleman should have made to an assembly of his neighbours upon a subject on which they were all well agreed. Certainly the feeling of those present in favour of the candidate required no stimulus.

" The new Member was to give a dinner to the electors at three o'clock. In the meantime Sir Walter strolled round the ancient Abbey. It amused me on this and on one or two other occasions, when he was in frequented places, to see the curiosity with which some zealous stranger would hover about his line of walk or ride, to catch a view of him, though a distant one—for it was always done with caution and respect; and he was not disturbed—perhaps not displeased—by it. The dinner party was in number, I suppose, eighty or ninety, and the festival passed off with great spirit. The croupier, Mr Baillie of

Jerviswood, who had nominated the candidate in the morning, proposed, at its proper time, in a few energetic words, the health of Sir Walter Scott. All hearts were ' thirsty for the noble pledge ;' the health was caught up with enthusiasm ; and any one who looked round must have seen with pleasure that the popularity of Sir Walter Scott—European, and more than European as it was—had its most vigorous roots at the threshold of his own home. He made a speech in acknowledgment, and this time I was not disappointed. It was rich in humour and feeling, and graced by that engaging manner of which he had so peculiar a command. One passage I remembered, for its whimsical homeliness, long after the other, and perhaps better, parts of the speech had passed from my recollection. Mr Baillie had spoken of him as a man pre-eminent among those who had done honour and service to Scotland. He replied, that in what he had done for Scotland as a writer, he was no more entitled to the merit which had been ascribed to him than the servant who scours the ' brasses' to the credit of having made them ; that he perhaps had been a good housemaid to Scotland, and given the country a ' rubbing up ;' and in so doing might have deserved some praise for assiduity, and that was all. Afterwards, changing the subject, he spoke very beautifully and warmly of the re-elected candidate, who sat by him ; alluded to the hints which had been thrown out in the morning of a future opposition and *Reform*, and ended with some verses (I believe they were Burns's *parcé detorta*), pressing his hand upon the shoulder of Mr Scott as he uttered the concluding lines,

> ' But we ha' tried this Border lad,
> And we'll try him yet again.' *

" He sat down under a storm of applauses; and there were many present whose applause even he might excusably take some pride in. His eye, as he reposed himself after this little triumph, glowed with a hearty but chastened exultation on the scene before him; and when I met his look, it seemed to say — ' I am glad you should see how these things pass among us.'

" His constitution had in the preceding winter suffered one of those attacks which at last prematurely overthrew it. ' Such a shaking hands with death' (I am told he said) ' was formidable;' but there were few vestiges of it which might not be overlooked by those who were anxious not to see them; and he was more cheerful than I had sometimes found him in former years. On one of our carriage excursions, shortly after the Jedburgh dinner, his spirits actually rose to the pitch of singing, an accomplishment I

* See Burns's ballad of *The Five Carlines* — an election squib.

had never before heard him exhibit except in chorus. We had been to Selkirk and Bowhill, and were returning homewards in one of those days so inspiriting in a hill country, when, after heavy rains, the summer bursts forth again in its full splendour. Sir Walter was in his best congenial humour. As we looked up to Carterhaugh, his conversation ran naturally upon Tamlane and Fair Janet, and the ballad recounting their adventures; then it ran upon the *Dii agrestes*, ghosts and wizards, Border anecdotes and history, the bar, his own adventures as advocate and as sheriff; and then returning to ballads, it fell upon the old ditty of Tom o' the Linn, or Thomas O'Linn, which is popular alike, I believe, in Scotland, and in some parts of England, and of which I as well as he had boyish recollections. As we compared versions he could not forbear, in the gaiety of his heart, giving out two or three of the stanzas in song. I cannot say that I ever heard this famous lyric sung to a very regular melody, but his *set* of it was extraordinary.

" Another little incident in this morning's drive is worth remembering. We crossed several fords, and after the rain they were wide and deep. A little, long, wise-looking, rough terrier, named Spice, which ran after us, had a cough, and as often as we came to a water, Spice, by the special order of her master, was let into the carriage till we had crossed. His tenderness to his brute dependants was a striking point in the general benignity of his character. He seemed to consult not only their bodily welfare, but their feelings, in the human sense. He was a gentleman even to his dogs. His roughest rebuke to little Spice, when she was inclined to play the wag with a sheep, was, ' Ha! fie! fie!' It must be owned that his ' tail' (as his retinue of dogs was called at Abbotsford), though very docile and unobtrusive animals in the house, were sometimes a little wild in their frolics out of doors. One day when I was walking with Sir Walter and Miss Scott, we passed a cottage, at the door of which sat on one side a child, and on the other a slumbering cat. Nimrod bounded from us in great gaiety, and the unsuspecting cat had scarcely time to squall before she was demolished. The poor child set up a dismal wail. Miss Scott was naturally much distressed, and Sir Walter a good deal out of countenance. However, he put an end to the subject by saying, with an assumed stubbornness, ' Well! the cat is worried;' but his purse was in his hand; Miss Scott was despatched to the house, and I am very sure it was not his fault if the cat had a poor funeral. In the confusion of the moment, I am afraid the culprit went off without even a reprimand.

" Except in this trifling instance (and it could hardly be called an exception), I cannot recollect seeing Sir Walter Scott surprised out of his habitual equanimity. Never, I believe, during the opportunities I had of observing him, did I hear from him an acrimonious tone, or see a shade of ill-humour on his features. In a phlegmatic person this serenity might have been less remarkable, but it was surprising in one whose mind was so susceptible, and whose voice and countenance were so full of expression. It was attributable, I think, to a rare combination of qualities;—thoroughly cultivated manners, great kindness of disposition, great patience and self-control, an excellent flow of spirits, and lastly, that steadfastness of nerve, which, even in the inferior animals, often renders the most powerful and resolute creature the most placid and forbearing. Once, when he was exhibiting some weapons, a gentleman, after differing from him as to the comparative merits of two sword-blades, inadvertently flourished one of them almost into Sir Walter's eye. I looked quickly towards him, but could not see in his face the least sign of shrinking, or the least approach to a frown. No one, however, could for a moment infer from this evenness of manner and temper, that he was a man with whom an intentional liberty could be taken; and I suppose very few persons during his life ever thought of making the experiment. If it happened at any time that some trivial *etourderie* in conversation required at his hand a slight application of the rein, his gentle *explaining* tone was an appeal to good taste which no common wilfulness could have withstood.

" Two or three times at most during my knowledge of him do I recollect hearing him utter a downright oath, and then it was not in passion or upon personal provocation, nor was the anathema levelled at any individual. It was rather a concise expression of sentiment, than a malediction. In one instance it was launched at certain improvers of the town of Edinburgh ; in another it was bestowed very evenly upon all political parties in France, shortly after the *glorious days* of July 1830."

As one consequence of these " glorious days," the unfortunate Charles X. was invited by the English Government to resume his old quarters at Holyrood ; and among many other things that about this time vexed and mortified Scott, none gave him more pain than to hear that the popular feeling in Edinburgh had been so much exacerbated against the fallen monarch (especially by an ungenerous article in the great literary organ of the place), that his reception there was likely to be rough and insulting. Sir Walter thought that on such an occasion his voice might, perhaps, be listened to. He knew his countrymen well in their strength, as well as in their weakness, and put forth this touching appeal to their better feelings, in Ballantyne's newspaper for the 20th of October:—

" We are enabled to announce, from authority, that Charles of Bourbon, the ex-King of France, is about to become once more our fellow-citizen, though probably for only a limited space, and is presently about to repair to Edinburgh, in order again to inhabit the apartments which he long ago occupied in Holyrood House. This temporary arrangement, it is said, has been made in compliance with his own request, with which our benevolent Monarch immediately complied, willing to consult, in every respect possible, the feelings of a Prince under the pressure of misfortunes, which are perhaps the more severe, if incurred through bad advice, error, or rashness. The attendants of the late sovereign will be reduced to the least possible number, and consist chiefly of ladies and children, and his style of life will be strictly retired. In these circumstances, it would be unworthy of us as Scotsmen, or as men, if this most unfortunate family should meet a word or look from the meanest individual tending to aggravate feelings, which must be at present so acute as to receive injury from insults which in other times could be passed with perfect disregard.

" His late opponents in his kingdom have gained the applause of Europe for the generosity with which th'ey have used their victory, and the respect which they have paid to themselves in moderation toward an enemy. It would be a gross contrast to that part of their conduct which has been most generally applauded, were we, who are strangers to the strife, to affect a deeper resentment than those it concerned closely.

" Those who can recollect the former residence of this unhappy Prince in our northern capital, cannot but remember the unobtrusive and quiet manner in which his little court was then conducted; and now, still further restricted and diminished, he may naturally expect to be received with civility and respect by a nation whose good-will he has done nothing to forfeit. Whatever may have been his errors towards his own subjects, we cannot but remember, in his adversity, that he did not in his prosperity forget that Edinburgh had extended her hospitality towards him, but, at the period when the fires consumed so much of the city, sent a princely benefaction to the sufferers, with a letter which made it more valuable, by stating the feelings towards the city of the then royal donor. We also state, without hazard of contradiction, that his attention to individuals connected with this city was uniformly and handsomely rendered to those entitled to claim them. But he never did or could display a more flattering confidence, than when he shows that the recollections of his former asylum here have inclined him a second time to return to the place where he then found refuge.

" If there can be any who retain angry or invidious recollections of late events in France, they ought to remark that the ex-Monarch has, by his abdication, renounced the conflict into which, perhaps, he was engaged by bad advisers ; that he can no longer be the object of resentment to the brave, but remains to all the most striking emblem of the mutability of human affairs which our mutable times have afforded He may say, with our own deposed Richard—

> ' With mine own tears I washed away my balm,
> With mine own hands I gave away my crown,
> With my own tongue deny mine sacred state.' *

He brings among us his ' grey discrowned head ;' and in ' a nation of gentlemen,' as we were emphatically termed by the very highest authority,† it is impossible, I trust, to find a man mean enough to insult the slightest hair of it.

" It is impossible to omit stating, that if angry recollections or keen party feelings should make any person consider the exiled and deposed Monarch as a subject of resentment, no token of such feelings could be exhibited without the greater part of the pain be-

---

* *King Richard II Act IV. Scene 1.*

† This was the expression of King George IV. at the close of the first day he spent in Scotland.

ing felt by the helpless females, of whom the Duchess of Angouleme, in particular, has been so long distinguished by her courage and her misfortunes.

" The person who writes these few lines is leaving his native city, never to return as a permanent resident. He has some reason to be proud of distinctions received from his fellow-citizens; and he has not the slightest doubt that the taste and good feeling of those whom he will still term so, will dictate to them the quiet, civil, and respectful tone of feeling, which will do honour both to their heads and their hearts, which have seldom been appealed to in vain.

" The Frenchman Melinet, in mentioning the refuge afforded by Edinburgh to Henry VI. in his distress, records it as the most hospitable town in Europe. It is a testimony to be proud of, and sincerely do I hope there is little danger of forfeiting it upon the present occasion."

The effect of this manly admonition was even more complete than the writer had anticipated. The royal exiles were received with perfect decorum, which their modest bearing to all classes, and unobtrusive, though magnificent benevolence to the poor, ere long converted into a feeling of deep and affectionate respectfulness. During their stay in Scotland, the King took more than one opportunity of conveying to Sir Walter his gratitude for this salutary interference on his behalf.   The ladies of the royal family had a curiosity to see Abbotsford, but being aware of his reduced health and wealth, took care to visit the place when he was known to be from home. Several French noblemen of the train, however, paid him their respects personally. I remember with particular pleasure a couple of days that the Duke of Laval-Montmorency spent with him: he was also much gratified with a visit from Marshal Bourmont, though unfortunately that came after his aliments had much advanced. The Marshal was accompanied by the Baron d'Haussez, one of the Polignac Ministry, whose published account of his residence in this country contains no specimen of vain imbecility more pitiable than the page he gives to Abbotsford. So far from comprehending anything of his host's character or conversation, the Baron had not even eyes to observe that he was in a sorely dilapidated condition of bodily health. The reader will perceive by and by, that he had had another *fit* only a few days before he received these strangers; and that, moreover, he was engaged at the moment in a most painful correspondence with his printer and bookseller.

I conclude this chapter with a letter to Lady Louisa Stuart, who had, it seems, formed some erroneous guesses about the purport of the forthcoming Letters on Demonology and Witchcraft. That volume had been some weeks out of hand — but, for booksellers' reasons, it was not published until Christmas.

> "*To the Right Hon. Lady Louisa Stuart.*

> "Abbotsford, October 31, 1830.

"My Dear Lady Louisa,

"I come before your Ladyship for once, in the character of Not Guilty. I am a wronged man, who deny, with Lady Teazle, *the butler and the coach-horse.* Positively, in sending a blow to explode old and worn-out follies, I could not think I was aiding and abetting those of this—at least I had no purpose of doing so. Your Ladyship cannot think me such an owl as to pay more respect to animal magnetism, or scullology—I forget its learned name—or any other *ology* of the present day. The sailors have an uncouth proverb that every man must eat a peck of dirt in the course of his life, and thereby reconcile themselves to swallow unpalatable messes. Even so say I: every age must swallow a certain deal of superstitious nonsense; only, observing the variety which nature seems to study through all her works, each generation takes its nonsense, as heralds say, *with a difference.* I was early behind the scenes, having been in childhood patient of no less a man than the celebrated Dr Graham, the great quack of that olden day. I had—being, as Sir Hugh Evans says, a fine sprag boy—a shrewd idea that his magnetism was all humbug; but Dr Graham, though he used a different method, was as much admired in his day as any of the French fops. I did once think of turning on the modern mummers, but I did not want to be engaged in so senseless a controversy, which would, nevertheless, have occupied some time and trouble. The inference was pretty plain, that the same reasons which explode the machinery of witches and ghosts proper to our ancestors, must be destructive of the supernatural nonsense of our own days.

" Your acquaintance with Shakspeare is intimate, and you remember why and when it is said—

'He words me, girl, he words me.' *

Our modern men of the day have done this to the country. They have devised a new phraseology to convert good into evil, and evil into good, and the ass's ears of John Bull are gulled with it as if words alone made crime or virtue. Have they a mind to excuse the tyranny of Buonaparte? why, the Lord love you, he only squeezed into his government a grain too much of civilisation. The fault of Robespierre was too active liberalism—a noble error. Thus the most blood-thirsty anarchy is glossed over by opening the account under a new name. The varnish

* *Antony and Cleopatra, Act V. Scene 2.*

might be easily scraped off all this trumpery; and I think my friends *the brave Belges* are like to lead to the conclusion that the old names of murder and fire-raising are still in fashion. But. what is worse. the natural connexion between the higher and lower classes is broken. The former reside abroad, and become gradually, but certainly, strangers to their country's laws, habits, and character. The tenant sees nothing of them but the creditor for rent, following on the heels of the creditor for taxes. Our Ministers dissolve the yeomanry, almost the last tie which held the laird and the tenant together. The best and worthiest are squabbling together, like a mutinous crew in a sinking vessel, who make the question, not how they are to get her off the rocks, but by whose fault she came on them. In short—but I will not pursue any further the picture more frightful than any apparition in my Demonology. Would to God I could believe it ideal! I have confidence still in the Duke of Wellington, but even he has sacrificed to the great deity of humbug, and what shall we say to meaner and more ordinary minds? God avert evil! and, what is next best, in mercy remove those who could only witness without preventing it! Perhaps I am somewhat despondent in all this. But totally retired from the world as I now am, depression is a natural consequence of so calamitous a prospect as politics now present. The only probable course of safety would be a confederacy between the good and the honest; and they are so much divided by petty feuds, that I see little chance of it.

" I will send this under Lord Montagu's frank, for it is no matter how long such a roll of lamentation may be in reaching your Ladyship. I do not think it at all likely that I shall be in London next spring, although I suffer Sophia to think so. I remain, in all my bad humour, ever your Ladyship's most obedient and faithful humble servant,

WALTER SCOTT."

END OF VOL. IX.